THE
BLUE EDGE
OF
MIDNIGHT

THE
BLUE EDGE
OF
MIDNIGHT

JONATHON KING

BCA

LONDON   NEW YORK   SYDNEY   TORONTO

This edition published 2002
by BCA
by arrangement with Orion
an imprint of the Orion Publishing Group Ltd

CN 106970

Printed and bound in Great Britain by
Mackays of Chatham plc, Chatham, Kent

*This is for my friend Bob Stowe, who left
this world too soon, and can't be forgotten.*

THE
BLUE EDGE
OF
MIDNIGHT

CHAPTER 1

I was a mile upriver, my feet planted on the stained concrete dam, back bent to the task of yanking my canoe over the abutment. It was past midnight and a three-quarter moon hung in the South Florida sky. In the spillover behind me, tea-colored water from the falls burbled and swirled, roiling up against itself and then spinning off in curls and spirals until going flat and black again downstream. Ahead I could see the outlines of thick tree limbs and dripping vine and the slow curve of water bending around a corner before it disappeared into darkness.

When I moved onto this river more than a year ago, my city eyes were nearly useless. My night vision had always been aided by street lamps, storefront displays, and headlights that swept the streets, crosshatching each other to create a web of light at every intersection. I'd spent my life on the Philadelphia streets, watching, gauging the hard flat shadows, interpreting the light from a door left ajar, waiting for a streak from a flashlight, anticipating the flare of a match strike. Out here, fifteen miles inland from the Atlantic Ocean in a swamped lowland forest, it took me a month to train my eyes to navigate in the night's natural light.

Tonight, in moonlight, the river was lit up like an avenue. When I got the canoe floated in the upstream pool, I braced myself with both hands on the rails at either side, balanced my right foot in the middle, steadied myself in a three-point stance, and pushed off onto quiet water.

I settled into the stern seat and pulled six or seven strokes to get upstream from the falls and then readied myself. The mile from my stilted shack had just been a warm-up. Now I'd get into the heavy work that had become my nightly ritual. This time of year in South Florida, high summer when the afternoon rains came like a rhythm, this ancient river to the Everglades spread its banks into the cypress and sabal palms and flooded the sawgrass and pond apple trees until the place looked more like a drowning forest than a tributary. It was also the time of year when a man with a head full of sour memories could power a canoe up the river's middle and muscle and sweat through yet another impossible night.

I tucked my right foot under the seat, propped my left forward against a rib, and was just pulling my first serious strokes when my eyes picked up a glow ahead in the root tangle of a big cypress.

Trash, I thought, pulling two strokes hard in that direction. Even out here you ran into civilization's callousness. But the package seemed too tight as I glided closer. Canvas, I could tell now from the cream-color of the cloth.

I took one more stroke and drifted up to what now appeared to be a bundle the size of a small duffel bag. The package was wedged softly into a crook of moss-covered root by the current. I reached out and prodded it with my paddle, loosening the hidden end from the shadows. When it finally slid out onto free water, moonlight caught it and settled on the calm, dead face of a child.

Air from deep in my throat held and then broke like a bubble in my mouth and I heard my own words come out in a whisper:

"Sweet Jesus. Not again."

* * *

For a dozen years I'd been a cop in Philadelphia. I got in at the smooth-faced age of nineteen without my father's blessing. He was a cop. He didn't want me to follow. I went against his wishes, which had become a habit by then, and got through the academy the same way I'd gotten through school. I rode the system, did just enough to satisfy, didn't stand out, but tried always to stand up. My mother, bless her soul, called it a sin.

"Talent," she said, "is God's gift to you. What you do with it, is your gift back to him."

According to her, my talent was brains. My sin was using only half of them.

Police work came easy to me. At six feet three inches tall, and a little over two hundred pounds, I'd played some undistinguished football in high school and my friend Frankie O'Hara used to drag me into his father's South Philly gym once in a while to act as a stand-in sparring partner. My strength there was that I didn't mind getting hit. A shot in the face never bothered me much. How that trait worked with my other "talent," my mother could never explain. But the combination of a cloaked intelligence, some size, and an indifference to a crack on the nose made police work easy for me.

In my years on the force I'd climbed a bit of a ladder, taken some special assignments, worked for a short time in the detective bureau. I'd passed the sergeant's exam a couple of times. But misunderstandings with management and "Officer Freeman's seeming total lack of ambition" found me walking a downtown beat on the four-to-twelve shift. It was fine with me until the night I shot a child in the back.

* * *

It was near the end of my shift. I was standing out of a cold drizzle at Murphy's Newsstand, a little step-in shop next to a deli just off Broad Street. Murph peddled the daily newspapers, three shelves of magazines holding the monthly array of faked-up cleavage, and probably the most important item of his business, the daily racing forms. With some thirty years on the street, Murph was the most sour and skeptical human being I'd ever met. He was a huge lump of a man who sat for hours at a time on a four-legged stool with what seemed like half of his weight dripping over the sides of the small circular cushion. He had a fat face that folded in on itself like a two-week-old Halloween pumpkin and you couldn't tell the color of his small slit eyes. He was never without a cigar planted in the corner of his mouth.

"Max, you're a fuckin' idiot you stay on a job what wit da way they been stickin' it to ya," was his standard conversation with me every night for two years. He had a voice like gravel shuffling around in the bottom of a cardboard box. And he called everyone from the mayor to his own mother a "fuckin' idiot," so you didn't take it personally.

On that night he was grumbling over the day's results from Garden State Raceway when my radio started crackling with a report of a silent alarm at C&M's Stop and Shop on Thirteenth Street, just around the corner. I reached down to turn up the volume and Murph rolled the cigar with his tongue and that's when we heard the snap of small caliber gunfire in the distance. The old vendor looked straight into my face and for the first time in two years I could see that his eyes were a pale, clear blue.

"Casamir," he croaked as I started out the open door, my hand already going to the holster strap on my 9mm.

It doesn't take long for adrenaline to flush into your blood when you hear gunshots. As a cop in the city I had heard too many. And each time I had to fight the immediate urge to turn and walk the other way.

I was halfway to the corner and my normally slow heartbeat was banging in my chest. I was trying to set up a scene in my head of Casamir's place; second storefront around the corner, glass doors flush against the wall, dingy fluorescent lighting inside, Casamir with his too-big smile and that pissy little taped-handled .25 behind the counter. I wasn't thinking about the rain-slick sidewalk or the lack of decent cover when I made the corner and tried to plant my foot and went skidding out in full view of some kid's gun barrel.

Snap.

I heard the crack of his pistol but barely registered the sharp smack against my neck and I came up on one knee, brought up the 9mm and saw the kid standing thirty feet away, a black hole of a gun barrel as his only eye. I was staring into that hole when I picked up the movement of something coming out of Casamir's door and then *Snap*, another round went off.

I hesitated for one bad instant, and then pulled the trigger. My weapon jumped. My eyes instinctively blinked. Chaos competed for only a second. And then the street went quiet.

The first kid went down without so much as a whimper. Casamir's .25 had sounded the third report of the night and caught the shooter in the street flush in the temple. My round hit the second boy, the one who had jumped out the door just as I hesitated. The 9mm slug caught him in the back between his skinny shoulder blades and he dropped. Unlike the Hollywood version, the kid didn't get blown back from the impact. He didn't get spun around. He didn't slowly crumple to his knees or try to reach out and call someone's name. He just melted.

The noise of my own gun was ringing in my ears and I must have been getting up because the angle of the scene was changing, but I didn't know how my knees were working.

Casamir was standing over the bodies by the time I made it thirty feet. He looked up at me, the old .25 hanging from his hand.

"Max?" he said, confused at my presence. His face was blank. His smile was gone. Maybe forever.

The first boy was facedown, the pistol that he had fired, first at Casamir and then at me, had clattered off into the gutter. The younger boy, mine, lay oddly twisted, his clothes, all baggy and black, seemed comically empty. But his face was turned up, his open eyes gone cloudy through long, childlike lashes. He couldn't have been more than twelve.

I was staring into that face when Murph, trailing from the newsstand, stepped up to my side and looked at me and then down at the kid.

"Fuckin' idiot," he says. But I wasn't sure which one of us he was talking about.

I was still staring into the boy's face, trying to breathe through a liquid burbling in my throat, and then I heard Casamir repeating my name: "Max? Max?" And I looked up and he was staring at me and pointing to his neck and saying, "Max. You are shot." And suddenly that night, and that world, went softly black.

CHAPTER 2

"**S**weet Jesus. Not again."

On the river I am still looking at the child's face, glowing in the moonlight, bobbing in the water, and my first reaction is to help. My second is to get the hell out. My third is to calm down.

The sound of a billion chirping insects is overpowering the silence. I draw a breath full of warm humid air and force myself to think. I'm a mile from my shack and a good two and a half miles from the ranger station. I'm staring at a dead child and a crime scene. I'm a cop too long, despite bailing out of the title two years ago, and if my isolation has taught me anything it is that you can't flush everything out of your head for good.

I start organizing, running through a list. The bundle was wedged up into the roots of the cypress tree but it could have been pushed there by the current, or placed there on purpose. The body is neatly and tightly wrapped, but the face is exposed. Why? Why does it need to look out? The skin is so pale that it looks preserved, but who knows what effect the brackish water has had? And if it's been floating upright, the settling blood could already be drawn down from the face.

The sailcloth of the bundle is a rip-stop nylon. Too clean, I think. Too new. I start to reach out and hook it with my paddle but I look at the face again and stop. Crime scene, I say to myself. Let the crime scene guys do it. It's not going anywhere. Go call it in.

It's two and a half miles, downstream, at least a hard hour to the ranger station at Thompson's Point. Cleve Wilson, the senior ranger, would be there on his monthly, twenty-four-hour live-in shift. I spin the canoe and start back north, heading for the falls. In eight or ten deep strokes I pick up speed and then lean back and launch myself over the four-foot dam, whumping down onto the lower river, kicking a spray up on either side. On the bob up, I grab another purchase of thick water with the paddle and pull back on it and shoot the canoe forward. The face of a dead child is chasing me again.

In seconds I fall into the stroke. Efficient, full, with a swift lift at the end. Same power, same pull, same finish. I glide through the wet forest, backpaddling only to make the quick corners, swing stroking only to pull around the rounder ones. In minutes I am running with sweat but don't even try to wipe it from my eyes, just whip the droplets with a head snap and keep digging. I know the route by memory and in forty minutes the river widens out and starts its curve east toward the ocean. The canopy of cypress opens up and then falls behind me. The moon is following. I ignore the burn building in my back and shoulders and keep my eyes focused on the next dark silhouette of mangroves bulling out in the water that indicates a bend in the river, and cut straight for it. Moving point to point, I just keep working it.

What I had wanted when I came down here was something mindless and physically daunting and simple. I'd bought this specially made Voyager canoe, a classic wood design that was modern but made in the old-fashioned style with its ribs and wood rails. I'd plunked it down in this river and paddled the hell out of it. I had heard athletes, long-distance runners and swimmers, say they could get into a zone where they could work without thought. Just settle into a pace and tune out the world.

But I couldn't do it. I found out soon into my isolation that it wasn't going to work that way for me. Rhythm or no rhythm. Quiet or no quiet. I'm a grinder. And the rocks that went into my head after I shot a kid in front of a late-night convenience store were going to tumble and tumble and I wasn't going to forget. Maybe I'd wear the sharp edges off after time. Maybe I'd round off the corners. But I wasn't going to forget.

* * *

The last thing I recalled that night in Philadelphia was Casamir's words, "You are shot." Then I mimicked his own hand going to his neck and found my own was wet and sticky with a soup of sweat and blood. I swabbed at the muscle below my ear with my fingertips and felt nothing until my index finger slipped into a hole that didn't belong there. I either blacked out or just plain fainted.

When I woke up at Philadelphia's Thomas Jefferson Hospital, I started grinding. I knew they must have had me loaded up with a morphine drip and all the other procedural narcotics, but I didn't come out groggy, I came out analyzing.

My first thought was paralysis and I was afraid to move because I wasn't sure I wanted to know. I stared up at the ceiling and then started working my eyes to the white corners and down to a light fixture and then to a television screen mounted high on the opposite wall and then to my left on the curtain rod and to the right a mirror that I couldn't look into.

I concentrated on what I could feel and picked up the cool stiffness of the sheet against my legs and chest and was encouraged enough to move my right hand. "Thank Him for small miracles." I could hear my mother's old mantra and my hand went across to the left side of my neck and felt the bandage, thick and gauzy and wrapped all the way around. When I tried to move my head, pain shot straight into my temples and I knew from the tingle that my vertebra were probably intact.

I was taking an accounting of fingers and toes when District Chief Osborne walked into my room, followed by my father's brother-in-law, Sergeant Keith O'Brien, and someone in a dark suit that should have had "Beancounter" written up and down one of the legs like they do on sweatsuits from the universities that say "Hurricanes" or "Quakers."

"Freeman. Good to see you awake, man."

I'd never met the district chief in the dozen years I'd been on the force and was sure he'd never known my name until early this morning when a dispatcher woke him out of a warm sleep in his home in comfortable East Falls. He was a big man, broad in the shoulders and the belly, and was wearing some kind of paisley button-down shirt and had tossed on a navy sport coat to look both official and hurried. He had gray flecked hair and a bulbous nose that was starting to show the spider web of reddish veins from too much whiskey for too many years.

"Surgeons tell us you're one lucky officer, Freeman," he said. "They say a couple inches the other way could have been fatal."

Of course a few inches the other way and I wouldn't have been hit at all, but being such a lucky officer, I decided to hold on to that charm and not respond, even if I could. I hadn't yet attempted to speak. My throat felt thick and swollen as if I'd been to the dentist and the guy had pumped me full of novocaine all the way down to my collarbone.

I swung my eyes over to my uncle, who'd taken a deferential step back from the chief. Since he was studying either the end of the bed or the top of his shoes, I took a clue.

"They say you're out of the woods now. So don't you worry. But as soon as you're ready, we'll need a statement," said Osborne, tipping his head to the beancounter as part of the "we" but not introducing him.

There was an awkward silence. You can't have an interview with a mute man. You can't say congratulations to a shot cop. You can't say "good job" to an officer who just killed a child.

"We'll check back, Freeman," Osborne finally said, reaching out until he realized my hand wasn't going to move, and then issuing what seemed to be a consolation pat on the side of the bed instead. The chief and the guy I would later dance with in his role as human resource director walked to the door, had a few short sentences with Sgt. O'Brien and left.

My uncle Keith came to the bedside, making eye contact for the first time. Giving me the Irish twinkle and waiting a good safe period before flashing his more consistent fire.

"Assholes," he said, not elaborating on who he was giving the title to and letting it sit wide ranging. "How're ya, boy?" he finally said.

When I tried to answer, I couldn't get even a croak through the novocaine-like block. My right hand went again to the left side of my neck, a movement that was already imprinted in my post-surgical psyche.

"A through and through," he said, nodding his head to the right.

"Punk kid threw a .22 at you before you got off the knock-down. The EMS guys said the slug went straight through muscle, missed the windpipe and the carotid artery."

He told me how the slug had passed through my neck leaving an entrance wound as clean as a paper punch. The exit wound was twice as large and raggedy. The lead had then pucked into the brick façade of the Thirteenth Street Cleaners, chunking out a thimble-sized hole with spatters of Max Freeman's blood around it.

"Fuckin' kid was a real sharpshooter," he said before catching the look in my eye. Keith was like the majority of cops in Philadelphia and on every department in the country. In twenty-five years he had never pulled his gun in the line of duty. If the department hadn't instituted a mandatory range qualification a few years back, the rounds in his old-style revolver would still be rusted in the chamber. But he had seen the results of shootings. He'd known officers who had killed and seen them change. Nobody took it without changing.

"Both of 'em DOS," he said. "Crime scene guys bagged them right on the sidewalk."

He hesitated, looking away.

"Twelve and sixteen years old. Both from North Philly. Down doing Center City for the night."

He went on how the newspapers and radio talk shows were already howling about their new discovery this month that kids were carrying guns. He said a witness across the street on Chestnut was screaming that I took the first shot, cut the kid down without a warning. He said Internal Affairs had my gun and would be all over the shooting investigation, but being wounded and all, I didn't have to worry.

He was talking, but I had only been hearing, not listening. My eyes had gone to the ceiling again, my right hand to the bandage on my neck.

* * *

I must have been forty strokes shy of the landing at Thompson's Point when the spotlight beams hit me full in the face. I had covered the last mile and a half in nearly thirty minutes and had kept a consistent seventy strokes a minute the entire time.

My gray T-shirt was black with sweat and I had worked through a stitch in my side that had started stabbing me after the first fifteen minutes.

I kept cranking into the light when a voice called out and two more cones of light swung onto me. I never slowed, just kept the rhythm until I felt the bottom of my canoe hit the boat ramp gravel.

"Shoot fire, Max! Slow down, boy!"

Cleve Wilson's was the first face I could make out as he walked down the ramp to greet me.

"We was just about to head up your way," he said with an uncharacteristic hitch in his voice and cutting his eyes to either side of the dock.

Shaking the sweat out of my eyes I brought the rest of the five-person ramp party into focus. There were four men and a woman. Two of the men were thick in the chest and waist and were dressed in the brown uniform of the Florida Highway Patrol. The other two seemed thin, and both were dressed in canvas pants and oxford shirts rolled up at the sleeves. The younger one cursed in Spanish when the river water lapped up onto his loafers.

The woman was as tall as the other four and I picked up the glint of blond hair in the flashlight beam, but averted my eyes. The night was already full of too much memory. I didn't want to think about the rattle that that wisp of hair put into my heart.

I looked back at Cleve and registered the hesitation in his face. I was already trying to figure out how they'd already heard about the child's body when he started in.

"We was just heading up to the dam," he said. "These folks got some sort of tip that there might be some kind of clue to an investigation they got going."

Cleve was putting on his old Florida Cracker voice, the one

he'd used with me for the first month I knew him. It was his way of gathering intelligence, by hiding his own and letting others mistakenly try to send things over his head. He was about to make introductions when the oxford shirts did it on their own.

Detectives Mark Hammonds and Vincente Diaz, county sheriff's investigators on a joint task force with the Florida Department of Law Enforcement. When Hammonds stepped up he used the practiced firm handshake of a businessman and the old interviewer's trick of staring straight into your eyes like he could see the truth hanging back in there where you couldn't hide it. I'd used the look myself many times. I held his gaze until he flinched, then I took half a step back. Hammonds was the kind who made sure you knew he was in charge without using the words. He was a thin man in his fifties, tired around the eyes, but he squared his shoulders and like so many in his position seemed to will himself to appear bigger.

Diaz was quicker with the handshake. He was a clean-cut, young-looking Hispanic and couldn't help himself from being amiable. If cops had junior executives, he would be it. Eager to learn, eager to please. He had big, white, square teeth and even though he tried, he couldn't keep from smiling a little bit.

The woman refused to step closer to the riverbank and when Hammonds introduced her as a Detective Richards from Fort Lauderdale, I too kept my ground. We nodded our acquaintance. She stood with her arms folded as if she were cold, even on a night when the air was hanging warm and gauzy at the water's edge. Her perfume drifted by on a swirl of river wind and seemed distinctly out of place. When I turned to talk to the others I could feel her eyes on my back.

"So somebody already called this in?" I finally said, directing the question to Cleve while I bent to pull my canoe higher up on the ramp.

"Called what in?" Hammonds said.

"You've got a crime scene out there," I said but I could tell immediately that even though it wasn't unexpected news, it still caught all of them hard. Hammonds' lips went tight together and Diaz winced. I felt the woman take an instinctive step closer.

"What kind of scene, Mr. Freeman?" Hammonds said.

"A dead child. Wrapped up. Just above the dam."

Cleve was the only one in the group that registered any true shock.

"Jesus, Max," he said, looking at the faces around him.

"Let's get a team out here," Hammonds said to no one in particular as he looked out over the water, his block chin tipped up into the air.

CHAPTER 3

Within an hour they knew what I knew and I was left
guessing. That's the way conversations go with good
investigators. Even in supposedly friendly interviews. You answer their questions, offer your observations, try to be cooper-
ative. They nod their heads, encourage the dialogue, make nice,
and give you squat. By the time you walk away you feel like
your pockets are empty and you just made a really bad deal
with a door-to-door salesman. No wonder lawyers tell you to
just say no and close the door.

The only line I'd been able to read between their questioning was that this wasn't the first kid they'd found. There had
been others. I couldn't tell how many or where. I also knew I
was a suspect. The first person who comes across the body in
a homicide always is. I didn't have to be told not to leave the
state.

In two hours a crime scene truck was parked on the boat
ramp and Cleve was loading up his park service Boston Whaler.
Hammonds had decided not to wait for daylight. Cleve had
tied a spare canoe to the stern cleat. In this high water, and with
his knowledge of the river, he could get them up to the dam.
From there they would have to take the other boat up to the

body. Hammonds, Diaz and two others climbed into the Whaler and Cleve started it up with a rumble, got the men to cast off his lines and then chunked it into gear and slowly motored out onto the river.

The woman detective stayed at the ramp, talking to two crime scene technicians and into a cell phone at the same time. When she finally snapped the portable shut and took a step toward me, I stood up from my interview spot on the dock and gave her my back.

"I'm going home," I said over my shoulder, waiting for an objection that never came.

I dragged my canoe into the water. Out to the west I could see Cleve's portable spotlight flickering in the mangroves. I'd be far behind. As I pushed out and settled in for a first stroke, I stole a look over my shoulder and saw the woman standing back, four feet from the water line, arms crossed over her chest, following me with her eyes.

As I paddled, the knots in my shoulders from the hours of sitting and answering questions started to work themselves out. It was still a good hour from sunrise. The river was now unnaturally quiet. I could pick up the low undulations of Cleve's outboard even though they had to be a mile ahead. But the motorboat's passing at this hour had effectively turned off the millions of live sounds along the banks and in the thick mangrove islands. The frogs and insects had shut up, wary of the man-made noise and movement, and fallen into the survival cover of silence. I'd interrupted their natural rhythm with my nightly paddling. But as I'd learned to smooth my passage, and perhaps as the river world got accustomed to my months of slapping through the night, it had simply adapted. Even the lower species do that.

I got back into my own rhythm: a reach, a pull through, finish with a light kick. A soft slurring of black water. I was grinding again. The dead child's face was in my head, mixing with the kid on a Philadelphia sidewalk. The FDLE team would have to spend some time up at the scene. But what were their options other than recovery? You couldn't cordon off a river. And despite the overblown tales of forensics, you weren't going to lift prints from the trees.

But I knew they'd pass right by the old stilted research shack I was living in, and while the weathered, hundred-year-old Florida pine construction caused the place to nearly disappear into the cypress forest, I wondered if they would squeeze the location out of Cleve. Would he swing them up through the overgrown channel to my porch? Would they rummage through the place without a warrant like I had done myself not so many years ago as a cop? It was illegal, but when we knew we had a chance to find evidence on some mope and wanted either to find something to convince us or find something to clear him and get him off the list, we did it. It was called efficiency in the face of urgency. Sometimes people, even the innocent, get used.

If they found something that took me off their list it would be a relief, but the idea of Hammonds sorting through my cabin caused me to pick up the tempo and I started driving the canoe hard.

By the time I reached the entrance to the forested section of the river, the first hint of dawn was peeling back the darkness in the eastern sky. But only a dozen or so strokes into the cypress canopy the air went wet and thick and too dark for the uninitiated. The FDLE crew must have started questioning their decision not to wait for daylight the minute they motored up into this blackness. A man can adjust, but can never be natural in such a place. He has genetically bypassed it, developed different sight, hearing and scent. But like someone only partially blind, I could make it back through my neighborhood by reading the unseen landmarks, feeling the current, the swirl of eddies, the familiar pools.

A half mile in I slowed at the pond apple outcrop, felt for the slight shift in water drifting west, and let it lead me. Two column-like cypress trees marked my entryway. A shallow-water entrance took me back fifty yards off the main river to a small dock platform. From there, steps climbed up to my back door. There was no one in sight. Not an unnatural sound save my own.

I looped a line from the dock around the bow seat and climbed out onto the landing. Then I bent to the first step of the staircase and under the glint of dawn looked carefully for a pattern in the moisture. No careless feet. The surface was undisturbed. Shortly after I'd moved in here, a friend suggested I hook up some kind of alarm system. He was convinced I'd be the target for uninvited explorers and bone-headed adventurers who might think that any cabin this remote belonged to anyone who could find it. I thought about it, but after several months of being here, I dismissed the idea. By listening and absorbing every sound, I reasoned, I would hear anyone sloshing and grunting and disturbing the flow of the place.

If I wasn't here, an alarm system wasn't going to stop anyone with an intent to break in anyway. It wasn't your typical neighborhood. Who was going to come running if an alarm went off? And even if someone broke in, there was little inside of value to take.

The cabin had been built at the turn of the century by a rich Palm Beach industrialist who used it as a vacation hunting lodge. It was abandoned in the 1950s and then rediscovered by scientists, who, bent on mapping the patterns of moving water in the Everglades, used it as a research station. When their grants dried up it was abandoned again. When the stock market and the economy tumbled in the oil crisis of the 1970s, the family that held deed to it put it on the market. The friend who set me up in it didn't go into its ownership. He simply arranged to collect $1,000 a month from my investment portfolio, and paid the bill.

I didn't argue the price. In the odd way of the world, the shooting in Philadelphia had left me with both damage and opportunity.

* * *

For ten days after my shooting on Chestnut Street I'd been silent, unable to get words through my swollen throat. Then I faked my inability to speak for another week.

The media stir that buzzed with the deaths of two boys quickly moved on to the next video disaster they could spin up onto the six o'clock news. Officers I worked with or had been friendly with called me to see how I was and to say that the shooting was clean. Once the crime scene and shoot team guys had documented that the first kid's gun had been fired, and Casamir's recollection of the events didn't waver, they quickly closed the investigation.

I still had to sit through the playing of the inside surveillance tape and watch as the second kid leaped out of the store and disappeared from the camera frame. Only I had seen him catch my bullet. Everyone else only looked at the aftermath and called it a justified use of force, a clean shooting. But it was my shooting.

After seeing the obligatory shrinks and counselors and department managers, the most valuable appointment I had was with the human resources wonk who recited my options, which included a large lump sum disability payment if I should decide to quit.

My uncle Keith, a cop along with my father for more than twenty-five years, blew a slow whistling breath through his teeth at the number of zeros in the payout.

I took the check and tried to wash out the memory. In the mornings I ran for hours along the uneven concrete of Front Street in the river breeze off the Delaware. In the afternoons I shot baskets alone at Jefferson Square playground or hung at Frankie O'Hara's gym and took my turns getting pummeled by local fighters. At night I walked, streetlight to streetlight, sometimes looking up to find I'd gone miles without realizing it, having to concentrate on a corner street sign for several seconds to determine where I'd wandered to.

One night I found myself in front of the Thirteenth Street Cleaners, staring at a thimble-sized pockmark in the wall, trying to see my own spattered blood deep in the grimy brick.

The next day I honored my mother's memory and this time used my brain. I contacted a lawyer in West Palm Beach, Florida. His family name had been scratched into my mother's address book decades ago. She and the matriarch of his family had some kind of never-discussed relationship. The lawyer was the woman's son, and my own mother had often urged me to "just meet him. He's a bright boy you could learn from."

I can't remember how he managed to convince me to fly south to see him. Perhaps it was the confidence and pure, simple logic in his voice. It wasn't condescending. It wasn't presumptuous. It wasn't overtly high-minded. He was the one who set me up in the research shack when I told him I wanted someplace isolated and completely different from where I'd come from. He's the one who arranged to use my departmental payout to buy into the ground floor of a new South Florida Internet research site. For the first time in a long time, he became the one person I trusted, and it paid off.

Out on the river I heard the burble of Cleve's outboard, the noise growing louder as he ferried Hammonds and his team back to the boat ramp. They'd have the child's body with them now, still wrapped tight until they got it to some morgue and the forensics guys could go over it.

As they went by less than 150 feet away through the cypress, I heard Cleve slightly rev the engine, letting me know he'd kept my place a secret, for now. But I knew I'd be back in a squad room soon enough, answering more questions. And I also knew I needed to talk to my lawyer before I let that happen.

CHAPTER 4

I was on the interstate, back in the fumes, back in the dull bake of the sun on concrete, back in the aggressive hurry up, back in the world.

I'd spent the morning staring out at the wet forest, watching the sun leak through the canopy and spackle the ferns and pond apple leaves and haircap moss below. I hadn't given nature much thought before coming here. I only studied the nature of humans on the Philadelphia streets, and it wasn't anything out of the sociology department at the University of Pennsylvania. People did things for pretty basic reasons and it has been that way for a lot longer than most of us will admit. We haven't changed much since we first gathered as tribes. Just the stuff around us changed. Hunger and fear, love and jealousy, greed and hate still rule us. You could put that down in the middle of the swamp or at the corner of Broad and Passyunk and it was still going to be the same.

I'd made a pot of black coffee on the wood stove in my shack and then sat at my empty table, sipping. Then I packed up a gym bag with clothes and a shaving kit and paddled back down to the ranger station where I used the phone to call my lawyer. Cleve was nowhere in sight.

"Gone up to headquarters," said his assistant, a young crew-cut kid who always seemed to have a crease in his uniform and a chip on his shoulder. The only time he seemed civil was when he was asking me if he could borrow the pickup truck I left parked in the visitor's lot for days at a time. "Didn't say when he'd be back," the kid said, obviously miffed at being called in to cover. "What the hell happened this morning?"

I looked at him like an adult offended by his demanding tone and his use of profanity, and answered with the same flat voice I always used with him. "I have no idea."

I went to the campsite restrooms where I showered and shaved, and then tossed my bag into my truck and headed south for the Palm Beach County Courthouse. And now I was bunched in with traffic, fighting with the other daily warriors for a moving spot on the highway.

After an hour of working along the middle lanes of I-95 at something approaching the speed limit, I slid onto the Clematis Street exit and crawled through traffic until I found the parking lot I always used when I came to the city. The old guy who worked the lot always recognized my midnight blue F-150 even if it had been two months since I'd been back. He always had a spot for me. I always had a twenty-dollar bill for him.

The temperature here felt ten degrees hotter than the river. As I walked the four blocks to the courthouse I could feel the beads of sweat sliding down the middle of my back. I was dressed in my civilized clothes: khaki trousers, a short-sleeved and unironed white cotton shirt and a pair of beaten Docksides. It was a look I adopted from the boat captains I'd seen in the few restaurants I'd visited, or in some hall of bureaucracy where they gathered for permits or licensing. It might seem shabby by northern standards, but was acceptable almost anywhere in South Florida. It was also the polar opposite of the look on Billy Manchester.

As I crossed the street onto the block that held the new county courthouse, I could see Billy waiting for me in the shade of a newly transplanted, half-matured Washington palm.

Standing with one hand in his pocket and the other cradling a manila envelope, he was looking off in the opposite direction and was, as usual, impeccable. He was dressed in an off-white linen suit that must have been a thousand-dollar Ferragamo and seemed brilliant next to his dark skin. His silk tie was pulled up tight to his freshly shaved throat, and his hair was closely cropped to the shape of his skull. He had one of those sharp-angled, perfect profiles you rarely see outside of the made-up world of television or movies, and at five foot eleven and a trim 160, that's probably where you'd think you'd seen him before.

As I approached I saw two young women in summery suits pass purposely through Billy's line of sight and flash two equally purposeful smiles. He grinned and tipped his head and just as they began to change course toward him, he gracefully turned to me, extended his hand and deflected the ladies without a trace of discourtesy. As the women floated off I wondered how he did it, but not why.

"M-M-Max," he said in greeting. "Y-You are l-l-looking healthy. L-Let's eat."

* * *

Billy Manchester is the most intelligent person I have ever met. And when I first talked to him on the phone I had an immediate intuition that he would not screw me.

After feeling him out a bit and after I explained the Philadelphia street shooting, we talked several times long distance about cop procedures, civil court possibilities, investment and tax laws. I never felt he was pumping me. In fact, it was more like him spilling valuable information to me. Still, I checked him out. Law degree from Temple University. Business degree from Wharton. Published dozens of times in professional law journals. No record of a lecture series.

He had all the credentials for academia, but was never a teacher. He had all the paper for a brilliant trial lawyer, but never tried a case I could find.

I had a friend at the *Philadelphia Daily News* run a clip search for me and found little. As a young man Billy had gained some attention as a kid from the inner city with a bright academic future. There was a piece about him and a prominent North Philadelphia public school chess club winning some prestigious tournament. A clip on his graduation at the top of his class from Temple's law school. No mention of his parents.

How our mothers, a black woman from North Philadelphia and the white South Philly wife of a career cop, came to be friends, neither of us knew. We'd been raised in widely different ethnic neighborhoods. But we seemed to share a similar theory on the disparities in skin color and customs we grew up with: We knew it was there. You dealt with it when you had to. But most of the time, it only got in the way of things that mattered.

After more than a dozen phone conversations, Billy persuaded me to come to Florida.

When he met me at the airport the first time, his *GQ* appearance made me hesitate. Way too slick for the voice, I thought. Then he looked unblinking into my face with his steady brown eyes and issued what I would learn was his standard greeting: "M-Max. Y-You are l-l-looking healthy."

After I got over the disbelief and the quick feeling that I'd somehow been conned, Billy haltingly explained that he was a tension stutterer. Over the phone or even from the other side of a wall, his speech was as straight and flawless as the head of a debate team. But face-to-face conversation was a constant struggle. His stuttering was so profound even the most basic words jammed up behind his tongue. But he was as serious and sincere as I had first judged him to be and he put me up in his beachfront tower apartment for weeks until he found the research shack for me. We made an odd pair: a successful black attorney transplanted to the south and a white Philadelphia cop trying to escape the city. But I learned to depend on his judgment and knowledge, and I figured it was going to serve me now.

As we walked east through the heat rising up from the sun-bright sidewalks down Clematis Street, I explained again to him about the events of the night before. He'd said little when I'd called him earlier. But I knew from the envelope under his arm that he'd been busy. When we reached the corner of Flagler Avenue, Billy steered me to a shaded outdoor table on the patio of La Nuestra Café. I saw a hurried movement from the waiter who had one of those "No, no, no that's reserved" looks on his face until he recognized Billy and then became effusive in his service.

Billy waited until he had a tall iced tea sitting before him and I had a sweating bottle of Rolling Rock in my hand. Then he put the envelope on the table between us.

In his phone conversations Billy was clear and logical and brilliantly straightforward. Face to face the stutter only made him more so.

"M-Max," he said, his eyes narrowing and going the color of black-brushed steel. "You are in s-s-some shit."

* * *

In the envelope was a stack of printouts dated weeks ago that Billy had copied off the computer Web sites of the three largest daily newspapers in South Florida. They lacked the typical, shouting headlines that the actual papers would have displayed, but the simple text was hammer enough.

The body of Melissa Marks, the South Florida kindergartener reported missing last week, was found Monday in a remote area of Broward County's western Everglades.

Investigators said the cause of the six-year-old's death was not yet known, but they believe the girl is the third victim in this summer's string of bizarre abductions and murders of children that have terrified South Florida communities over the past three months.

"We think the same person or persons are responsible for this and the previous atrocities," said spokesman Jim Hardcastle of the Florida Department of Law Enforcement, which has been coordinating a multi-agency task force that includes three county sheriff's offices and the Federal Bureau of Investigation.

"We are continuing a massive investigation into these homicides and are committed to finding those responsible."

Hardcastle declined to give any details of how police were able to locate Marks' body and would only say that it was found in a remote area about thirteen miles west of U.S. 27, which is the unofficial border of the still-wild Everglades and the suburban communities of Broward County.

Marks had been missing from her home in the new development of Sunset Place since last Sunday, when her parents reported to police that the girl had disappeared from their home in the middle of the night. The child had been asleep in her bedroom and was discovered missing by her mother who had awakened to give her daughter medicine for a recent illness.

Despite an almost immediate and widespread search by neighbors and police with helicopters and dogs, no trace of the child was found until Monday's discovery.

The disappearance and death is eerily similar to the two earlier cases in which a seven-year-old boy from the western community of Palmetto Isles and a five-year-old girl from Palm Ridge were abducted in June and July. Their bodies were also found in remote wilderness areas.

Investigators refused to comment on the causes of death and also declined to give details on how they were able to locate those bodies within days after the children were taken.

I shuffled through the printouts, all dating back to the first child abduction. The follow-up stories documented the FBI's involvement, the futile searches for clues, the shattered parents, speculations, and not surprising, fear.

My throat had gone dry and the printout paper felt dusty between my fingers. Billy had purposely left out any reproduction of photographs that I knew would have been published: The smiling elementary school snapshots, the pictures of parents standing bleary-eyed and dazed at funerals, the flower collections and rain-soaked cards and farewells at some public spot.

As I read, the sun crept onto our table and Billy, sitting silent with his legs crossed, waved away the waiter twice. I finally looked up and he met my gaze and without a hint of humor said: "You don't g-get out m-much. Do you?"

The uproar that the killings created hadn't gotten onto my river or through my self-imposed wall against the world. As I stared out at the asphalt street, Billy filled me in on his inside information on the cases that had buzzed through the courthouse and law offices for weeks.

The investigators were keeping the details, especially the cause of death, as close as they could. They also had not revealed how they knew where to look for the bodies they had found. But somehow they'd gotten onto my river and were probably less than a couple of hours from finding the child I'd discovered. Now they had me attached to that killing. It was only good police work to consider me a suspect.

I was staring out across the street again, my fingers lightly touching the scar on my neck. I hated circumstances. A logical world can't stand them, and an overcrowded world can't avoid them.

Had the body floated down into the spot where I found it from some point upriver? The source of the tributary was a broad shallow slough that drained into the cypress swamp and was also fed by a canal opening that helped drain the Glades. Had the body been wedged at that particular spot on purpose? Did someone know about my nightly forays? Did someone know I'd find it?

Over the tops of the buildings a thick stack of thunderheads was creeping out of the western sky, roiling up as they sucked moisture out of the Glades and pushed toward the coast. But the ocean breezes held them back. Here the sun still glinted hot and bright off the chrome on a line of cars that filled the street and then flushed away each time the stoplight changed.

"If you're th-thinking of t-talking to them, don't," Billy said.

I just shook my head. He knew I was thinking like a cop. He knew I would be thinking about Hammonds' team and their struggle with a high-profile case.

He finally waved the waiter over and while it was my turn to hold a response, he ordered a cold penne pasta salad and, looking at me with a slightly raised eyebrow, took my silence as license to double the order for two. Billy knew I was existing on canned meat and fruit and the occasional skillet-fried tarpon from the river. He automatically tried to influence my diet when he had the chance.

His advice not to talk to Hammonds and his team meant he was asking me to hold on to my right to remain silent. It was something I hated when I was a cop, and because of that experience I knew how valuable it was from the other side of the fence.

"They've got to be pulling in every favor and chit they can to get this one off the board," I said. "How the hell do you keep four dead kids off the front page and the brass off your ass?"

I knew the pressure to solve a case like this would be tremendous. They would already have looked hard at family members with the first abduction. That's standard homicide procedure, especially when kids are involved. But according to the newspaper clips Billy pulled, none of the first three families had any connection with each other except that they all lived in new neighborhoods close to the edge of the Glades. Whether there was some hidden link between them that was being held back from the press was a guess. If it was not true, that left only the outsider theories. In between bites we talked about the possibilities.

Billy had been mildly intrigued by the case since the second child was found. Television news was all over it. The press conferences with broken, tearful parents pleading for the return of their children. The reward offers. The inevitable squeeze on the child-molesting suspects. And in this case, the tangible fear among the public. It was just the kind of thing I wanted to know nothing about. But even if I followed Billy's advice and kept my silence, we both knew I was in it now. I was the first person outside the families with a connection, no matter how tenuous. The cops were going to jump on that. The only question was how hard.

After Billy paid and tipped the waiter enough to make his whole lunch shift worthwhile, we walked back to the courthouse through a rising heat I could feel through the soles of my shoes. The asphalt and concrete were like stove burners. The storm curtain had been slowed by the breeze, but its graying face was massing up now as the heat of the city rose up its nose.

"You are p-probably going to g-get a visit soon," Billy said as he reached into a pocket of his suit and slipped out a thin cell phone and extended it to me.

"It's charged up. C-Call me," he said, smiling and serious. "Not next m-month either."

I shook his hand, thanked him, and watched him walk away.

Three blocks later, the sweat was soaking my waistband and my feet actually felt damp. I got to the parking lot and I could see from the way the attendant looked down at his own shoes that something was wrong. When he took my ticket he looked up with a shrug, but with eyes that I swear were beginning to tear.

"I don't know how," he started to say as we walked toward the corner of the lot where I could see my truck parked in a front row. "I didn't see no kids or nothing. I didn't hear nothing either."

I let him lead me around to the driver's side where he stepped back with his palms turned out and issued an audible sigh.

Starting just behind the cab was a deep gouge in the paint about pocket high that ran almost to the middle of the front fender. Someone had used a key or screwdriver. When I bent to touch it, there were still tiny curlicues of midnight-blue paint spiraling off the line. The attendant wouldn't meet my eyes. He just stared at the scratch, trying to wish it away.

I was thinking about a time when I was doing a six-month shift with the metropolitan investigative unit in Philly. The squad of detectives was formed to watch organized crime figures. Once, after spending two days following Phil "The Lobster" Testoro between his South Philly rowhouse and his suite in an Atlantic City hotel, Kevin Morrison, the guy I was partnered up with, got out of our unmarked car and strolled through the parking garage we were in. Checking for witnesses first, he approached Testoro's Lincoln Continental, pulled out his keys and ran a serious sine wave down the length of the Town Car and then coolly returned. I sat without comment for five full minutes before Morrison, without looking at me, said: "Let him know we're watching."

Now I touched the gouge on my truck and scanned the sidewalks and street corners, futilely I knew, for an unmarked car with a couple of bored men in the front seat. Then I shook my head, said "Not your fault" to the attendant and got in the truck, cranked up the air conditioning and headed back to my river.

CHAPTER 5

By the time I pulled into the visitor's parking lot at the ranger station I had a too familiar tightness across my head, a band of pain that strapped from temple to temple and pressed into the bone with a pressure that you tried not to think about because dwelling on it only seemed to screw it down. It's what the traffic did to me. Even at mid-afternoon it had been bumper to bumper and down here the proximity of fenders had no effect on speed. Everything still moved on the interstate at sixty mph. I wasn't comfortable in it. In the streets of inner city Philadelphia, traffic was slowed by constraint. Unless you used the Schuylkill Expressway or shot over the bridges to New Jersey, speed was not an option. Down here I'd learned to use as many alternate routes as I could find when I ventured out, but when I took the interstate I stayed in the middle lanes and tried to fit in with the lemmings. It still gave me a headache.

Cleve was at the boat ramp, looking up at the piled, sooty clouds that were now directly overhead. One good rip of lightning and the whole front would split open and the rain would drop "like pissin' on a flat rock," the old ranger would say. The humid wind from the east was being sucked west, pulling at our pants legs and shirtsleeves but doing little to dry the film of sweat on my back.

"Give me the willies," Cleve said, still looking up at the coming storm but no doubt seeing the tiny wrapped body from this morning. "Wasn't like that boy with the gator."

Cleve had told me the story the first week I'd arrived. An eight-year-old had been canoeing the river with his family and they stopped along one of the drier banks to get out and stretch. The boy decided to cool off in a slightly deeper pool where the water swirled and spun back before continuing downstream. Whether the male alligator had already been in the hole or had been alerted by the movement, no one knew.

The animal got the boy's head in its jaws and pulled the child under, trying to drown its prey. When the boy's father realized what had happened he jumped to his son's aid, clubbing the gator's head and snout with a paddle until the beast let loose. It had taken too long to get the injured child through the wilderness to a spot where a helicopter could airlift him out. He died later at the trauma center.

Cleve had been at the pickup site, tending the boy's head wounds while his family looked on.

"I've seen what nature can do," he said, finally shaking himself from the past to look me in the eye. "But this one wasn't nature and those boys knew it."

He then told me of his trip up the river early that morning with Hammonds and his crime scene team. They'd barely said a word on the way out. Cleve knew how most people reacted to a trip out here, with relaxed conversation and obvious questions. Instead, Hammonds' boys were quiet and preoccupied with a device they kept out of sight in the stern of the Whaler. They only engaged him with queries about access spots, where the headwaters started, the nearest roadways or bridges. And the location of my place and how often he saw me coming and going.

"You couldn't see the channel to your shack, but I couldn't lie," Cleve said, cutting his eyes to gauge my reaction.

"Don't worry about it," I said.

When Cleve got them to the dam, he had to untether the canoe and float it on the upper river. It would only hold three, so Hammonds and one crime scene photographer climbed in with him. The wrapped body was right where I'd told them. The photographer snapped away as Cleve inched them up to the spot. The ranger saw Hammonds check one more time on the gadget he brought from the Whaler before they lifted the child's body out of the tangle of cypress root. The men said nothing on the ride back, and never looked at the black, zippered body bag into which they'd slid the bundle.

"It was damned eerie," Cleve said.

The rest of the team was waiting at the dock when they got in and loaded the body. Before they pulled out, Hammonds told Cleve they might need him again, without elaboration.

"I don't see why," he said, looking up at the heavy clouds and then helping me settle my canoe in the water. "They won't need me to guide them to that spot again now that they got that GPS reading."

* * *

I almost beat the storm back to my shack. I was well under the cypress canopy when the first muffled rumble of thunder tumbled out of the west. The first light wave of rain got caught up in the tops of the trees and I was just lashing the canoe to my dock when fat drops started smacking through the leaves. By the time I got to the top of the stairs the sound had risen to a rush.

Inside I stripped off my wet shirt and tossed my gym bag near the bed. The first time I experienced a South Florida downpour out here it scared the hell out of me. The roar in the trees mixed with the sharp drumming on my tin roof made me cover my ears. After several months I'd gotten used to it.

I rekindled my stove fire, scooped out coffee from a three-pound can, and sat at the table to wait for my old metal pot to boil.

The table had been left behind by the research scientists and was the size of a large door. It had been repeatedly chipped and gouged and there was no telling what they had spilled or stacked or dissected on it. Large swathes of varnish had been worn or corroded away and the wood was dark where fluids unknown had seeped in and stained the fiber. It had been used hard, as had most of the shack's furnishings.

Along one wall there was a set of bunk beds with one good plastic-covered mattress that I'd moved from the top to the bottom. Two mismatched pine armoires stood in a row against another wall and may have been used for clothes or scientific equipment. I used one for my clothes and in the other I stacked a growing collection of books. I'd brought some with me, mostly travel narratives by Paul Theroux and Jonathan Raban, books that I used to climb into to leave the Philadelphia streets for at least a few hours. The rainy night a sergeant caught me in the subway alcove at the Walnut and Locust station reading Theroux's *The Kingdom by the Sea* was yet another small tumble in my career. When Billy found out I was a reader he started adding to my pile with history books on Florida and the Caribbean.

"You have to know where you are to be comfortable in a place," he'd said.

Along the length of a third wall was a row of cupboards and a butcher block countertop with an old pre-electric ice box at one end and a slop sink positioned at the other. I used the counter for food preparation but Cleve speculated that the researchers probably used it to stretch out the southern water snakes, the cottonmouths and pygmy rattlesnakes, for measuring and tagging. I had thanked him very much for his insight, especially after the day three months ago when I almost stepped on a Florida green water snake that had curled up on my doorstep, obviously returning for a refitting.

The only modern concession in the place was the walled-off bathroom in the far corner in which the research crew had installed a marine toilet in deference to the local ecology. It also probably helped the accuracy of their water-sample studies.

As my coffeepot began to rattle with the motion of boiling water, a chirping sound poked through the din of rain. It wasn't until the third ring that I realized it was Billy's cell phone going off in my bag. I dug it out, sat on the edge of the bunk bed and punched it on.

"Yeah?"

"Global Positioning System," he said, his voice smooth and unblinking on the other end. The phenomenon of Billy's come and go stutter always struck me.

"You were reading my mind again, counselor."

"Now that I've got more than just a passing interest in these killings, I pulled some favors. The task force is using GPS readings to find the bodies of the victims," he said, and then launched into a technical description of the directional technology that used satellites to extrapolate coordinates and locate a spot as small as a square foot anywhere on the planet.

Years ago GPS technology got passed from the military out to the civilian world to the great benefit of ocean shipping and sailing navigation. Even on a moving boat you could figure out exactly where you were by using the satellites. Recently the GPS had miniaturized to hand-held size. Mountain climbers and even half-serious hikers and hunters were using them. Cleve had already figured that was what Hammonds used this morning and I'd been grinding it over since pushing off to paddle home.

Billy's info smoothed the stone. Hammonds wasn't marking the spot in order to look for a pattern like I'd thought. He was confirming the coordinates he already had.

"The killer has been leaving them GPS addresses," Billy said over the phone. "That's why Hammonds was already on his way when you hit the boat ramp. If you hadn't found the body, they would have an hour later."

"My luck," I said.

I thought of Hammonds, staring into my eyes at the boat landing, trying to see a flinch of deception. I'd had first contact with the body of the fourth victim of a serial killer. I obviously lived, for reasons he didn't yet know, out on the edge of the Glades, away and apart from society. I was adept with a canoe, one of the few ways, I now knew, to get to the remote places where the previous three dead children had been found.

"Yes. Well, it's also good defense strategy," said my lawyer. "Why would a killer direct the cops right to his own backyard and then tip them before they even got there?"

"So he'd get caught," I said. The line went quiet for several long seconds. "I'll talk to you later, Billy. Thanks."

That night after the rain stopped I lay in bed, picking out the individual sounds of the river, the dripping water off my roof, an isolated slosh of some night prey scuttling away from a hunting owl or water snake. When I first moved in here the silence of the place set up a palpable cone around my city ears. It was like the feeling you get when you pull your car to a stop after a long night trip and shut off the engine and just sit there in stunning quiet. In the city those were infrequent moments. Here they were nearly constant.

A breeze sifted through the trees and into my louvered windows but the rain-soaked air was close and thick. Still, the thin sheen of sweat on my chest and legs picked up any air that moved and did its cool evaporation. I was not uncomfortable, but when I closed my eyes I could see the pale face of the child, milky eyes in the moonlight. The image was crowding out my old nightmare. I reached up and touched the scar at my throat and at some point deep in the night, I fell off to sleep.

* * *

At 10:00 A.M. the next day the race was on along I-95. As I headed south a steady stream of BMWs, Honda Civics, high-colored convertibles and pickups with metal gang boxes rushed past me on the inside lane. The eighteen-wheelers, fuel tankers and step vans boxed me in on the inside. If you weren't doing ten over the speed limit, you were in the way. If you got frustrated and said the hell with it and pushed it to eighty in the passing lane you still weren't immune. Someone doing eighty-five would eventually tailgate you until you moved over. The lesson was simple: be aggressive and pay no attention to the rules. It's how you got there ahead of the schmucks.

Four hours earlier the birds had awakened me. The anhingas and herons were early fishermen. The ibis and egrets fluttered in after daybreak. In the rising sunlight I made more coffee, stood on the staircase looking up through the cypress and decided to go on my own to Hammonds' task force offices. When I called Billy, he tried to talk me out of it with that unerring logic of his, but I knew how jammed the investigators had to be. If I could get them off my scent, maybe they'd save some time and turn some other strategy, some corner. Billy countered in his lawyerly best: "Don't offer."

If you've never been in the system, the old law enforcement saw that says "If you're innocent, what's there to be afraid of?" makes a certain sense. I've used the line myself when interviewing suspects. But the truth is not always simple. I've seen rape convictions, based on the absolute certainty of the woman attacked, overturned by DNA. I've seen death-row inmates who gave confessions end up being cleared with the arrest of another. And I've seen prosecutors jailed for obstruction in cases they had believed in so deeply that they became blinded to the truth.

I'd also seen the floating face of a dead child. If I was a suspect, Hammonds' team would have already pulled my Philadelphia file and at least started tracking my move, my money, my life since the night I shot a boy in the back on a rainy street corner. Maybe they'd already dismissed me. But there had been something in the investigator's face that said no.

As I drove I refused to join the interstate aggression game and hung in the middle lane all the way south into Broward County. It was my habit to keep a wide margin between my front bumper and the trunk in front of me, but down here that's like creating a parking space in a desirable lot. Somebody behind you always wants the space. They'd pass, move in, I'd fall back. I got leapfrogged all the way to Broward Boulevard and took the exit west.

From the off ramp I could see the county sheriff's office rising up like a sandstone and mirror box in the middle of an unusually tidy junk yard. Its six stories dwarfed the run-down collection of strip shopping centers, ancient cinderblock apartment houses and low-rent businesses spread out around it. The new headquarters had been built in the middle of a traditionally black neighborhood. They hoped the new presence would change the area, but all the building had changed was the block it stood on. Back in the 1960s the interstate had speared through the community, splitting what cohesion the neighborhoods had once built. After that the poverty, crime, and apathy of government did its own erosion. The blocks around headquarters had been called "The Danger Zone" by the cops who patrolled the area. It had the highest incidence of burglaries, robberies and homicides in the county. The officers called the roaming neighborhood dogs "zone deer." They called the yellow-eyed drug dealers by name. They called themselves the zookeepers. It reminded me of too many parts of Philadelphia. It took me back home.

I pulled my truck all the way to the back of the parking lot and found an empty spot in the shade of a bottlebrush tree. I made sure the scratched side was facing away from the building and got out in the sparkling heat. It was before noon and already eighty-four degrees. The asphalt was like a burner turned low. In the two minutes it took to walk to the front entrance and get through the double doors I could feel the sweat start in my hair. Inside it quickly evaporated in the envelope of air conditioning.

The lobby was circular with a rotunda-like ceiling soaring all the way to the top. The floor was a dark green faux marble and the stone crawled up the sides of a round reception desk and spread flat on the counter. Even at my six foot three, the desk top came to my chest. The only hint that I wasn't standing in the lobby of a downtown bank was the uniformed officer looking down at me with one of those developed demeanors that says bored and too busy at the same time.

I asked for Hammonds' office and she pushed a clipboard with a sign-in sheet and a plastic visitor's badge at me.

"Fourth floor," she said, pointing at the bank of elevators.

On four I had to use a phone to get a secretary to buzz me through to a reception area lined with beige doors and offices with glass halfway down the walls. It was a far cry from the overwaxed and stale interior of the Philadelphia police headquarters that we had called the roundhouse. But the atmosphere was the same. The furtive glances, the busy work, the "anybody know this guy?" nods. No one up here was in uniform and they all seemed content to let me chill. When Hammonds' secretary asked me to take a seat, I thanked her and paced instead.

From the waiting area I could see into two offices. Behind the glass in one, the guys with ties shuffled back and forth between waist-high cubicles. In the other, an open desk dominated a room lined with file cabinets. Two wood-veneered doors were closed and positioned on the far wall. As I paced, one of the doors opened and the woman detective, Richards, walked out and headed for the desk.

She was dressed in a cream-colored skirt and a long-sleeved, silk-looking blouse that fluttered as she moved. Her blond hair was up in some kind of knot and pulled severely behind her head. She was wearing high heels that made her look even taller than she appeared at the boat ramp. Aerobics, I thought, assessing the tight calf muscles in her long legs. She never looked up as she moved from the desk top to the row of files and the sense of athleticism was obvious. Twice she glided past a paper shredder and wastebasket without moving her eyes from the document she was reading. Once she spun away from the desk and then, without breaking stride, hip checked an open file drawer that banged shut hard enough to rattle the glass. Dancer and hockey player, I thought and then turned to see the secretary watching me.

"Mr. Hammonds is right this way," she said. Whether it was from the embarrassed flush in my face or not, the tight grin on her face said "Caught ya."

Hammonds' office was like the rest of the place, indistinguishable from any other modern business I'd ever been in. His broad desk sat at an angle guarding one corner. Bookcases lined one wall, file cabinets the other. Two cushioned chairs were positioned in front of the desk. When I came in Hammonds remained seated, reading a file for several seconds before carefully closing it and rising to acknowledge me.

"Mr. Freeman. Please, sit down. What can I do for you?"

Again he used the eye contact, but I was the one who flinched this time.

"You've got a tough one," I said. "I wanted to see if there was anything I could do to get out of the way so you could get on with it."

Hammonds kept the lock on my eyes. Always the professional. Never let emotion slip into the language or demeanor.

"Is that right?"

Again we let silence pass between us.

"Look, I used to be a cop in Philadelphia," I said, giving in. "You're working this string of child killings, so I wanted to let you know so you could take me out of the mix and get on with your investigation."

Hammonds still didn't blink, and just as I was second-guessing my decision to come here, there was a light rap at the door and Detective Diaz with the smile walked in. He was followed by Richards.

"You've met the detectives, Mr. Freeman. They have been on this from the beginning. I'd like them to sit in," Hammonds said, leaving out the "if you don't mind."

Diaz stepped in with the collegial handshake. Richards had put on a jacket that matched her skirt. She nodded, crossed her arms and moved behind one of the chairs.

"Mr. Freeman was just offering to help us," Hammonds said, looking back into my face, waiting.

"Look. I was in law enforcement. I know how some of this works," I started. "Call up for my records and you can save some time."

"We know about your record, Mr. Freeman," Hammonds said, putting the tips of his fingers on the file on his desk. "Twelve years and then it looks like you kind of went off the deep end."

I had never read what they'd finally put in my personnel file, how they worded the shooting, how the shrinks had described my mindset after hours of counseling, what they thought of my walking away from a job that was in my blood and had long been in my family.

"Yeah, a little," I finally said, looking down for the first time. All three of them moved almost imperceptibly closer.

"Should we get a recorder in here, Mr. Freeman?" the woman asked.

I looked up into Hammonds' face. His cheeks seemed hollow. Puffy bags sagged under dark eyes that held no emotion.

"This was not a good idea," I said and rose to my feet and started out. No one tried to stop me. I was pulling open the door when Hammonds spoke:

"What's it feel like to kill a child, Mr. Freeman?"

I left the door standing open and walked away, giving all three of them my back.

* * *

When I passed through the front doors the heat felt like a fog wrapping around my face and arms and clogging my nose. The air conditioning had set me shivering. Back outside the afternoon bake started me sweating again. I was halfway across the parking lot when I heard my name.

"Mr. Freeman. Mr. Freeman. Wait. Please!"

Diaz was nearly skipping to catch up. I turned to acknowledge him but kept moving toward my truck. He came alongside and blew out a quick breath.

"You gotta excuse Hammonds. He's wired a little tight these days," the young detective said, sticking his fingers down in his pockets despite the heat.

"I'll give him that," I said, unlocking my truck door.

"These murders got everybody on edge. The bosses, the

politicians, the civilians. The feds are pushing and threatening to take over if we don't show something soon. Everybody wants the killer and Hammonds is the one that has to keep saying we haven't even got a good suspect."

"And he still hasn't," I said, opening the door.

"Hey, I made some checks up north myself. No one said you went signal twenty after that shooting with the kids."

"Is that right?"

Diaz was looking at the long jagged scratch running through the paint on my truck and shaking his head.

"But no one knew you'd come down here either. They just said you took a payout and disappeared."

"Yeah, well, that was the idea," I said, closing my door and starting the engine. Diaz stepped back as I pulled out of the space, his hands still in his pockets.

I was cursing under my breath as I pulled out into traffic. Always listen to your lawyer. Especially if he's your friend. I'd done myself no good here. But at least I knew where I stood. They were desperate and had me on the target board and it was going to take a lot more than a Mr. Nice Guy smile to get me off it.

When I pulled up behind a line of cars on the ramp to the interstate the traffic was as insistent as it had been at ten o'clock and would be at five and at eight tonight. There were no lazy Southern afternoons here.

As my line lurched again with the cycle of the light, I caught sight of a newspaper hawker working his way down the row.

"Slain Palm Beach Child No. 4" read the headline. When the guy got close I rolled down the window. He looked in and I saw that he had a fat face that folded in on itself and a spit-soaked cigar planted in the side of his mouth. I did a double take and then handed him a dollar. He passed the paper in and when he started to dig for change I waved him off.

I held the paper against the steering wheel and read the secondary headline.

POLICE LINK KILLING OF GLADESIDE KINDERGARTENER TO MOONLIGHT MURDERER

VISITATION SERVICE FOR ALISSA GAINEY SET FOR TODAY

I scanned the front-page story, shuffled to the page inside where it continued, and found mention of the funeral home where the girl's visitation was being held. The blast of a horn snapped my head up. The line was moving. I swung onto the northbound ramp, squeezed my way onto the interstate and settled into the middle lane, staring into the line of cars in front of me.

In Philadelphia I had still been in the hospital when they buried the twelve-year-old I shot. I'd read the follow-up stories in the *Daily News* that identified him as a sixth grader in the North Philadelphia neighborhood near Temple University, that his family was churchgoing, that a collection was being taken up. I'd asked the nurse to get me an envelope and while she was gone I'd climbed out of bed, retrieved my wallet and emptied it. Later I scratched the name of the church on the envelope and wrapped the money inside with a piece of paper with the name of the fund on it. Another shift nurse promised she'd get it mailed. Despite being raised in my mother's Catholic home I am not a prayerful man. But I prayed for Lavernious Coleman. And I prayed that no nosy reporter would find out about the donation. And I prayed a little bit for myself.

When I got to Forest Hills Boulevard, I got off at the exit and headed west. After four or five miles, I started looking for the approximate numbers on the neat new shopping complexes and the low, discrete business marquees. They were trying to avoid creating another neon trash alley like those that plagued so much of South Florida's sprawl. Maybe it was neater, in a gameboard kind of way, but it somehow made me nervous.

I found Chapel Avenue and followed a curving two-lane avenue with a grass-and-palm-lined divider until I saw the inevitable white Doric columns. The architectural necessity of that classic touch on funeral homes was lost on me. Maybe it had something to do with the pearly gates, a hopeful hint for those left behind. The street was lined with sedans and SUVs. An attendant was directing the overflow to a parking area behind the building. I turned into a lot across the street, backed into a spot and left the engine and air conditioner running.

There was a television news truck parked a block down. Its telescoping antenna had not been raised, but I could see that the van's side door was open and at least one reporter and her crew were working the sidewalk. I watched them stop a couple in their thirties with a small child in tow and ask, I assumed, about the little girl who now lay inside surrounded by flowers and grief.

I picked up the newspaper and read about the child I'd found on the river.

According to the news account, Alissa Gainey, like the others, had been taken after dark—this time from the enclosed pool area of her home where her parents had set up a lighted play area. " 'She had her little plastic kitchen out there, her table and dolls. She spent hours out there, just playing,' said a tearful Deborah Gainey. 'She was already in her pajamas. Her little blanket was gone. She never put it down. Oh God, she's gone.' "

The story said the mother had been just inside the sliding-glass doors, writing out household bills. She hadn't heard a sound. The doors to the screened patio had been locked. The killer had neatly sliced through the thin screening with a razor or sharp knife. The mother had discovered Alissa missing when she went to call her in for the night.

"The Gaineys' Gladeside home is in a newly built community of single-family homes that was completed two years ago. The location, a mile from the official berm area that acts as a buffer to the Everglades, is similar to those neighborhoods where the previous child abductions have taken place."

Beside the age of the victims, their homes in the suburbs seemed the only other common trait in the cases so far. It didn't narrow things down much.

I was new to Florida but I knew enough about the modern-day range wars. Despite its growing poplation, everyone from the big builders to the workaday carpenters to the little guy waiting to open his dream bagel shop looked out on those acres and acres of open sawgrass and said: "Just a little more. What's the big deal?"

It had been going on like that for a hundred years and the environmentalists had fought it for a hundred years. The developers had ruthlessly bid and outbid each other for open land as they pushed out into the Everglades. The landowners either refused to sell on principle or milked the demand for the highest price they could get. And the home builders had to sell every unit to make a profit over the costs. There was plenty of money involved. Tons.

I looked up from the paper and the flow of couples, dressed in dark and respectable suits, was increasing in and out of the funeral home's double doors. I watched as the news crew approached a middle-aged man whose face flushed with anger as he pointed his finger into the face of the young woman reporter and backed her off the sidewalk. A uniformed officer seemed to appear from nowhere and slip between them. The reporter was whining, the mourner moved on.

I turned back to my paper and stared at the inside photograph of Alissa, a blond, thin-limbed child, posing for a school picture in a cornflower-blue dress, her hair in braided pigtails. She had been a quiet, intelligent and friendly student, according to a quote from her kindergarten teacher. The story said she was an only child.

I thought about Mrs. Gainey's mention of her daughter's blanket and wondered if it had been wrapped inside the canvas package I'd found her in. Had the killer taken anything personal with the other children, a sick keepsake, a memento of conquest? Or was it all business with him? I thought about the news printouts that Billy had given me at the restaurant. The quiet stealth was incredibly risky. I'd worked child abductions from playgrounds, busy department stores and parking lots, but never from a home, unless it was parent related.

A sudden sharp rapping on my window scared the hell out of me. The newspaper snapped in my hands, tearing the middle section. Standing outside was a cop, dressed in the same city uniform as the one that had stepped in between the reporter and the irate mourner. I rolled down the window.

"Afternoon, sir," the officer said. "You here for the viewing?"

"Uh, yeah. Uh, I mean, no, not really," I muttered. The question had caught me off guard. I really didn't know why I was here.

The cop was young, probably a rookie working the visitation to keep the nosy public moving. He took several seconds to sweep the inside of the truck, look at my clothes and then stare at my face with enough concentration to run the likeness through his head.

"I, uh, was going to go in and pay my respects, but, you know, I didn't feel right," I stammered.

"OK. Well, you're going to have to move on," the officer said.

I nodded, tossed the newspaper into the passenger seat and put the truck in gear. The young officer stood back, taking in the look of the truck, the scar down the side. As I pulled away, I knew he was taking down my license tag number.

CHAPTER 6

I was back at the ranger station by mid-afternoon and the sun was burning a dull white through a high cover of cloud. The river glowed a flat pewter color and lay unruffled off the boat ramp. Cleve's young assistant was on duty but made no effort to come out and speak as I flipped my canoe upright and loaded my bags in. He was probably pissed that I hadn't filled him in on the discovery of the body when I'd seen him two days ago. He was a kid. He'd get over it.

I stepped into the boat, pushed out onto the windless river and set to stroking, fixing on the tall bald cypress that marked my first turn to the west. The water was empty. Tomorrow was the weekend and would bring a handful of boaters and a few kayakers who would follow the river past my shack. But today it was mine. Without a wind to fight, I stayed in the middle of the channel moving easily against a soft outgoing tidal current. The only sound was the low gulp and slice of my stroke. In the top of a dead cypress an osprey stood on the edge of his stick nest and surveyed the water with yellow eyes. An osprey is a raptor that fishes the coastal estuaries with a quiet efficiency, plucking its prey out of the water with needle-sharp talons. When I first saw one I mistook it for an eagle, but Cleve corrected me and pointed out the difference in color and wing shape and size. He added that the great national symbol was no match for the smaller osprey.

"I've seen them drive a bald eagle out of the sky if they thought it was threatening their nest. An eagle is a scavenger. He'll take an easy dead meal any day. But an osprey's a true hunter."

The bird watched me pass as I left a slow spreading wake that would quickly clear and leave his market for fishing undisturbed.

When I reached my small platform dock the light was leaking out of the trees and canopy. The cloud cover had broken up in the west, and the falling sun was shooting red-tinged beams through the few remaining cirrus strings. Before going in I stripped off my clothes and took a rain barrel shower on the porch. The research crew, or maybe even the rich hunting-camp owners, had rigged an oak barrel just below the roof line and fed the gutter system into it so there was always fresh rainwater. A hose with a nozzle was fitted into the bottom of the barrel, and gravity fed the water when the hose was unclamped. It was no match for the showers at the ranger station, but it washed away a layer of sweat and took an edge off the humidity.

Inside I started a fresh pot of coffee and then pulled on an old T-shirt and a pair of shorts. I poured a cup and then sat in my straight-backed chair at the oversized oak table. The light inside had turned a honey color, and I took a long sip of coffee and watched the rippling pattern of weak sun on the far wall.

It was a single, less than rustic room and as I sat in the wooden chair with my heels up on the table, I could tell something was wrong in it.

* * *

I had spent a lot of time in this place, most of it in silence, much of it in this chair. A single small room can be memorized by a man who sits and feels it hour after hour, month after month. And such a memory can easily be alerted by the presence of someone else.

Good forensics cops say no one can come into a room and not change it. Dust comes in a person's wake. A man's weight depresses something. The bacteria of his bad breath, the pheromones of his natural skin oils drift in the air. Something had changed here.

I tilted my head back and stared at the louvered cupola at the very top of my arched ceiling. It was the Old Florida design that let hot air rise and escape and I imagined seeing altered air actually collecting up there. A shaft of light was now pouring through my western window. In its beam I could see floating dust particles. I followed their drift to the floor and there, on the pinewood slats, was a thinly visible footprint in the glow of sunlight.

I looked foolishly around as if someone might be behind me and then lowered myself out of the chair and moved to the print on my hands and knees. There were no tread markings, no boot pattern. The print was flat like something a slipper or moccasin might make. I had come in barefoot from the shower. When I put my own naked foot next to the print, I guessed the size at a 9 or 10. Out of the patch of light no others were visible.

I got up and started searching in the corner where the print was pointing and began going over every inch of the room, from floor to as high as I could reach or climb, in every corner, drawer, cupboard and container. Someone had been here and either taken something or left something behind.

After forty-five minutes of searching I found it. On the back edge of the top bunk mattress, my intruder had made a razor cut. Probing inside I felt a hard plastic box the size of a large cell phone. When I pulled it out, I had a GPS unit in my hand.

"Son of a bitch," I said aloud, placing the unit on the table and sitting down to stare at it.

Outside early night sounds were starting. I could hear the herons and egrets squawking as they settled into the trees to roost. The leopard and pig frogs were beginning their low grunting.

The cops or the killer? I thought. Somebody planted it and I was being set up.

By now the room was going dusky. I got up, lit the kerosene lamp and retrieved Billy's cell phone from my gym bag. It didn't matter who made the plant, a team with a warrant would have to be on its way. I couldn't be here when they arrived. And neither could the GPS. I looked at the piece of incriminating technology, and then made a call. The other end was answered on the third ring.

"Station twelve, Ranger Stanton speaking, may I help you?"

The kid was still there. It took me a second to remember his first name.

"Hey, Mike, this is Max Freeman out at the research shack."

"Yeah?" he said flatly, probably adjusting the chip on his shoulder.

"Look, I need a favor, Mike."

"Yeah, well, I'm just packing up, Mr. Freeman. My shift is already done."

"Right," I said, trying to put an unrushed tone to my voice. "But I was thinking that since I wasn't planning on using my truck for a couple of days you might like to use it for the weekend, you know, since its just sitting there."

"Yeah?"

I had definitely lifted the kid's spirits and used the right bait.

"Sure. But I need a favor. Cleve said you're pretty good with cars and I thought you might help me out with that scratch on the driver's side."

"Man, I seen that, Mr. Freeman. That's a sin, man. Hey, I got a buddy who can compound that right out. You know, I can take care of that easy," he said with true enthusiasm.

My hook was set.

"Great. Why don't you take it home with you now. Cleve has a key in his desk drawer. It's the one with the yellow Pep Boys tag on it."

Right there under his nose all the time. But the kid's joy seemed unaffected.

"OK. Got it, Mr. Freeman. When do you need it back?"

"How about Monday or Tuesday?"

"I got a Tuesday morning shift," he answered.

"Sounds good."

The kid thanked me again and I punched the off button and knew that, one, the law hadn't gotten to the boat ramp yet. And two, the kid would be revving that V-8 and be out of there in record time.

Next I dialed Billy's private number and he clicked in before the second ring.

"Yes."

"Hey, Billy."

"Max? It's unlike you to call when the sun is down."

"I need to see you."

"OK. Shall I meet you at the ranger station?"

Billy could sense my urgency and was instantly turning up his efficiency.

"No. I need you to pick me up at the southern access park, the one along Seminole Drive."

"All right."

"It's going to take me an hour to paddle up there."

"Anything you want to tell me now?"

"No. I'll see you there."

I turned off the phone and stuck it into my bag. I knew I was being paranoid, but I wasn't going to discuss the GPS unit over the phone. I'd spent very little time with the electronic surveillance guys in Philly but the stories that got passed around about cell-phone intercepts were legion.

I quickly dressed in a pair of thin canvas pants and a dark long-sleeved shirt. I stuffed some other clothes into my travel bag and put on my black, soft-soled Reeboks. I then pulled out a plastic Ziploc bag that I used for storing salt and sugar. I put the GPS unit inside, sealed it, and then wrapped it tight in a piece of dark oilcloth I used to keep things dry in the canoe. If I met anyone along the way and had to dump the unit in the river, it might stay until I could come back for it later.

Before walking out the door I slathered some insect repellant on my face, neck and wrists and put out the lamp. My night ritual began again.

I headed upriver, slow at first, breathing in the thick smell of marsh and wet cypress. It was dark and this time the waxing moon was shrouded in high cloud. But even in that uneven light I could follow the water trail south into the current. Within a few minutes my eyes adjusted and I could pick out the edges of the root tangle and tree boughs. I'd been this route so many times I could almost time the upcoming curves and turns around the cypress knees and fallen logs. Still, I kept glancing behind me, expecting to see the beams from spotlights swinging through the vegetation in search of my shack.

I'd tucked the wrapped GPS under my seat so I could get to it quickly and wedge it into a root hole if I had to. Maybe they'd wait until morning. Hammonds and his crew had already had a taste of the night out here. The word would have gotten around. Serving a warrant in unfamiliar territory is full of the same unpleasant possibilities whether you're in a place like this or in some dark tenement house in the city. You don't know what's coming around the corners. You don't know what kind of reaction you're going to get from someone when you tell them you're the man, and all their rights to be secure and private in their own home have just been flushed. I didn't like doing it myself as a cop and I didn't like the idea of it being done to me now.

I picked up the sound of the water spilling over the dam ten minutes before I got there. The current strengthened and I had to drive the bow in to get around the eddies to the concrete abutment. I yanked the canoe up and onto the upper river and started again.

As I passed the spot where I'd found the dead child, the moon broke through a gap in the clouds and raised the light. Somewhere in the canopy a barred owl let out its double set of notes.

Hoo. Hoo.

It was the first time I'd heard that species on the river. Who indeed, I thought.

* * *

When I reached the access park, Billy was waiting, sitting in his car along the entrance road with his engine and lights off. The park was deserted at this hour. The place is used almost exclusively by canoeists and kayakers, and calling it a park is giving it too much glory. There is a single canoe concession that rents boats and paddles. The owner is a tobacco-spitting transplant from Georgia who is long gone by 5:00 P.M. when all his rentals are due back in. A single bare bulb glowed over his makeshift office and I pulled my canoe up into the pool of light knowing that tomorrow he'd recognize it and keep it safe until I returned.

Billy didn't see me until I walked into the light, and then he came over to help me with my bags.

"Will handling evidence get you in trouble?" I asked, holding out the GPS bundle.

"Only if w-we go to c-court. And if this is w-what I think it is, w-we better not go to court."

As we drove east to the ocean I filled Billy in on my discovery of the footprint and the unit. We were both thinking, "Setup." But who? The cops or the killer? We ground out the possibilities.

Hammonds' crew was under tremendous pressure to find a suspect. But no matter how I rolled it, I couldn't see them getting desperate enough to plant the GPS. The feds could be jumping the gun to try and snatch credit away from the locals, but why not just let Hammonds fall flat on his own? Either could have gotten a GPS unit easily enough. And they pretty much knew the location of the shack from Cleve. But how do they get out there and slip in and leave the thing without being seen or without leaving a trace? Cops are not the most subtle actors on their feet, I knew from experience. They also don't like to muck up the chance of making a clean case against a suspect that they still have on the hook. And when you put my discovery of the body, the psych report from Philly and my canoe access to the wilderness Glades together, they already had a pretty good barb in me.

On the other hand, if the killer planted it, he was taking a hell of a chance.

He could easily know the water. Might even have known the shack. He could have come in from the west out of the Everglades, but he would have had to be watching to see me leave. So why hadn't he called in an anonymous tip right away?

If he'd planted it after I left this morning, he could have called Hammonds' group and they could have escorted me back from their offices themselves.

"W-Warrants are hard to g-get signed on a Friday," Billy said, working the puzzle with me. "Even f-federal warrants. But they c-c-could be there now."

As we drove over I-95 on the Atlantic Boulevard overpass I caught a glimpse of the moon opening up over the ocean through the clouds. If the killer had put the cops on to me, he would have been there too, watching from somewhere in the forest, waiting, like a good hunter, to see his trap sprung. Was he still there? Or would he have followed me out? Was he following now? As Billy pulled onto A1A and headed south to his oceanfront apartment building, I cussed myself for being paranoid but looked back at the traffic behind us as we pulled into the entrance of the Atlantic Towers.

CHAPTER 7

I had spent two weeks in Billy's penthouse apartment when I first moved to Florida. But a place like this never fails to amaze.

The elevator stopped at the twelfth and highest floor and opened onto an alcove that was all his own. A handsome set of double oak doors stood at one end. Billy snapped down the European brass handles and pushed the doors wide to swing my bags through. He punched a single button on a wall panel and the huge, fan-shaped living area glowed in subdued recessed lighting. The thick carpet and textured walls were done in subtle shades of deep greens and blues. The wide leather couches and chairs were dark but offset with some kind of blond wood tables that kept the place from feeling heavy. Sculptures in onyx stone and brushed stainless steel glowed in the indirect light and several paintings adorned the walls. On the south wall was my favorite, an oil by the seventeenth-century Flemish painter Hieronymous Bosch called *The Wanderer*, which I had pondered for hours during my first stay.

But the dominant feature of the place was the bank of floor-to-ceiling glass doors that spanned the east wall and opened onto the ocean. Billy opened the center panels knowing I couldn't resist. I stepped out onto the patio and into a salt-tinged sea breeze that poured into my nose and made me feel young. The ocean was black. In the distance I could pick out points of light from freighters or maybe night fishermen. Even in darkness you could feel the expanse. For someone who'd lived his whole life in the boxed-in, high-walled grid of the city, this was a foreign land. Billy had told me when he first moved to South Florida and began making "real money," he'd determined that he would never live on the ground floor again. He had done too much time on the cracked sidewalks and asphalt streets of Philadelphia. Once he'd made it out, he craved vistas above the shadows. I understood, but it still felt too high to me, too exposed.

Billy let me stand quiet at the railing for several minutes before calling out "Drink?" from his kitchen.

I grinned, knowing he was already pouring my favorite Boodles gin over ice. When I came back inside he had the drink and the oilcloth package sitting on the wide kitchen bar counter. I took a seat on a stool and a sip from the glass.

"Y-Your m-move," he said, taking a drink of chardonnay from a crystal wineglass.

I unwrapped the GPS unit and now it was Billy's turn to show his own anxious excitement.

"M-May I?" he said, extending his palms and when I nodded, he scooped up the unit and headed through an open door on the west wall that led to his home office. Inside I knew he had an array of computers and modems and a wall of law and research books. I stayed at the kitchen counter, drinking gin and watching *The Wanderer* while he tinkered. Outside I could hear the rhythmic wash of ocean waves, inside the irregular tapping of computer keystrokes.

"You're right about the setup. You can call up the previous settings logged into the unit," Billy called out through the door of the office. "There are four. And I called up a geological survey map from a Web site and the last one matches your spot on the river. The others are out in the Everglades and could easily be where the other bodies were found."

Billy was talking from the other side of the wall. The physical barrier had removed his stutter.

"If the investigators found this in your place, it would have been some heavy evidence. They would have had no choice but to stick you in jail."

"No doubt the killer knew that too," I said, loud enough for him to hear.

"We're not dealing with some backwoods hick or pissed off frontiersman trying to fight off the new settlers. This guy's got a plan," he answered.

Billy's use of the word "we're" meant he'd stepped over the line from sitting back and denying my involvement to actively pursuing a theory on who and why someone was killing children along the edge of the Everglades.

As I sipped my drink at the counter, he told me how he'd contacted friends in the medical examiner's office who must have owed him big time. He'd learned how the children had been killed.

The first victim had been poisoned and the toxin was analyzed and found to be rattlesnake venom. According to Billy's source, the stuff had been pumped into the kid through two puncture wounds in the child's leg. The wounds had looked remarkably like an actual bite. But the M.E. still wasn't sure whether the killer had let a real snake bite the child or had faked it and administered the dose himself. It could have been either way.

In the early 1900s, Billy explained, Florida was home to more rattlesnakes than any other state in the nation. As late as the 1940s professional snake men cleared them off newly purchased land. Charging by the head, they frequently poured gasoline down the gopher holes where the snakes nested and then snatched them up when they fled the fumes. A small industry had grown up around the sale of the snake skins like so many of the pelt and plumage trades that once thrived in Florida. And in more recent years, a small medical industry had found a niche in milking the rattlesnake venom to use for creating antitoxins. It was not a difficult procedure if you had the know-how and the guts to perform it.

The second child, according to Billy's man, died of a single slash across the throat. The cut was created by a thick, three-inch-long claw that forensics experts identified as coming from a large wildcat, possibly a Florida panther. The claw, shiny and yellowed, had been found wrapped up with the body. A body, Billy said, wrapped in the same way I had described the child on the river last night. The Florida panther had long been on the endangered species list, hunted by the early settlers and then penned in by shrinking open territory.

The third child had been drowned, but when the medical examiners studied the water left in the lungs they found an impossibly large concentration of chemical fertilizer, a pollution level far higher than any river or canal or lake sample in the region.

"This guy is definitely sending messages," Billy said.

"So why try to put it on me?" I said.

"Who knows? Maybe Hammonds' team was getting too close. Maybe it got too hot. The guy is obviously familiar with the Glades. Maybe he knew about you living out there and snatched an opportunity."

"I don't think Hammonds is close at all."

There was a silence from the other room. I didn't want to admit to Billy that I'd gone against his advice and been to Hammonds' office. I changed the subject.

"So you start killing kids with a half-assed attempt to make at least the cause of death look natural, but then you leave messages all over the damn Everglades so the cops can find exactly what you did and where. Why? Just to scare the hell out of everybody?"

A few years ago I'd read about a series of tourist attacks in Miami and at a rest stop in northern Florida. It hit the tourism industry pretty hard at first, but now it had become an old memory, and not even that for the hordes of new visitors.

"The real estate people are already freaking out," Billy answered. The sound of keystrokes continued in the other room. "There are at least a dozen new developments under construction out along the Glades border and the publicity is killing sales. You're talking about losing millions of dollars if they dried up, not to mention the construction industry jobs that would go down the drain."

"So somebody that's pissed off at carpenters and land developers starts killing kids? Come on," I said.

"Development has been the lifeblood of the South Florida economy for a hundred years. When the beach communities started filling up, it pushed west into the wetlands. They drained the Glades with canals and changed the entire lay of the natural land," Billy said. "The Seminole Indians hated it. The environmentalists fought it. But it's still going on."

"The Audubon Society turns to serial killing?" I said, my voice loaded with cynicism.

"There are wackos in every group. You know that."

I remembered the West Philadelphia neighborhood where John Africa's so-called back-to-nature group MOVE barricaded themselves in an inner city compound and railed against the authorities for crimes against the people. Back to nature in the middle of one of the biggest and oldest cities in the country. Make sense of that.

With bullhorns, the group's members had begun bellowing at passersby about their right to freedom and the destruction everyone around them was wreaking on the planet. In their naturalist mode, MOVE didn't believe in garbage pickup, or the modernity of basic hygiene. Their compound began to stink. Neighbors complained. The health department issued orders, which MOVE ignored. More neighbors complained, soon about children living in filth, unkempt and possibly in danger. MOVE refused to let anyone on the property. They barricaded the place. They were armed.

My father was working twelve-hour shifts outside the West Philly home and told us at breakfast that the frustration was growing thick as a fog around the place. Finally, the police tried to make an arrest. Gunshots were exchanged. Next thing we knew the mayor cleared a plan to drop a bomb on MOVE's bunker. Years later we heard that the demolition expert put three separate charges together, each strong enough to do the job. Someone put all three in one bag and let the package go from a helicopter. We saw the whole damned block go up in flames. Eleven people were killed, including four children. Sixty-one homes were destroyed.

Yeah, I knew there could be wackos all right, on both sides.

Billy came out of the office and laid the GPS unit and a printout of a topographical survey on the countertop. I flattened out the map while he filled both of our glasses. He had marked three red Xs on the longitude and latitude intersects. I recognized the shape of my river and the spot above the old dam. The other Xs were in similar territory, remote, out on wilderness land far from any road or trail.

While Billy pulled his typical kitchen magic in putting together dinner, I walked back out to the patio and stood looking at black ocean, listening to the shushing of waves below and thinking of children lying dead in the moonlight.

CHAPTER 8

The next morning I jolted awake. The mattress was too soft. The air too cold. I didn't know where the hell I was.

I propped myself up on my elbows, focusing on the off-white wall in front of me until I recognized Billy's guest bedroom. After eating Billy's superb Spanish omelets last night, we'd stayed up drinking on the patio, staring out at an invisible horizon and hashing out scenarios. Billy answered my ignorant questions about the Everglades, and admitted he was far from expert. But he knew people, Billy always knew people, that he could introduce me to. Some were guides, he said, men who knew their way in and out of the rivers and wetlands and isolated hammocks. They also knew a lot of the people who lived out on the edge of civilization, the recluses and the ones who had moved away from society.

I turned my head to look at him when he said recluses. In a way, he knew he was describing me.

"I w-will arrange a meeting," he'd said, tipping his glass. "G-Good night."

Now I was feeling the aftereffects of gin and air conditioning. My head was full of cotton and my throat was as dry as parchment. I dressed, went into the kitchen and downed three aspirin with a glass of water. Billy had left a note next to a bowl of sliced fruit on the counter. He'd gone to his office and would call at noon. A fresh pot of coffee was waiting and I poured a cup and went out on the patio. In the early sun the ocean stretched out like the sky itself. From this high up the horizon gave the illusion that you could actually see the curve of the earth. An easterly breeze put a corduroy pattern on the ocean's surface and about halfway out to the horizon the water turned a deeper, oddly tinged shade of blue. The wind had been blowing from the east for two days and the Gulf Stream had shifted closer to shore. The Stream was a huge river of warm ocean water that began as a loop current in the Gulf of Mexico and then funneled up between the tip of Florida and Cuba. At a steady three knots, the vast stream pushed northward along the coast of the United States, its flow so enormous that its water would eventually mix with the North Atlantic and reach the British Isles.

The edge of the Stream was always shifting, and when the wind blew east, it slid closer to the Florida coast. Boatmen here could tell when they crossed into it by the color of the water, a deep, translucent blue unlike any other color on the planet. Scientists say that the water of the Stream is so clear that it affords three times the visibility of the water in a typical hotel swimming pool, and since its depth ranges to some six hundred feet, it is like looking into a blue outer space.

Billy had taken me sailing on his thirty-five-foot Morgan during my first few days here and when he knifed the boat into the Stream, I stared at that color in disbelief. It had an unreal way of drawing you deep into a place where you forgot your surroundings, your petty material anchors and your constant grindings. For an hour I lay on the bow deck, staring into its depths. I was sure that if I reached over and scooped it up I would have a handful of blue in my palms.

After my third cup of coffee I pulled myself away from the patio, laced up a pair of running shoes and took the elevator down. The doorman in the lobby greeted me by name:

"Nice to see you again, Mr. Freeman. Enjoy your run."

I skirted the oceanfront pool and slogged through the sand to the high tide mark. I stretched out on the hard pack and then did three miles. The first cleared my head, the second leeched the gin from my pores and the third killed me. I finished back in front of Billy's tower, took my shoes and sweat-soaked shirt off and waded into the surf. There I lay back and closed my eyes in the sun and let the warm waves wash over me for twenty minutes before heading back up. An attendant at the pool handed me a towel. The doorman in the lobby handed me a sealed manila envelope.

"Just arrived for you, Mr. Freeman."

I turned the package in my hands. Large enough for a subpoena. But it held no markings.

"From Mr. Manchester?" I asked.

"No, sir. It arrived by courier, sir."

In the elevator I punched in Billy's code and then ripped open the envelope. I shook the contents out into my hand. Slightly bent at the corners, where the rivets had been popped, was the aluminum logo tag from a Voyager canoe. I recognized the stamped serial numbers as my own. The tag had been pried from the bow of my boat. I held the rectangle of metal by its edges and spun it. No markings. No message. A bell rang when the elevator reached the penthouse. I stepped out and stood shivering in the air conditioning.

* * *

I shaved, showered, and was working on a new pot of coffee when Billy called me past noon. Last night I'd been insistent about learning more about the areas where the other children had been found. Billy was calling to give me the name of a pilot in Broward County who was an Everglades guide and gave fly-over tours of the wetlands. He would also know most of the other guides as well as the hunters and fishermen who spent serious time there.

"His name is Fred Gunther and don't be put off if he's a little tight," Billy said. "These killings have a lot of people spooked. I get a feeling even the guides are looking over their shoulders."

He gave me the address of a hangar at a small private airport.

"Use my other car in the parking garage. The keys are in my desk."

I didn't tell him about the canoe tag. I'd dropped it back in the envelope and tucked it in a bag along with the GPS unit, knowing I was stockpiling evidence that was either going to save me, or put me on a deep shit list with Mr. Hammonds. I had already brought Billy into it by showing him the GPS. I was getting a cop's prickly feeling on the back of my neck and between my shoulder blades. I wasn't going to bring my friend in any further. An hour later I was on the interstate in Billy's Jeep Grand Cherokee, watching the rearview mirror as much as the traffic in front of me.

I followed Billy's directions off I-95 and west on Cypress Boulevard. There were no cypress trees anywhere near the roadway. Instead it was lined with strip malls packed with places like Lynn's Designer Nails, E-Z Liquors and Chang's Szechuan Chinese. On the corners stood self-serve gas stations where a single clerk took cash through a drawer from the one out of four customers who didn't pay with a credit card at the pump.

Farther west the commercial zones were broken by twenty-five-year-old housing developments. Small block homes stood row upon row with patches of green lawn separated by chain link or the occasional wood fence. Trade the palm trees for maples and the white roof tiles for shingles and it could be Lindenwold, New Jersey.

When I got onto the airport's Perimeter Road, I looked for number thirty-six, Avics Aviation. Halfway around I found the sign on a gun-metal gray hangar and pulled into a spot at the side where I could see several small planes parked on the cracked tarmac. Bent under the wing of a single-prop Cessna was a big man dressed in loose khaki trousers and a white polo shirt. He was rummaging through a side baggage compartment. I watched him for a few minutes as he moved easily about the plane, ducking under struts and checking various spots on the exterior.

I got out of the Jeep, walked through a curtain of midday heat and called out "Hello" over the mechanical pitch of a plane moving to taxi out toward the runway. I yelled my greeting again and the big man snapped his head up, missing a nearby strut and then sliding smoothly under the wing before standing full up to face me. He was not a clumsy man.

"I'm looking for Fred Gunther?"

"That'd be me."

"Max Freeman," I said, extending my hand. "Billy Manchester suggested I might talk a bit with you?"

"He did," answered Gunther, tipping down his sunglasses to look at me with pale green eyes.

He reached out and his massive palm seemed to swallow my own. His fingers were like thick swollen sausages tied at the knuckles and his skin was as dry and slick as waxed paper. I had never seen a hand so big.

"Come on inside outta this heat."

I followed him to the hangar, matching his pace and figuring his shoe size to be about a twelve and certainly not smaller.

Inside the hangar Gunther led me to a small, half-windowed office along the east wall. He closed the flimsy wood door behind us, took a seat behind a metal desk and nodded at the threadbare couch. The heat that followed us in tripped the wall-mounted air conditioner and set it to rumbling. I declined the stained couch and pulled a straight-backed chair up next to his desk.

The room held the odor of grease and high-test fuel. There were two calendars on the wall behind Gunther, one of a bikini-clad woman holding some sort of shiny tool and the other a shot of a big bass leaping from clear water.

"Billy did some favors for me a couple of years ago when some tour clients tried to sue me over a big misunderstanding. So I owe him," Gunther said, propping his elbows on the desk and dropping his ham-sized hands in front of him. "But I don't mind telling you, I'm not real comfortable. People out in the Glades are getting awfully touchy about this kid killing stuff. Especially when folks start saying it might be Gladesmen trying to scare off the developers."

"Where did you hear that?"

"Word gets around when lawmen come out asking questions and mentioning license renewals and county tax assessments," Gunther said.

Hammonds, I thought. His team, the FBI, they would all be squeezing every option they could. But did they really think it was some backwoods crazy poaching suburban kids on the edge of the Glades?

"Well, I don't know what Billy told you, but I'm really only interested in learning a little more about the landscape," I said.

Gunther looked down at his hands and then up into my face like he was going to apologize for not being able to help me.

"Mr. Manchester said you used to be a cop?"

"Used to be. I got shot in the neck and quit," I said, even surprising myself with my openness.

The big man's face seemed to change on hearing my admission, as if a gunshot wound made a difference.

"Well, then," he said, checking his watch. "My four-thirty client stood me up. Let's go flying."

Outside, ripples of heat shimmered off the runway as we walked to the plane. Gunther came around to the passenger side to show me how to twist down the door handle. He had just popped open the door when the distinctive double *hoo* notes of a barred owl sounded from behind us. Gunther snapped his head around and scanned the line of Australian pines on the other side of the roadway.

"Never heard one of those in daylight before," he said. "And never around here."

He stared a few seconds longer, shrugged his thick shoulders and then dipped under the wing to circle around to his side. I climbed in, shut my door, and stared off into the trees.

* * *

It wasn't until Gunther put us into a hardbanked turn that I truly started to worry. All during the startup, the taxiing and takeoff, I had been mesmerized by the pilot's movements. The snicking of switches and radio checks, the dialing of gauges and maneuvering of levers. His big hands moved across the panel and cockpit with an impressive grace and economy.

But I had never been in a small plane before and when we went into the first steep bank and climbed into the western sky, that old stomach-on-a-roller-coaster feeling got me. Gunther must have seen the changing pallor of my face.

"Pick out a spot on the horizon and focus," he said over the tinny-sounding headphones. "It's like a small boat on the ocean, but without the wave motion."

I locked onto a radio tower in the distance and started gaining some confidence in the steady engine drone, and the vibration humming through the cockpit. In the distance a few clumps of cloud moved across the blue background like ragged sails. It was one of those rare summer days when the thunderheads were not boiling. The afternoon sun was glinting off objects below. I finally shifted my view down and watched the sprawl move under us. We were following a concrete road that lay below. I watched the small white roofs of the old developments start to show a newness. Then, farther west, they turned larger and the barrel tiles turned them orange and terra-cotta. The neighborhood streets were laid out in curving, circular patterns to fight the feel of living in a boxy grid. The homes bloomed around a series of lakes and when I asked Gunther about them he explained that they were created by the giant backhoes that scooped up the ancient limestone and then dumped it on the building sites to give some solid foundation for the housing. The holes left behind lowered the water level and were then gussied up to look semi-natural.

"Waterfront property out of a swamp," he said. It was impossible to pick up any hint of derision in his voice over the headphones.

We flew on with little change below for fifteen minutes and then Gunther nodded ahead and announced, "There's the border, for now."

In the distance I could pick up the color change first. Then it sharpened at a highway running north and south. The barrel-tiled roofs and commercial plazas abruptly ended and an open field of rust-colored grasses began.

The enormity stunned me at first. The land spread out, unaltered, as far as you could see. When we passed over the roadway the terrain below lost all boundaries and was held only by the horizon. Kansas was my first thought. I'd never been west, but schoolbook descriptions of flat fields of golden grain had to come from a view like this.

Gunther eased the plane down to a lower altitude and I could pick up more detail. The sawgrass was less uniform and the green tinge of lower growth seeped through. In spots the sun reflected off streaks of exposed water, the first reminder that this was not solid ground and that a huge sheet of water covered mile after mile, and everything grew up through that liquid layer.

Without my realizing it, Gunther had turned us north and seemed to be heading for a dark green clump growing on the horizon. As we got closer I could see it was a stand of trees, sitting like an island in a sawgrass ocean.

"Hardwood hammock," Gunther said as we approached and then circled the stand. I recognized the twisting gumbo-limbo and pigeon plum trees that dotted parts of my own riverbank.

"It would take an airboat or maybe, in high water, a Glade skiff to get out here," Gunther said. When I didn't respond, he looked over at me.

"This is where they found the first kid's body."

He took the plane out of its bank and steered us back south. The sun had yellowed and was starting to backlight a new band of streaky high clouds.

"The second one was down off a prairie creek near the National Park. The third was farther north, in one of the canals to Lake Okeechobee. And I guess you know about the fourth one."

I looked over at him, watching the pilot's hard profile against the light of his side window. Billy had obviously explained more than Gunther had let on.

"So who would know how to get to those spots?" I said, dipping into an area he had opened up.

"Look. You have to understand there's a lot of characters out here. Folks whose fathers and grandfathers lived a rough existence since the 1920s. They stayed away from the coast and traded progress for what they considered freedom, and it wasn't always legal," he said. "Hell, I'm considered an outsider, but I've sat around with these guys and heard them talk about sniping off the wardens and the tax men and land speculators if they threatened what they consider to be their Glades."

"So it could be a native, somebody who knows the land out here and maybe went off the deep end?" I said.

"Maybe. But even the guides like me, and the hunters and fishermen who live on the coast and come out here all the time, could get out to those spots. Hell, even the environmentalists get out here. And they're not always wrapped too tight when it comes to fighting development."

Both of us fell silent. Gunther seemed to be the one focused on a distant point to keep from getting queasy.

"It's a long way from drinking and talking about it and actually going out and killing kids to scare people away," he finally said.

By now the sun was going orange and beginning to spin streaks of purple and red through the low clouds. We passed over a fish camp that sat isolated in the grass with a dock that stuck out into a clear-water channel. I could see the beaten-down paths in the sawgrass from airboats spoking out from the weathered building.

Gunther was banking toward the east when the first cough sounded. When the second one changed the thrumming sound of the engine I looked over at the pilot whose fingers were now moving to try and catch up to the beat.

"What the hell?" was all he said.

The third cough came with a lurch and the nose of the

Cessna dipped. Gunther never said another word but I could tell from the tight web creasing at the corner of his eyes that we were going down. The horizon suddenly tilted as Gunther tried to horse the plane back toward the fishing camp. Blue sky turned to sun-tinged grass. I had time to grab a handful of the console in front of me. I never even heard the thump of impact.

CHAPTER 9

I might have been out ten seconds or ten minutes. Or maybe my brain just shut down with shock and I hadn't been unconscious at all. But Gunther was.

When my sight kicked back on I could see the big man wrapped hard around the steering yoke, his head up against the windshield and leaking a string of blood that ran down through his eyebrow and onto a cheek.

I tried to reach out to him, but I was half hanging in the seat harness, all my weight pushed forward with the angle of the cockpit. We had pitched into the Glades and speared into the water and black muck. The propeller and most of the engine had disappeared, buried in front of us. The wings at either side looked like they'd simply dropped flat out of the sky and lay floating on the bent stalks of sawgrass, resting on the pile. But in the cockpit, water was settling knee high around both of our legs and when I looked down at Gunther's leg, I could see the glisten of white bone that had ripped through his trousers at the middle of his thigh. Compound fracture, I thought. And God knows what else.

I tried to do a quick assessment of myself. I could move my feet, but when I tried to twist my shoulders a pain screeched through my lower chest. I had been punched at Frankie O'Hara's gym with enough wicked hooks to the body to know that I'd at least bruised a few ribs but hoped I hadn't cracked any. I took shallow breaths and after several seconds I reached out and got a good brace with the left arm on the console and pushed my weight off the harness. I fumbled with the buckle but got it loose and then got solid footing on the angled cock-pit floor. I leaned back on the edge of my seat and then reached over to get my fingertips on Gunther's neck artery. A pulse. Thready, but a pulse. The pilot had not even reached for the radio when we'd felt the first jolts from the engine. I looked at it now, folded into the crush console and partly submerged in rising water. Useless.

I had to get myself out. I had to get him out. And we were already losing daylight. Who was ever going to find us out here? Who even knew we were out here?

One step at a time, I told myself. "Ya can't book 'em till ya catch 'em," Sergeant McGinnis had said in the police academy. "And can't catch 'em till ya find 'em."

"And can't find 'em if they're dead," one of the smartass rookies would always whisper.

I used my right hand to twist down my handle and pushed loose the passenger door. Each movement sent a spike of pain up my side, but I was able to crawl up on the seat cushion and pull myself out onto the wing. I stood. My left knee was creaky. An ankle throbbed. Over the wall of sawgrass I could see the roofline of the fish camp in silhouette against the pink glow of sunset that still lightened the horizon. Gunther had brought us to within 150 yards or so. I didn't know how I'd get him the rest of the way.

I crab walked across the fuselage to the other wing and wrenched open the pilot's door. Gunther's seat belt was either unhooked or had snapped. If he had a neck injury, I couldn't help it now. We were both soaking wet. It was getting dark and even a seventy-five-degree South Florida night was going to play hell with our body temperatures. Gunther had an open fracture and was probably bleeding internally. I'd taken enough emergency medical courses as a cop to know we were in deep shit. I looked again at Gunther. He was 230 pounds and unconscious. Even if I could get him out, I'd never be able to carry him 150 yards. I got that old cop feeling of hearing shots and wanting to go the other way. Fight or flee. Self preservation. The sky still glowed in the west. I bent over, got a grip under the pilot's arms and started pulling.

* * *

It took another twenty minutes to get him out. My rib cage screamed. Part of me was glad the big man was out cold. At least he couldn't consciously feel the pain of his broken femur as I jerked him out onto the wing. He groaned only once and I saw his eyes roll up. I bent my face to his mouth and felt the whisper of breath on my cheek. Still breathing. I sat, resting and trying to figure out my next move.

"OK, Fred. What's next?" I said out loud. If I was taking him, it had to be a joint effort. If I wanted him to live, I had to convince myself he could. I knew that if I didn't believe it, I'd give up.

I stood and took another bearing on the fading roofline of the fish camp and tried to imagine the route in my head. Once we were down in the sawgrass there'd be no sight line. The straight edge of the wing pointed just to the right of the building, about fifteen degrees off. I could use that at first.

I eased myself down at the crook of the wing and the fuselage and onto the matted sawgrass. The footing was shaky, but I sank only knee deep into water. But when I stepped away from the flattened grass I was suddenly up to my waist. The bottom felt slick and doughy and sucked at my Reeboks when I took a step. I'd never be able to drag Gunther through this. I stood there, warm water filling my jeans, staring down at the water and grinding. The grass was my enemy. Could I avoid it? No. The muck was my enemy. Could I avoid it? No. The water and Gunther's weight were my enemy.

Float him, I thought. It was the only way.

Would a plane this size have a raft? Doubtful. And I hadn't seen anything that resembled a life vest in the cockpit. I worked my way back to the fuselage and found the handle to the side compartment where I'd seen Gunther rummaging when I first pulled up at his hangar. The recessed handle twisted out and I popped the door and wrenched it open. Inside the space was dark and I had to reach in and start pulling out whatever I could reach: a rolled-up length of canvas tarpaulin, some fishing gear, a sleeping bag jammed deep in one corner, and a large zippered black bag with a U.S. Diver's logo on the side.

I hesitated only a second to look at the new cream-colored canvas tarp, then pulled the bag into the opening and unzipped it. A mask and snorkel, a breathing regulator and mouthpiece, a set of huge fins, a sleeveless wetsuit top and the piece of luck I was hoping for, a buoyancy compensator.

"You're a scuba diver, Fred," I said aloud. Gunther probably ferried clients down the Keys, where the only living coral reefs in the continental U.S. lay just off shore.

I'd seen the guys from rescue-and-recovery use scuba equipment in Philadelphia, watched them slip down the banks of the Delaware River one morning in their slick black wetsuits and ease themselves into the water looking for the remains of a homicide victim. Strapped across their chests and attached to the air tanks were buoyancy compensators, inflatable vests that they could fill with air or empty out, to keep them afloat or let them dive.

I took the vest and wetsuit out of Fred's bag and climbed back onto the wing.

"OK, Fred. We're going on a hike, man. Help me out with this and I promise we're gonna make it."

I checked Gunther's pulse. Maybe I was kidding myself, but it seemed stronger. I wrestled his arms into the vest and clipped it over his chest. I found a stem labeled "manual inflate" and started blowing. My ribs screeched twice with each breath, when I sucked in air and when I blew it out. Ten minutes of pain got it done.

I then took up the wetsuit jacket and slipped it under the big man's broken thigh. Looking for something to wrap it with, I stripped off the pilot's belt. Attached to it was a leather scabbard. I unsnapped it and took out his knife. The blade was small and oddly curved but was so sharp it sliced easily through the rubber and cloth of the wetsuit. I trimmed it and then cinched it around the leg using the belt to secure it. I was cutting the corded shoestrings from his boots to help tie the jacket when I fumbled the knife and it plunked into the water below and out of sight. I cursed its loss for no apparent reason.

"OK, Fred. Moment of truth, my friend."

I pulled the big man to the crook of the fuselage and let his legs dangle. I got back down into the water and with both feet planted on the matted sawgrass, inched Gunther off the wing and let him slide down my chest and thighs and into the water. I laid him out. The inflated vest kept his massive chest up. Even the wrapped rubberized wetsuit seemed to float his injured leg some.

By now we'd lost most of the light. The sky had gone dusky and a few early stars had already popped. My night eyes had adjusted and the white plane held a slight glow. I took a bearing on the wing edge, fifteen degrees, and stepped deeper into the water.

"Just like a night paddle, Fred," I said, looking at Gunther's pale face. "Let's muscle through."

* * *

I don't know how much time passed. We were in hell on earth. You can't keep track of eternity.

Every step into the grass wall was a process. I would sweep at the high, saw-toothed blades with one arm and try to find some half-solid purchase with my forward foot. Then, with my left hand gripped on the shoulder strap of the inflatable vest, I would pull Gunther forward and try to plant another foot in the muck below. I was sweating before we started and three steps into the wall the mosquitoes began to swarm around my face and arms. I could feel them in my hair, knew that the few I splattered with a swat on my neck were instantly replaced. They were so thick I drew an occasional group into my mouth with a breath. I would flail at them with my free hand. Then sweep the grass, move the foot, yank Gunther forward eighteen inches, move the other foot, flail the insects, and begin again. Early on I stumbled and fell, going under over my head in the water and discovered it gave at least a few seconds of relief from the mosquitoes, so I took to voluntarily dunking my head every few steps. Oddly, the insects didn't seem to light on Gunther. Maybe they could sense the odor of imminent death. Maybe the stink of my own sweat and animal oils drew them away from him.

I checked the pilot's pulse. Still there.

"Stay with me, buddy. Work with me," I said, then swept the grass, moved the foot, yanked him forward . . .

I quickly lost sight of the plane. I thought I could establish a line and then use my own created trail to keep it straight. But once we were enclosed in grass and darkness it was impossible to know if we were making headway toward the camp or skewing off to either side. Above me the first few stars had multiplied into a thousand and twice my heart jumped when a breeze momentarily split the grass and a beam of light seemed to flash through. I thought it was a search light at first, only to realize it was a low moon starting to climb the eastern sky, sending its beams flickering through the Glades. I kept moving.

The night was pulling the warmth out of the water. My legs were cold as it leached away body heat. I tried to concentrate but was losing focus. Gunther had groaned a couple of times when I yanked at the flotation vest. He was slipping in and out. At times the water was so shallow I was able to get good footing and fall forward to gain three feet. In deeper water every lunge brought us less than one. I tried counting the pulls, closing my eyes to concentrate on twenty pulls, then resting, then doing twenty more. As I weakened the moon came full into view above the grass, hanging in the air like a soiled silver dollar. The pain in my ribs became a dull mass. I could no longer feel the razor cuts on my arms and face from the sharp sawgrass. I reduced my pulls to ten at a time between resting.

I tried to think of the paddling, the rhythm and strokes of the canoe. I tried to think of running, pushing through the ache, and then cussed myself for putting in three miles this morning and how that strength could have helped me now. I tried to use the stars as some kind of guide to keep a straight course. I'd lost count of the pulls long ago.

I'd quit sweating but couldn't remember why that was a bad thing. I'd lost any sense of the mosquitoes and then cut my pulls to five at a time and quit talking to Gunther. I thought, more than a couple of times, of leaving the pilot behind.

I was giving up when I swung my arm into the grass again and the back of my hand thunked into something solid. The pain seemed to snap a few brain cells alive.

A piling, I thought, prying my other hand from a cramp-locked grip on Gunther and then using both to feel the squared pole in front of me. I reached up and touched the wood like a blind man. There was a platform above that sloped down in the opposite direction like some sort of ramp. I yanked Gunther around. I got a step up onto solid wood and dragged his chest out of the water. Once he was secure I crawled up the planks toward the moon.

We'd hit the camp off to the south at a short boat ramp that must be used to drag up canoes or skiffs. In the moonlight the weathered wood of the structure glowed like dull bone and the surrounding horizon of sawgrass took on the color of ash. I stumbled along the dock, my legs stiff and barely holding. At the main cabin the door to one side was unlocked and it swung open on crusted hinges.

Inside it was darker, but like in my own shack, I could make out shapes of a table and bunks against one wall. I found a slick blue rain tarp folded on top of an old trunk and carried it back outside to where Gunther lay. He groaned again when I pulled him onto the flattened tarp.

"Bedtime, Fred," I said, and then twisted two corners together and somehow dragged him up the ramp and into the cabin. Inside I pulled a mattress from one bed to the floor and after deflating the vest and prying him out of it, I rolled the pilot onto the mattress and covered him with every blanket I could reach.

I finally sat on the edge of the bunk, breathing hard and shallow as if only half of my lungs were working. I was caked with mud from the crotch down. A filmy mixture of blood and water covered my arms. My face felt swollen from the insect bites.

Moonlight was pouring through an old-style four-pane window. Gunther's face was turned up to the ceiling. I didn't know if he was alive or dead. I stared at the spot on his neck where a pulse would be but I could not move myself to it. I didn't even feel myself fall back into the bed.

* * *

I could feel the helicopter blades, more than hear them, a whumping of air that rattled the wood walls around me. In my half dream I could feel the knock of boots on hardwood floors, the hard steps vibrating into my cracked ribs and curiously tickling the bone.

I could feel the words, sharp and urgent medical terms jumping out of men's mouths, and then I was rising up out of warm water. Up out of pain. I'd spent enough time in hell. It was time to leave.

CHAPTER 10

When I woke up the stiff coolness of the sheets was against my legs and chest so I raised my right hand and it went to the left side of my neck. There were no bandages this time, only the smooth dime-sized scar. I was in a hospital bed but I had not dreamed eighteen months in Florida.

I tried to open my eyes but the lids felt like they were stuck with a dry, cracked paste and when I finally forced them, it felt like sandpaper scraping across my corneas. Billy Manchester was standing at the end of the bed, his arms folded across his chest.

"Good m-morning, Max."

I blinked a few more times and tried to swallow but couldn't find any moisture in my cheeks.

"Counselor," I finally croaked.

"Y-You are alive."

The reassurance was a light attempt at humor, but I wasn't sure how close to reality.

"Was there any doubt?"

"I wasn't here w-when they brought you in. But d-dehydration and exposure are d-dangerous conditions."

"How long?"

"You w-were in and out of c-consciousness most of yester-day and l-last night," Billy said, pouring a glass of water from a bedside pitcher and putting in a straw before telling the story.

When I hadn't showed up at his tower by late Saturday night and he couldn't get an answer on the cell phone or at Gunther's office, Billy had called the sheriff's office. When he told them of my planned meeting with Gunther, they patched him in with a search-and-rescue unit that was already working reports that Gunther and his plane were missing.

The pilot's family had been to the hangar. Billy confirmed his ownership of the Jeep parked next to the tarmac. At 11:00 Sunday morning a private pilot radioed his sighting of a downed plane near the Everglades fishing camp. Within an hour a ranger in an airboat was at the camp and was met by an emergency helicopter. A chopper with a pontoon landed in the swamp and airlifted us out.

"Gunther?"

"He's alive. But he m-might lose his l-leg."

I reached for the water glass and sipped at the straw. My arms looked swollen and the thousands of fine lacerations from the sawgrass had been coated with some kind of clear antisep-tic cream. Billy had started to pace.

"Your n-name is all over the news. They had to ch-chase one reporter off this floor already today."

The ranger who first arrived at the fish camp had surveyed the area after we'd been airlifted. He'd followed the mashed sawgrass trail we'd left leading back to the plane. He'd told reporters he wouldn't have believed it possible if he hadn't seen it with his own eyes. The press was clamoring for a bedside interview. Billy, as my attorney, had issued a single, unstuttered "No."

I knew how uncomfortable Billy would be in front of cam-eras and tape recorders. But his anxious pacing meant more than that.

When he'd gone to get his Jeep late Sunday afternoon after they stabilized me, he'd dismissed the taxi driver and gotten inside the truck. He was pulling out in reverse when he saw the message in his rearview mirror and stopped and got out to walk around back and read it. The words were drawn in a slight film of dust on the back window: "Don't Fuck With Mother Nature."

Somewhere back in my cobwebbed brain I plucked out the memory of the owl voice hooing from a stand of pines.

"I c-called Hammonds. He said his c-crime scene technicians would go over it."

"And the plane?" I said.

"I know s-someone at the FAA."

I had no doubt they'd find some sign of tampering when they went through the wreckage.

Billy was still pacing.

"Hammonds is outside," he said. "They w-want to talk. I told him only w-with me p-present."

I looked at Billy's eyes and when they locked onto mine, I knew he'd found out about my stupid visit to Hammonds' office without him. I nodded.

"B-Be careful. You're not off the h-hook yet," he said, going to get the detectives.

Hammonds came in first, followed by Diaz and Richards. Diaz nodded and I swear came close to winking. Richards took up a spot against the far wall, brushed a strand of blond hair from her face and crossed her arms.

Hammonds stood at the end of the bed. The model of professionalism. He was wearing a charcoal suit, his tie pulled tight. But there was a slump in his shoulders that I doubt was there three months ago.

"I'm a little dismayed that an ex-cop who took it upon himself to bail out of a law enforcement career comes down here and starts getting his fingers stuck in a serial killer investigation," Hammonds started, pulling no punches despite the situation.

"We're agreed," I said, my voice still dry and barely audible.

"We served a warrant on your place Saturday morning," he said.

"On a tip?"

Hammonds looked quickly at Diaz, who just shrugged.

"On an anonymous tip that we might find an important piece of electronics that could be vital to our investigation."

"And?"

"Came up empty. And disappointed," Hammonds said, holding my gaze.

"Maybe you'd find a better suspect by looking for somebody who knows about planes. At least enough to bring them down," I said, feeling a flush of anger making its way through my medication.

"We're already on that. In fact your friend Mr. Gunther was on our screen before you got there."

"As a suspect?" I said, looking over at Billy.

"As a person with a wide circle of friends who know the Everglades, some of whom have strong views about it."

"From what I understand that's a big circle," I said.

"Your involvement with him makes it a somewhat smaller circle."

"Oh, I see," I said, now feeling the blood rise in my chest. "I get *involved* with this guy in a series of child killings and then we decide on a suicide pact and crash our plane in your godforsaken Everglades. But then after we're busted up and Gunther's half dead, we change our minds and I drag his ass all night through the swamp and then roll over in the fucking middle of nowhere with the near zero chance of somebody finding us before we both shrivel up into fish bait."

Hammonds' eyes did not leave my face. His expression never changed.

"If that's your best fucking theory, *Detective,* no wonder you're still chasing this asshole."

My outburst silenced the room and plunged me into a dry coughing fit that ripped at my insides. Billy tried to get a sip of water into me. No one said anything for several seconds.

I looked at Richards who stood staring at the jiggling bag of saline that fed into my arm. Her eyes were red-rimmed and held a deep ache. I'd seen that look before, reflecting back at me in a medicine cabinet mirror in my own Philadelphia home.

"Do you really think I did this?" I said, looking at her.

She started to speak but then turned away and quickly walked out the door. Diaz cleared his throat and took a step forward.

"She was at the kid's funeral all morning, the one you found," he said before Hammonds cut him off.

"Mr. Freeman." His voice was unaffected by my tirade. "We are still seeking that electronic device. And Mr. Manchester has indicated that our search may not be futile."

I looked again at Billy, who was silent.

"If you are inclined, give Detective Diaz here a call," Hammonds said and then turned and walked out of the room.

Diaz reached out and put a business card on the bed. This time he actually did wink before leaving. I closed my eyes, exhausted again, and let the silence sit in the room. I could feel my heartbeat under the sheets. I thought I could feel the saline dripping into my vein.

"We should give him the GPS?" I said without opening my eyes.

"I think it w-would be p-prudent. They might track it b-by its serial number. They could g-get lucky."

Billy's sense of protecting me had shifted from legal to physical. The killer had made a turn when he sabotaged Gunther's plane. He'd expanded his threat and his target field. There were no windows in the room, only the off-white walls. It made the space look starkly empty.

"What's with the woman?" I asked Billy, surprising even myself when the question slipped out of my mouth.

"My guess is sh-she has let herself get too close, " Billy answered. "You know h-how the ch-child you found died?"

I had missed a few days of news.

"Dehydration," he said. "She was d-deprived of water. Probably f-for days."

I kept my eyes shut. I had watched Richards when she came in the room, could smell her perfume. I'd seen her move her fingers to her hair and tuck the loose strand behind her ear and the movement raked my insides more than any fractured rib could have.

"Billy," I said. "Get me out of here, OK?"

CHAPTER 11

It was the first time I'd seen her close up. She was crouched in the shadows, holding an assault rifle, breathing in that same deep rhythmic way of hers that I would watch for years afterward in our morning bed.

That day we were inside an abandoned Philadelphia elementary school. The electricity was long since gone, pulled out by the demolition contractors who in a few weeks would knock down the thirty-year-old structure and scoop it off the corner near Lehigh Avenue in Kensington. The only light came in through the partially boarded windows and streamed through the haze of dust that seemed to float from the old recessed tile ceilings.

The Philadelphia Police SWAT team used the building for exercises, practicing how to handle interior room sweeps in the empty hallways and classrooms. Meg had been with them for eighteen months. She was a patrol cop. A good one. Tough when she needed to be and friendly enough when she wanted to be. At least that was the word around the roundhouse. She was also a hell of a good shot with a sniper rifle and that's why she was working with the Special Weapons And Tactics team.

I was there on an invite from Tommy Gibbons, a guy I'd

known since we were in the police academy who'd asked me to stop in and observe this particular training gig. Gibbons had been trying to get me to apply for a SWAT spot for a couple of years. My lack of ambition bothered him. His constant state of enthusiasm bothered me. Somehow, we were friends.

"Come on, Max. Just come out and watch," he'd said, interrupting a perfectly fine glass of Schaefer on draft at McLaughlin's. "I know there's an intense guy under that dumb lineman look. I know it. You got what makes these guys tick, Max. Come on. Just come out and watch 'em work and see if you don't catch a bug."

I was into my third glass of beer. It was summertime. A thirty-year-old version of the Drifters singing "Up on the Roof" was on the jukebox. I was staring at the oak scrollwork on McLaughlin's famous hundred-year-old bar mirror and for some yet unknown reason said, "Yeah, OK."

So the next day I was leaning against an empty metal fire extinguisher box watching the team position themselves in the hallway for a drill on "room probes" and watching the woman who would capture and then severely stomp my previously lazy heart.

Megan Turner was dressed in black, armed and dangerous. There was something about her profile, the sharp straight nose, the small rise of her cheekbones, and her delicate but determined chin that made me stare despite myself. Yet even that first day it was her eyes that caught me. From a distance of fifteen feet their ice-blue color seemed to absorb the fractured light, reflect none of it, and perform the uncanny task of sending an emotional thought across a room. It was her eyes and her hair that day.

Meg had become the team sniper soon after her recruitment to the team on the strength of her ability to put five out of five .308-caliber rounds from a sniper rifle into the dimensions of a quarter at two hundred yards. Good sharpshooters say they aim for a spot just in front of the ear, right where a close side-burn might end. A .308 round there will kill a suspect instantly, before his reflexes can pull the trigger of his own gun.

But on this day Meg was playing backup, armed with an MP5 assault rifle and given the task of covering a teammate who was doing a mirror probe of a classroom.

As the six-person team took up their positions, she had settled in against a hallway corner. Although her eyes were already on the doorjamb of the target room, I could feel her peripheral vision taking me in. She was wearing a pair of black gloves with the fingers cut off and before locking herself into position, knowing I was watching, she consciously loosened a strand of her long honey-blond hair from her baseball cap and stroked it behind her ear. I would learn, much later, that it was a calculated move. And I fell instantly in love.

Once the drill started, she fixed her rifle sites on the door-jamb while her partner crawled quietly along the floor, inching like an awkward snake along the baseboard of a scarred and dirty wall. When he got to the open doorway, he pulled out a long-handled mirror similar to a dentist's tool and slipped it around the corner, squinting and tilting the reflection to search the room.

For thirty-two minutes the heat in the hallway climbed. And for thirty-two minutes I watched Megan Turner's concentration. The sweat started in tiny beads at line of her cap and I watched them build and then roll in strings down her brow and neck. The air grew thick and nearly impossible to draw in. She sighted her weapon and never flinched. I'd never seen such a display of total focus.

When the officer on the floor yelled "Clear" the sharp sound of his voice made me jump and bang my shoulder against the extinguisher box. Megan simply exhaled, a slight grin tugging at the corner of her mouth.

After the exercise the squad gathered in the parking lot where they stripped out of their dark clothing and bulletproof vests, dumped cups of water over their heads and inhaled Gatorade. I was hanging near Gibbons and one of the team leaders when Megan looked up and caught me watching her again.

"So what do you think, Freeman?" she said, and the voice seemed way to soft, far too feminine.

"Impressive," I said, surprised that she knew my name.

"Challenging enough for you?"

"Possibly."

"Love to have you."

Gibbons looked up with the rest of the team, but I didn't see them rolling their eyes. I was watching Meg loosen a strand of her now wet hair and stroke it into position behind her ear.

"Yeah," was all I could manage.

We dated for six months and I tried every day to figure out if I'd fallen for the toughness it took to hold the crosshairs of a sniper rifle on a suspect's head for several minutes, or her ability to cry after separating another kid from his junkie mother on yet another domestic violence call.

Both of the attributes fascinated and scared me.

How I got past that and asked her to marry me I still didn't know. I was not a commitment kind of guy, more out of apathy than avoidance. I didn't think of myself as a man who needed companionship. I'd never had a date in high school. I'd gone out with friends that friends had set up for me, but rarely made a move myself. Women unsettled me. I'd grown up in a male-dominated household and had little clue how the female psyche worked. I'd tried to study them from afar, to grind out answers to their odd emotional abilities, but had obviously failed. Even Megan was indecipherable. But her energy hooked me.

We got married in a relatively small ceremony in South

Philly. Her family side was huge and varied. My side was full of cops, mostly friends and family from my father's side. After the wedding we went to Atlantic City for a week. Meg discovered blackjack and the dealers and pit bosses loved her. She cussed when she lost and shrieked when she won and her smile and flashing blond hair made everyone at her table happy to be there. I often stood back from the green felt table, watching, touching her spine through the sheer fabric of her blouse just to remind her I was there.

For three years we kept a small townhouse apartment tucked away between the tight center city streets just north of Lombard. We went to the Walnut Street Theatre and she watched quietly and then drank loudly at the Irish pub across the alley. We took the Broad Street subway to the Vet to see the Phillies and I watched quietly and we both drank deeply at McLaughlin's afterward. When she worked out at the local Nautilus club, I left her alone. When I holed up with my books, she left me alone. When we made love, she was enthusiastic. I'm still not sure what I was.

Throughout the marriage, Meg stayed on the SWAT team. Sometimes, when she got called out in the middle of the night, I would show up in uniform and stand out on the perimeter, talking with the crowd-control guys, trying to picture her inside or up high on a rooftop, sighting in her sniper rifle. But the night she took out a suspect holding three hostages at gunpoint in Overbrook, I was on another call.

The guy had been chased by campus police after a robbery where he'd already wounded a security guard. He had slipped in behind three women, students at St. Joe's, as they walked into their dorm room, and then forced them into a lounge on the second floor, screaming that he would kill them if the cops tried to arrest him.

Meg's team was on call and as the uniform guys cleared the

dormitory to isolate the room, they took position. She was on the third floor of the student affairs building across the street with a clear view inside the lounge. Her teammates were silently creeping the halls while a hostage negotiator was getting an earful of cuss words on the only telephone in the room, a wall-mounted set that was directly in Meg Turner's sight line.

The negotiations were short. The fourth time the negotiator rang the phone in an attempt to keep the suspect talking, he pulled one of the women over to the phone with him. He had his gun to the girl's head and through Meg's telescopic sight, she could see his finger on the trigger and his face in full profile.

"You motherfuckers done called one damn time too many already and now you gone see what the hell it's gone cost . . ."

The man never finished his sentence. The .308 round exploded perfectly on his right sideburn. All three students were rescued unhurt.

Hours later, after my shift, after the SWAT crew had been debriefed and let loose, I found them at McLaughlin's. The place was full. The Phillies were in New York, getting whipped by the Mets on the overhead television. Off-duty cops were in every corner and clustered at the bar, sifting in and out among the members of the shooting team.

When I came in out of a light rain, I stood in the vestibule and could see her through the frosted glass. She sat at the end of the polished bar, her perfect profile caught by the light coming off the ancient mirror, her ice-blue eyes shining with that soft electric emotion I'd seen the very first day in the halls of the elementary school.

She wasn't drunk. She wasn't loud. She seemed to be carrying nothing extra in her head only hours after killing a man. She just looked damned beautiful. But her eyes this time were subtly moving on a blond, broad-shouldered member of one of the other Special Weapons teams. He was smiling widely and moving his hands in animated expression. I'd seen him before and some sense of his ambition caused me to avoid him.

I stayed behind the glass, watching her play him. The rain dripped off my jacket and pooled at my feet. I watched my wife take up her glass of draft, draw a sip, and then with her eyes on another man she loosened a strand of her long honey-blond hair and stroked it into position behind her ear.

CHAPTER 12

I am cold. In my dream I can hear water sluicing through concrete gutters. A swirling rain, caught in the wind that shears around the Wanamakers building, tunnels down Chestnut Street and whips against my face. Water is running black into the storm drains in center city Philadelphia and I am running, hard, my black Reeboks slapping the sheen of water on the sidewalk. I am breathing hard, gasping against the rain water pelting my face and I keep looking up to see the corner at Thirteenth Street, but I'm confused. Am I getting closer? Or farther away? Am I running at it? Or running way from it? Suddenly my foot hits a spot. I skid, lose my balance, start to fall.

The scraping sound of stiff plastic on concrete jars me awake and my eyes pop open and I am gripping the arms of a chaise lounge. I am on Billy's patio, sitting in the late-morning sun. I got to my feet and walked into the kitchen, trying to shake the dream out of my head. I cupped my hands under the faucet and splashed water into my face. I was back in the world.

Billy had gone to his office. He'd taken me out of the hospital two nights ago. With a few carefully folded fifty-dollar bills, he'd gotten help from hospital security to get me out a back entrance and avoid any lingering members of the media. He'd waited until after 9:00 P.M., after television's main broadcast hour, when the reporters would be easing back from any live standups they might have done.

"I'm a-afraid you've l-lost your anonymity," he'd said.

Billy of course was right. After the plane crash, my name was in the accident reports. Gunther was going to recover. And since the Glades ranger was going on about how I'd dragged the pilot to the dock, the instant inclination of the press was to do a hero story. In my favor was the fact that I had no address for them to find and no phone to call. No sound bites, no quotes, no hero.

But I also knew reporters weren't all slaves to the news cycle. Someone would have seen Hammonds and his team at the hospital and made a connection: What's the lead investigator of the child killings doing interviewing a guy who crashed a plane in the Everglades? Television might not care, but the newspapers would question whether or not to make a hero out of a guy being questioned about serial killings. The media didn't like stories that didn't fit into pigeonholes. How do you portray a cop who gets shot in the line of duty but kills a twelve-year-old in the process? I knew the drill. They'd back off to see "what develops." They might eventually move on. I hoped Hammonds would be smart enough to let them.

For a full, quiet day it had worked. I'd lain here, stretched out in the warm morning sun and then through the shady afternoon. Billy had mixed up some kind of hydrating mixture of watered-down fruit juice and vitamins. I'd been able to eat, bowls of brothy soup and then some thin pita bread. I drifted in and out of sleep with the ache in my ribs and the one in my dreams taking turns waking me.

This morning my body was stiff, but my head wasn't going to let me rest any longer. I got up and went inside and poured myself a cup of coffee, washed down a prescription Percocet with it, and looked out through the wall of windows at the thin line of the horizon. The coffee cup shook when I tried to raise it and I needed both hands to steady it. I was still wobbling despite the sleep and the medication. My skin was dry as paper and my lips were still swollen and cracked. The hot coffee stung them but I couldn't deny my habit. Diaz's card lay on the counter and I picked up the phone.

"You have reached the desk of Detective Vince Diaz, if you would like to leave . . ."

I waited for the damned beep.

"Look, Diaz. This is Max Freeman. I've been able to locate your piece of electronics. If you want to pick it up, call me." I left Billy's cell phone number, even though I knew the detective bureau would have a caller I.D. readout and probably already had Billy's private number. I looked at the digital clock on the stove. Diaz called back in eight minutes.

"Hey, Mr. Freeman, that's great. I'd like to come up as soon as possible. Get moving on that particular thing, all right?"

I gave him the address and told him he could call from the lobby when he arrived.

"Yeah, you kind of surprised us leaving the hospital so soon."

"About an hour?" I said.

"Yeah, sure, an hour."

I punched him off and dialed again.

"Ranger Station twelve, Cleve Wilson."

"Cleve. Max Freeman."

"Good God, Max. Where the hell you been?"

It might have been a question, or a statement of wonder.

"I've been a little busy Cleve, I'll fill you in when I get out there but I'm not sure when that will be."

"You know those detectives were back out here with a warrant. I had to show them to your place," he said and this time I could hear the apology in his voice. "But I went in with them, you know, just to watch if they messed things up."

"It's all right, Cleve. I appreciate it."

"And boy, they do not miss anything, if you know what I mean."

Cleve was a pro at understatement.

"Anything interest them in particular?"

"Well, they did perk up a bit when they found that nine millimeter of yours in the bottom of your duffel."

I had forgotten about the gun and sat there in Billy's kitchen wondering how I'd been able to let it slip far enough into the back of my mind as to finally let go of its memory, the feel and smell and sound of it echoing off the brick and glass of Thirteenth Street.

"But they didn't take it," Cleve said quickly, breaking the silence. "I heard one of them wondering if it was your old service issue. Then they put it back."

"Yeah? Well, thanks, Cleve. Like I said, I'll see you when I get back out there. I was actually calling to check on my truck."

"It's sitting here. The boy come back with it and since the scratch was gone and it was all shined up, I figured he was telling the truth about you letting him use it. But I've got the keys back in my desk."

"Thanks, Cleve."

I punched the phone off and finished my coffee while I watched the beginning of an afternoon rainstorm drive the sunbathers off the beach below.

* * *

I met Diaz in the lobby. I was carrying a small gym bag and a traveler's cup of coffee. I'd taken a shower and dressed in a pair of light cotton trousers and the loosest long-sleeved shirt I had. My skin was still tight and had started to flake off my forearms, either from the salve for the mosquito bites or from the dryness of dehydration. The Percocet had taken the edge off the ache in my bruised ribs.

Diaz was waiting under the watchful presence of the tower manager to whom he'd presented his I.D. before having me called. The manager bowed slightly when I thanked him, but continued his careful vigil as we drifted to a sitting area in an anteroom off the main entrance hall.

"Nice place," Diaz said, sitting down on the edge of a wing-back chair while looking up at the vaulted ceiling.

I took a seat on the adjoining couch and put the bag between my feet on the marble tiled floor.

"That for me?" he said.

"Look. I'll be straight with you. I don't want any of this coming back on Billy Manchester. I've got this and it's going straight to you. No one else in the middle or with knowledge," I said. Diaz was looking at his hands.

I'd been too paranoid and a hell of a lot more distrustful of the investigators to give up the GPS before. It was perfect evidence for a case against me, even if I was the one who handed it over. Now they were scraping, and more people, including me, were in the target zone. But I didn't want concealing evidence coming back on a man of Billy's position.

"I don't think that's going to be a problem. No one seemed to know your attorney around the shop, but when we started asking around the law world, everybody seemed to know him. *Connected* and *smart* were the words that kept coming back. And I think this is smart too," he added, looking up into my face.

I reached into the bag and brought out the GPS unit. It was rewrapped in plastic, and I told him how I'd found it, the cut mattress and the filmy footprint I'd found in my shack.

"All the locations of the bodies are logged into it," I said, passing the machine to Diaz. "That's how you found them, right?"

The detective looked up and I could tell he was turning a corner, and doing it behind Hammonds' back.

"You know what this is like. I saw your file out of Philly," he started. "This guy's been playing us and we're scratching at anything we can. It got to the point we were left waiting for a break, a mistake. And when you came paddling up out of the river we figured, hoped, you were the mistake."

I knew he was holding my eyes to see how I might react.

"Maybe we won't get anything off this by tracking the supplier and seller. Maybe it comes up empty again. But it's better than sitting around waiting for another kid to disappear."

"And maybe he's through with that," I said. "Maybe he's got a new target."

Diaz let the thought sit for a few empty seconds.

"Yeah, well. No offense, but if that's true, if he's after you instead of another kid, a lot of folks aren't necessarily going to see that as a step back."

I was still holding on to the straps of the gym bag, hesitating. When Diaz started to get up I reached in and took out a baggie containing the bent aluminum tag from my canoe and handed it to him.

"I think it's more true than you guys are willing to admit," I said, reaching into the bag for my second bit of concealed evidence.

* * *

Thirty minutes later we were in Diaz's unmarked sedan heading for the river. He'd been pissed when I told him what the tag was. It was the first time I'd seen him angry and he let some Spanish slip into his voice.

"Crime scene, man! *Mierda*, you know evidence and crime scene protocol!"

Now he'd calmed down as we headed for the access park where I'd left my canoe the night I ducked the warrant, and where the killer must have pulled the tag.

By then we'd agreed the chance of finding fingerprints on anything were remote and tracing the courier who delivered the tag was probably a dead end too.

"That's the way he sent the first set of GPS coordinates," Diaz said. "Straight to the sheriff's office."

Since then he'd altered his methods, even e-mailing the GPS numbers in from a computer terminal at a downtown Radio Shack. It didn't take an FBI profiler to figure out this wasn't some swamp rat survivalist taking shots at the encroaching city dwellers.

"He knows the Glades. He knows how to get in and out of these damn neighborhoods without being seen. He knows enough about the gadgets to use them. And he sure as hell knows how to play on everybody's fears," Diaz said. "Hell, we don't even know if it *is* only one damn guy."

The detective went quiet as we drove west. He'd already overstepped his bounds talking about the investigation. Seeing his frustration, I doubted they'd found anything to help them. But he was right about the crime scene protocol. They at least deserved to take a look.

I told Diaz where to make the turn off Seminole Drive and we curved out toward a line of cypress trees and then down the entrance road to the park. A warm drizzle was spattering the windshield and Diaz looked up through the glass, hesitating. But when I got out and started toward the river, he followed.

Ham Mathis was hovering around his canoe concession office, emptying out the ice water from the cooler where he kept cold drinks for his rental customers. He peeked out from under the hood of his yellow rain slicker and spat a brown string of tobacco juice into the wet grass when he saw me coming.

"Hey, Ham. How's it going?"

The old Georgian set the cooler down and looked up.

"Hey, Max," he answered, sneaking a look at Diaz coming up behind me. "I truly am sorry about your boat."

He let another string of juice fly and then led us around to the back of his trailer. There lay the carcass of my canoe.

"I pulled her 'round so's the customers wouldn't see her," he explained.

The boat was flipped on its gunwales like I'd left it, but someone had stomped her. Gapping holes in the center of the hull yawned like twisted black mouths in the rain. Each rib had been methodically snapped. It had taken a malicious effort to do that kind of damage to its tough outer skin.

I went around to the bow and checked the port side where the tag had been. The pulled rivets had left four small jagged holes behind.

All three of us just stared at the broken shell for several long minutes.

"That's how she was the other mornin' when I come in," Mathis finally said. "I ain't never had no vandalism out here before."

"Anything else damaged?" Diaz asked.

" 'Cept your paddle," Mathis answered, looking at me. "Snapped it like a twig and tossed it down the bank."

I showed Diaz where I'd set the canoe five nights before. We agreed there wasn't much of a chance of picking up any footprints or latents off the canoe skin. Mathis had called the county sheriff's office the morning he'd found the mess and a patrol deputy had come by and written up a report. When Diaz went into the small trailer with Mathis to get a reference number, I walked down to the river. The water had turned dark green in the fading light and was pocked with raindrops. Large circles grew in the spots under the cypress boughs where heavier drops fell from the branches. The air smelled thick and green, an odor I had never known until I came here from the city. A heron sat perched on a log on the opposite shore, searching the water for a meal. Suddenly it raised its head, then croaked its distinctive *keyow* and flew off as if something in the shadow behind had scared it. I stared into the dark patches but if something had flushed the bird, I couldn't pick it up.

"Angry?"

Diaz's voice startled me. He'd come down from the trailer and was standing behind me, fingers in his pockets and shoulders hunched against the drizzle.

"Guy that smashed that canoe didn't just want to let you know he was following. He was pissed," Diaz said.

"Yeah," I said, turning back to the river and looking into the shadows. "But not enough to show himself."

As we stood there Diaz's beeper went off and he retreated to his car to use his phone. A minute later he flashed his headlights and punched the horn. I yelled to Mathis that I'd come back later with my truck and he waved me off. When I climbed into Diaz's car he put the sedan in gear before I could close the door.

"That was dispatch," he said, setting his lips in a hard line. "They got another missing kid."

CHAPTER 13

Diaz spun a circle through the grass along the edge of the access road and the rubber yelped when he hit the Seminole Road pavement. As he sped east I knew he wasn't planning to drop me off.

He had his blue light on the dash by the time we made the interstate and despite the rain-slick roadway he hit the southbound entrance ramp hard. I kept my mouth shut and cinched up my seatbelt. I'd been on a few car chases in the city but despite how Mel Gibson and the boys make it look in the movies, you rarely get above fifty miles an hour on urban streets. When Diaz merged onto the interstate he was already doing sixty-five. When he got to the outside lane he pushed it to eighty-five and started talking.

"They got the call out from dispatch fifteen minutes ago, same as the last ones, some new housing development called Flamingo Lakes out in Westland," he said as if I knew the layout. He powered past a low ride Honda as the driver picked up Diaz's blue light in his rearview and jumped to an inside lane.

"We scrambled a unit out there and they already got a call out for a K-9 and a bloodhound unit. We used to wait for some kind of confirmation, but not anymore."

We surged up on the bumper of a sport utility vehicle, Diaz laid on the horn and slid halfway into the inside emergency pullover lane so the guy got the full view of the flashing blue light in his side mirror.

"*¡Muevete, hijo de puta!*"

The SUV finally found room to merge over and there was a line of six more cars in the lane ahead. Diaz stayed straddling the emergency lane and forced them all over like he had some sort of force field pushing out in front of him.

"Six-year-old girl," he said flatly as he pushed it to ninety miles an hour in the now open lane. "Playing in a fenced yard on the lake. This time he killed a dog on the way in."

I looked over at the detective's profile, saw his jaw muscles flexing and kept my silence.

Even at this speed it was a thirty-minute trip down into the next county. By the time we reached the entrance to Flamingo Lakes my calves were cramping from pushing my toes to the floorboards trying to put on my phantom brakes. After jumping off the interstate we'd swerved through suburban traffic going west, blew through six stoplights and caused a dozen cars to jam on their brakes.

When we turned onto the street I saw a spray of blue and red lights webbed at the end of a broad cul-de-sac. Diaz had to park a block away. I followed him in and we walked past two television trucks with their broadcast antennas up, a knot of huddled neighbors with cell phones, and a couple of K-9 patrol cars holding barking dogs. A big, boxy ambulance was backed into the driveway of the house at the end of the street. Letters on the mailbox spelled Alvarez. The place seemed too chaotic for a crime scene.

I walked a step behind Diaz, matching his stride as he nodded his way past several uniformed officers. No one gave me a second look. There were two plainclothes detective types just inside the entrance of the house, both talking into two-way cell phones, and we squeezed past.

Inside the house the energy hum changed. Every light in the big, two-story home seemed to be on, but it held the stark, empty feel of a nightclub thirty minutes after closing time. The décor was off-white and pastel and spotless. But the furniture—sectional couches and oversized chairs—had all been pulled out from the walls.

"Last time we had an abduction callout we were an hour into the search when the kid crawled out from behind a couch," Diaz whispered, as if reading my puzzled look. "She'd climbed back there and fallen asleep."

All conversation inside the house was consciously subdued. I followed Diaz into the kitchen and saw Detective Richards sitting at a polished wood table. Another woman sat next to her, elbows planted wide, her eyes in both palms, fingers thrust up into her dark hair. Richards had an arm resting lightly on the woman's shoulder and was touching her head, stroking her hair as she talked to her in low tones.

Diaz caught his partner's eye and mouthed the question: "Hammonds?"

Richards pointed a finger to the rear of the house and then looked directly into my eyes. Green or gray? I thought. She turned her attention back to the woman, a mother whose heart I could not and did not want to imagine. I followed Diaz through a set of French doors and out onto a patio.

In a corner of the backyard Hammonds stood within a huddle of men dressed just like him, suits minus the jackets, ties knotted, shoes tight and made for the city. I figured FBI, but Hammonds still seemed to be in charge, no matter how tenuously. He stood in the middle, his silvered hair glowing in lights blazing from two outside spotlights mounted high on the corners of the house. I stayed on the cut stone patio while Diaz went out to the group. I could see the low fence that surrounded the long sloping yard. An orange and blue plastic jungle gym and slide stood to one side. Next to it, a yellow crime scene blanket covered a large object on the grass. The dog.

When I looked up, Diaz was talking with Hammonds, who did not look in my direction, but nodded his head and handed Diaz a bulky, hand-held flashlight.

"The kid was out here playing in the yard while the mom was cleaning up dinner dishes," Diaz said when he came back, talking like he was briefing me.

"She didn't hear anything unusual, but the sun was going down, it was getting late so she comes out on the patio to call the kid inside and sees the dog lying there. She looks around. No kid. She freaks."

I followed as he moved to the back end of the yard.

"They got the fence up to keep the dog and the kid inside. They were safety conscious and worried about the lake."

We hopped the waist-high fence and Diaz flipped on the flashlight, sweeping it across the ground until it illuminated a row of small white markers standing like folded cards in the grass, each with a number printed on it.

"Patrol guys got here first and found the mom out here knee-deep in the water and came in after her so there's a lot of prints. But these?" he said, shining the light on a deep print next to marker number one. "Could they be the same as you saw in your place?"

I bent to the imprint. Then the next one. And the third, all left in a patch of shiny mud. They were the same size as far as I could tell. The third one showed clearly that it had no tread, just a smooth size nine.

Diaz swung the beam farther out into a sudden stand of cattails and water lily that spread out into the water. I asked him to swing the light left and saw the water grasses stop abruptly at what appeared to be the property line. Next door the neighbor's green St. Augustine lawn went uninterrupted into uncluttered open water.

"Weed sprayed," Diaz said, again reading the puzzle in my face. "The developers tried to sell this whole place as a man-made wetlands area to help appease the environmentalists. They let the indigenous stuff grow in the water and they even have workers come out and pull any non-Florida stuff out."

He sprayed the light back into the grasses leading out into the water from behind the victim's house.

"It's great for luring the birds but some of the owners don't like it. They think the water grass looks like weeds and ruins their view so they spray it all dead."

He swung the beam back to the footprints that disappeared into the lilies.

"So what about the prints?"

"Could be," I answered. "I thought the one at my place might be a moccasin or something. You know? No tread or anything. Just like these."

"Booties," Diaz said. I looked up.

"Booties. Like the kind windsurfers or scuba divers wear. They're like a black neoprene sock that pulls up over your foot. They use them to keep you from chafing your skin with the straps on dive fins or from stepping on shells and stuff in the water."

I nodded and stood staring at the prints, thinking about Fred Gunther's scuba equipment bag and the clean canvas tarp in the storage bin of his Cessna. The same kind of canvas that glowed in moonlight and had been wrapped tightly around Alissa Gainey's floating body.

We started back up to the house. Hammonds and his group were still in their loose circle and he still didn't look at me.

"So the guy comes in from the water. Maybe he lies out

there in the high grass, waiting for the chance, watching the kid and the mom."

Diaz was one of those detectives who had to run his theories out loud, hear his own voice to find a mistake in the sequence or logic. I knew a couple like that. I just listened.

"He comes out of cover as late as he can because he wants to use the darkness. He jumps the fence and snatches the kid, somehow keeps her from screaming and—boom. Back in the water and gone."

As Diaz talked, the mechanical whine of a helicopter began to build. I could see it swinging in from the east, a cone of brilliant light pouring into the neighborhood and now into the lake. The chopper stopped and hovered while the beam poked down into another crescent of cattails and maidencane at the shore line. One of the men in Hammonds' group was looking up and talking into his cell phone. The chopper banked and moved over us, the downdraft ruffling through our clothes. Next to the children's slide the wind had kicked up the crime scene tarp leaving the crooked rear leg and haunches of a big German shepherd exposed. The cream and black fur had already lost its natural luster.

"You forgot the dog," I said to Diaz, as the chopper moved off.

"Oh, yeah," he replied, looking for the first time at the dead animal. "He cut its throat with one slice. Somehow, before the thing had a chance to even yelp."

"He do this before, kill a pet?"

"No. In fact, the first one he came in the middle of the night and took the kid out a bedroom window. The family dog, a real yapper according to the father, never reacted."

"He's getting reckless."

"Or more pissed off," Diaz said.

When I looked up, Richards was standing on the patio,

watching us. She was wearing dark jeans and a white, short-sleeved shirt. The spotlights behind her put a halo around her blond hair and backlit the thin fabric of her blouse, putting the outline of her breasts and her tapered waist in silhouette. I turned away to look out over the black water of the lake while Diaz went to talk with her.

On the opposite side of the lake the chopper was working another spot, hovering like a mechanical dragonfly tethered by a glowing white filament. Hammonds would have patrol officers working the entire perimeter, asking neighbors if they'd seen a strange boat along the shore or a van parked along the streets that didn't seem to belong.

How did the killer move from out there in the wild to a place like this? How did he operate so smoothly in both? I'd known street criminals in Philadelphia, burglars and hustlers and dopers who knew the corners and cracks in the city so well you'd never find them in a rundown and never trace their movements. But drop them off just over the way in the pinewoods of South Jersey and they'd be lost forever, looking for a pay phone on a tree trunk.

This guy knew both worlds. And he had mastered the wall between them.

"Max?"

Diaz was beside me, and had crossed an uninvited line with the use of my first name. I followed him back up to the patio.

"Look, I'm gonna get this GPS thing and the canoe tag over to the lab guys. Maybe there's something more in the memory of this thing and we can always hope for a lucky fingerprint."

I nodded and started up toward the house with him. We stopped in front of Richards, her arms crossed in that classic this-is-my-space pose. But she looked directly into my face; her eyes had flecks of gold in the green irises.

"How's the mother?" I said.

"Her sister's with her," Richards answered. Her voice held a low smoker's rasp.

"You think of anything out there?" She tipped her head toward the lake.

"I'm not sure."

"If he's following you, and you get to him before we do," she said, "don't leave him standing."

I opened my mouth, and then closed it. It was the kind of thing that scared me about women. How did they move from one part of their head to the other so easily? Blow a suspect away one minute, hit on a guy at the bar the next? Comfort a grieving woman one minute, talk about killing a man the next?

"Let's go," Diaz said. "We drop this stuff off and I'll drive you back."

We started through the house and when I took a last look out the French doors, Richards was bent with one knee in the grass, pulling the yellow tarp back over the dog.

CHAPTER 14

I rode with Diaz to the county's forensics lab but stayed in the car in the empty, well-lit parking lot while he went inside. After twenty minutes the detective came out and begged off taking me all the way home. He assigned a young resource officer who looked like a high school student to drive me back.

"We're fresh on this one and I should be out working it," Diaz said. "I'll call you if we get anything off the, uh, evidence."

I said nothing during the trip back to Billy's. The kid took my lead and drove in silence. I'd called Billy on the cell phone to let him know where I'd been. The convenience of having the phone in my pocket was beginning to worry me. I'd carried a police radio with me for most of my working life but thought I'd left that behind.

When I got back the night manager cleared me with a phone call and when I walked into the apartment, Billy was working the kitchen. Two pink slabs of tuna steak were sizzling under his broiler and the odor of garlic bread was rising out of the oven. I hadn't eaten since a dose of my own bad oatmeal that morning and it was now nearly ten. I sat at the counter and Billy put a plate of sliced apple and a tall glass of water in front of me.

"Thanks, mom," I said. But the joke didn't go over well.

"What d-did they have d-down there?" he asked without turning from his work. "I ch-checked the online reports, b-but it was all standard p-press release stuff."

He tipped his chin at a video screen that was recessed in the wall above one end of the counter. A Web page for the local newspaper was up.

I told him about the prints leading into the water, the obvious presence of the FBI and the dead dog. While I talked he laid out the seasoned tuna on two plates with steamed okra and put the garlic bread between them. He ate standing up, thumbed a few buttons on the remote and the Web page screen turned into a live broadcast of the local news. The abduction was the lead story.

A young reporter with glasses was doing a standup in the neighborhood, motioning back to the two-story pink stucco home. The camera had to leave him and zoom to get a grainy shot from where the press had been cordoned off more than a block away. Back in the frame the reporter scribbled circles onto a pad while giving the name of the missing girl and making the leap to put her in with the other victims of what the media had taken to calling the "Moonlight Murderer."

"Another innocent victim silently swept away from her home leaving law enforcement with nothing to do but wait," blabbed the reporter. When coverage jumped to a photo of the child and an interview with one of her teachers, I got up and started making a fresh pot of coffee. I stood at the machine and listened to the lead reporter interview neighbors, asking them if they were now afraid for their own families. One said she was trying to sell her house and knew three other friends putting theirs on the market. A man spoke cryptically about "armed security" and "you do what you have to do."

Billy punched off the report and I sat back down.

"S-So if they l-let you inside, you are at l-least off their suspect list," he said, always the attorney.

"It helps that I was with one of their own detectives when the abduction happened," I said, sipping the coffee. "But once a suspect, always a suspect."

"W-Well, y-you've got one f-fan," Billy said, handing me a message slip from his office. Fred Gunther had called from the hospital, asking me to come in and see him.

"He say how he's doing?"

"Sounded d-depressed to me. They are still not sure about the leg."

"Say why he wants to see me?"

Billy shook his head.

"Maybe he just w-wants to th-thank you."

That night I dreamt of the city, of running from my mother's Philadelphia house near St. Agnes Hospital down Mifflin Street to Front and then north. The heat of the summer is stirring a soup of gutter dust and exhaust fumes and I am pointing my face out to the Delaware River hoping to catch a breeze from the Camden side. On the water, container ships are sliding down with the current and from the sidewalk I can only see their superstructures, moving like buildings on rollers. I hit the cobblestones past South Street and my ankles are twisting and my knees are aching but I ignore the pain and push on. I know there is a fountain up ahead in the park at Penn's Landing so I keep pounding with the goal of cool water splashed up in my face and down my shoulders but when I finally reach the wide, knee-high pool I bend to the clear water and cup my hands around the face of my own reflection but it is Lavernious Coleman's cheeks that I touch, his eyes, filmed and growing sightless. I try to pull my hands away but can't get them out, my fingers are stuck in the cattails and the duckweed of the Everglades and the sawgrass is trying to pull me down.

When I woke up I was sweating. I could hear my heart thumping under the sheets in Billy's guest room. I sat up and swung my feet to the floor and rubbed my face and knew there would be no more sleeping this night. On the patio the ocean was black and murmuring against the beach and I sat waiting for the first soft light of dawn to tinge the horizon.

* * *

I needed to get my truck. Needed to get back in my own vehicle, drive at my own pace. Feel like I had some control over something instead of depending on others and spinning whichever way they determined I should be yanked.

I took a cab to the ranger's station, over Billy's protestations, and got there about ten o'clock, just as Mike Stanton was loading up the Whaler for a run out on the river. My truck was parked in the visitor's lot under a light pole. The kid saw me get out of the taxi and pay the driver, but turned back to his work.

I walked to the truck, gave it a once-over and opened the driver's door. A cab full of heat and stale air spilled out. I tossed my bags in and walked across the lot to the boat ramp.

"Nice job on the scratch, Mike. How much do I owe you?"

"About fifty dollars, Mr. Freeman," he said, finally looking up at me. "My friends and I did it ourselves."

"She run all right for you?"

"Yeah, fine. 'Cept I have never been pulled over so many times in my life," he said.

I raised as much innocence into my face as I could.

"Four times in two days by cops asking all kinds of questions about who I was and where the owner of the truck was and had you left the state. It wasn't worth it so I just parked it."

"I'm sorry for the trouble," I said, handing the kid five twenties from my wallet. He took all five without comment.

"Oh, and Mr. Freeman," he said as I started to turn away. "Cleve said to tell you to use his canoe 'round the side there if you wanted. Said yours got busted up?"

"Thanks," I said without elaboration.

I walked back to my truck feeling guilty, knowing the kid must be just shaking his head.

The noon traffic was no different from any other part of the working day, but this time sanity sat behind the wheel. No blue light, no horn, total adherence to the laws of the state. It took me more than an hour to get to the hospital, and when I asked for the room of Fred Gunther, the elderly woman at the information desk gave me a visitor's badge and directed me to follow the blue stripe on the hallway floor.

I thought I had sworn off hospitals two years ago when I was wheelchaired out of Jefferson in Philadelphia with a bullethole in my neck and an appointment for a follow-up with a psychiatrist, neither of which I had asked for. Now I was on my second visit in five days. I hated hospitals, had watched my mother die in a hospital, eaten from the inside by cancer, refusing to end her pain with medication. Her knurled and leathery hand closed tight around my fingers, whispering a Catholic prayer with her final breath. I shook the vision. I hated hospitals. I moved through the hallways with pastel wallpaper, dodging staff dressed in blue and pink and green. It was a color-coordinated world with no place for black.

When I reached Gunther's room the door was open and he was alone. The media swirl had moved on to the next exclusive of the day. The big man was lying in bed, his eyes closed and his huge hands folded over his chest, fingers stacked in a pile. I scanned the length of the bedclothes and saw two lumps where both feet were covered. When I shifted my eyes back to his face, he was awake.

"How you doin'?" I said, covering some embarrassment.

"I've been better."

His voice was raspy and tired. I let him come full awake and watched him shift his weight using his powerful shoulders and arms.

"How much longer they going to keep you?"

"A while. They say I'll be able to keep the leg."

"I'm glad to hear it."

"Thanks to you."

I let that sit. Avoiding a trite response. We'd quickly run out of polite things to say.

"Could you close that door, Mr. Freeman?"

I shut the heavy door and when I came back the listlessness had left his face.

"I've had a lot of time to think," he started. "And I wasn't sure who to tell this to, but it seems that maybe you're the one."

I nodded and waited out his hesitation. It's a standard cop interviewing technique.

"I've got some friends, acquaintances really, out in the Glades who aren't exactly, uh, traditional folk. Some are natives. Some, like me, are just grown into the place and can't stand the way it's changing."

His voice had jumped a decibel and at least one notch of anxiety.

"So you said before," I replied, hoping to bring him back down but not shut him up.

"Before all this with the kids started, there was a history of protection from the outside among the folks who live out there. And it wasn't all pretty. A game warden was killed in the fifties. Some revenuers disappeared in the early days. We used to laugh about the old tales, but things had changed. Even the Seminoles were making money off the coastal folks, bringing them out onto the reservation to gamble at the Indian casino and all.

Hell, they even let them hold a damn rock concert for 60,000 kids out there on a New Year's."

I moved to the side of the bed. Closer. Just you and me, pal.

"So these acquaintances aren't laughing so much anymore?"

"Shit started happening. A group of overnight canoeists who weren't using a guide got vandalized in the middle of nowhere. Their water was stolen. The ribs of their boats smashed. Some hikers on the canal levee stumbled into a nest of rattlesnakes in a spot where no natural rattlesnake would set up territory."

"Anybody claim responsibility?"

"No one outright."

There was a wrestling match going on in Gunther's head between conscience and fear.

"I don't think the old-timers would stand for something like this, but you can't always tell with some of the younger ones," he said.

"You have any names?" I said, taking a chance of shutting him down.

Gunther sighed, blowing air out his nose and closing his eyes for several seconds. I thought I'd taken a step too far. Then he reached over for a message pad and pen and started writing.

"You go out to this place and ask for Nate Brown. I already talked to them and they'll sit down with you."

The pen wedged between Gunther's thick sausage fingers looked like a dark sliver stuck in his huge hand.

"How come you're telling me this instead of the cops?"

"These people don't talk to cops. They've been avoiding authority out there for a hundred years."

"So why open it up now?" I said, again pushing. His wan face suddenly gained a slight flush of color. A sharp clearness came into his eyes.

"Hell, boy! Somebody tried to kill us!"

We both listened to his anger echo through the room. I took the piece of paper from his hand.

"Mr. Gunther, somebody has already succeeded in killing four kids. Kids who were a lot more innocent than you or I."

He closed his eyes again, lying there in silence like I found him. I let the door click quietly shut when I went out.

CHAPTER 15

"**N**ate Brown? Never heard of him. But if you're heading out to the Loop Road area, you're on your way to a different world."

As I pulled out of the hospital parking lot Billy was on the cell phone giving me directions to the Loop Road Frontier Hotel, the name Gunther had written on the message pad where Nate Brown and this group of acquaintances had agreed to meet me.

As I headed south toward Miami, he also gave me the history of the place.

Only thirty miles from the high-rise glitter, urban blight, Hispanic-dominated politics and thoroughly modern city of Miami, lay a place outside the curve of progress and, in many ways, still outside the purview of the law.

The Loop Road had first been hacked out of the Everglades in the early 1900s by dreamers, men who thought they could simply plow through what they considered useless swampland and create a link between the thriving new cities of Miami on one coast of Florida and Tampa on the other side. They were men with money and power and not a little bravery. And they made some progress.

By dredging limestone from under the water and piling it up and tamping it down, they started a road. But as is often the case, men with more power and money scuttled their plan. A roadway was eventually built across the lower end of the peninsula, at a heavy price to the laborers who died cutting the way through. Men drowned in the vast fields of water. Others were maimed in dynamite blasts. Some simply disappeared in an ancient Glades muck that could suck a boot, a leg, a worker's torso down.

But when the road from Tampa to Miami was finally finished in 1946 and dubbed the Tamiami Trail, it had effectively bypassed the first attempted roadway. The original Loop Road would remain unfinished, a trail to nowhere. And a trail to nowhere, in the middle of nowhere, draws a unique breed of resident.

For half a century the Loop Road was little more than a jump-off point for alligator hunters, exotic plume hunters and not a few moonshiners. Even in the years when killing off endangered alligators and snowy egrets became illegal and prohibition kicked in, the Loop was still a jump-off for poachers and white lightning runners, bail jumpers and criminals who needed a place where few questions were asked and authority ignored.

"It has a long tradition of being a place apart," Billy said. "The people who live there don't like strangers, government, developers, and have a special disdain for the law."

By the time Billy finished his history lesson I'd gotten off the I-95 exit to Southwest Eighth Street and headed west.

"I'm not sure I'd go out there alone if I were you."

"Yeah. Thanks," I said, punching him off.

Within a few miles I'd lost the city, the bodegas, the strip shopping centers, even the stoplights. Out here there were stretches of small orange and avocado groves, acres of tropical tree farms and open stands of slash pine. In some places the narrow roads ran under ancient stands of oak draped in moss whose limbs stretched across the roadway to form dark green tunnels that reminded me of my river. I had to cut farther south and by the time I found Loop Road the late-afternoon thunderheads were gathering in the western sky, piling up and tumbling east.

The Loop Road Frontier Hotel seemed more a backcountry Southern roadhouse than a hotel. When I found it I pulled into a shell-covered parking lot that was a quarter full with old-model pickup trucks, a few dusty sedans and a semi-tractor with its grease-covered skid plate exposed. I turned off my truck and sat listening to the heat tick off the engine, wondering if this was a mistake.

Off to one side of the building's covered entrance three men, probably in their early twenties, stood in lazy conversation, bootheels up on the bumper of a dented Ford pickup. They were dressed in jeans and tight, dark-colored T-shirts and wore baseball caps with various logos stitched on the front. They were not unlike a hundred other groups of young and uninspired locals I'd moved off the street corners of Philadelphia in my years of foot patrol. I could see them cutting their eyes my way.

I got out, locked my door, and had started toward the building when the biggest of the trio called out: "Hey, Mr. Fancytruck. You lost?"

I know I should have ignored it. I know I could have walked on and let the laughter fall behind me. A life is full of should-haves and could-haves. Instead I stopped and turned to the group.

"I don't think so."

"Well, I think so," the big one said and stepped forward as I knew he would. I'd seen it too many times.

He was my height but thirty pounds heavier and most of it fat. His chunky face was topped by a 1950s style crewcut but in his left ear was a tight looped earring. His brown eyes held an alcoholic luster. Get drunk or high so your reflexes are off and your oxygen intake is impaired and then go out and pick a fight. Idiocy knows no boundaries, I thought to myself.

"You a cop?" he sneered, moving within striking range, braver than I expected.

"No," I said. "Do you need one?"

"We don't need no fucking cops out here," one of his buddies answered from his spot behind the big one. Neither of the others had moved off their fender.

"Good," I said, turning to move on when I heard the big one suck in a quick snort of air.

Even professional fighters give away their intentions with breathing patterns. It is a natural instinct to draw in a snatch of air before expending the tight energy used to deliver a blow or make a hard move. Everyone does it. Amateurs are just louder and sloppier.

When I heard the whistle of air I turned and spun inside his first roundhouse punch, aimed at the back of my head, and caught the blow instead on my left forearm. I had blocked a lot of punches in my hours at O'Hara's Gym and this one was no light shot. His second swing I caught on my right elbow and it felt like a baseball bat. The guy knew leverage and was throwing his weight behind his swings. But he was easy to read and I knew what was coming and covered up, my fists high next to my temples and elbows in to my ribs. Protect your head and heart, Frankie's dad had always coached, even to the pro boxers he trained.

With his friends rooting him on, the big boy kept throwing and I kept stepping inside, taking his best on my shoulders and arms. He was already breathing hard. I knew he'd burn himself out. Only once did he try to come in low and even though I blocked the shot with my elbow the force crunched into the ribs I'd bruised in the plane crash and the pain set a new fire in my chest.

Then one of the others decided to get in on it and came at me from the side and fired a skinny punch that caught me on the cheek and I knew this had to end before it turned into a stomping.

I circled the big one, moving away from his right hand and timed my own punch as perfectly as Frankie's dad had ever hoped to teach a rangy, whitebread football player from the neighborhood. Stepping inside just as he was drawing a deep breath, I planted my right foot and using the power of a thousand hours of river paddling and beach running I drove a short right fist into his chest. The blow caught him just below the sternum, right in the notch where the ribs meet, and the air came out of his throat like a bubble bursting on the surface of a lake.

He went down hard on the seat of his pants and sat there, arms flopped to his side, eyes open but sightless, looking like an old stuffed bear left useless in the corner of the room.

His friends were stunned and stood frozen, looking down at him while I turned and stepped up on the porch and without a word walked through the front door of the Loop Road Frontier.

* * *

Inside I stood in what passed for a lobby, leaned against a wall and shook. My knees were quivering, my hands trembled and I knew that if I could see them, the pupils of my eyes would be huge. Adrenaline. You couldn't avoid it. It's a biological reaction in every animal that ever hunted or was hunted. It surges through the blood to help you flee or fight. And it pumps regardless of the choice.

I paced a bit, flexing my hands open and closed and letting the feeling leech away. The entryway I was standing in was small and paneled in Dade County Pine similar to my river shack. But this was polished and gave off a dark glow in the light of a small chandelier hanging from the eight-foot ceiling. At an empty counter a placard with a ridge of dust along its top edge was propped up and read: No Rooms.

A hotel with no rooms. I didn't wonder. But I could hear the distinctive sound of clinking glassware around the corner and followed it to the expected barroom.

The room was dusky with heavy wood and dull sidelights on the walls sheathed in smoked yellow glass. A mahogany bar ran the length of one wall. It was backed by an impressive ten-foot-long mirror set in a scrolled wood frame that matched the hue of the mahogany. Two men sat at the bar. A broad circular table held four more and I could not see around into the darkest end of the room where booths and at least one other table sat. There were no windows to the outside.

I sat down on a stool and the bartender ignored me for a full five minutes. She was a thin woman with bleached blond hair pulled back in a tufted ponytail held by a red rubber band. She wore belted jeans with a cowboy buckle and the kind of white insulated shirt with three-quarter sleeves that up north we called long underwear. Finally she moved down the bar to me, a damp rag of a woman.

"Can I get ya?"

I had already checked the bar preference.

"Bud," I said.

"Three fifty."

Her face was white and stern. Her only makeup was a smear of lipstick and she kept her dull brown eyes turned away. She didn't move until I put a ten-dollar bill on the bar top and only then went to get me a cold bottle and a wet glass. She didn't even grunt when she made change. The other patrons two seats away never looked up from their cribbage game.

I propped my elbows on the bar. My arms and shoulders ached from the big boy's hammering. When I looked in the mirror across from me I could see swelling already lumping up the side of my face from the other one's cheap shot and I could feel where my teeth had gouged the inside of my mouth. I took a mouthful of beer, swished it around and swallowed the mixture of cold alcohol and blood. A sweating, shaking stranger with a fresh knot on his face didn't seem to draw even a second look from the regulars.

I swiveled around on the stool. An alligator skin that had to be eleven or twelve feet long was tacked on a side wall above a row of booths. A stuffed, mangy-looking bobcat was snarling from his perch above the coat rack. I drained the beer and figured that when the bartender got around to granting me another overpriced drink I'd take a chance and ask for Nate Brown.

My back was to the entrance when the boys from the parking lot came in. They'd apparently gulped a few more shots of courage from a bottle in their rusty truck. They shuffled up and took up positions around me. No one else bothered to look up.

"You're fuckin' meat," the skinny cheapshot announced. The big one stood back out of range, his face still a shade pale, his breathing still raggedy.

The men at the bar turned and rag woman crossed her arms and watched like they were viewing a half interesting rerun of an old TV episode.

"Get up, meat," the big boy rasped.

I tightened my grip on the beer bottle in my hand and felt suddenly tired, the adrenaline glands confused.

"Don't you boys go breakin' stuff in here again, Cory Brooker," the bartender offered, but made no move to come closer.

The circle tightened. Cheapshot sucked in his breath and his right arm started to come up. I was a split second from bringing my foot up into his crotch when a brown wizened hand reached in and clamped the boy's forearm. He tried to fight it but when he turned to see who had hold of him, he blanched and stepped back.

The owner of the hand stepped into the circle and all eyes fell on him. His close-cropped steel-gray hair bristled up from a deeply tanned scalp and his eyes were so pale as to be nearly colorless. He still had a grip on the skinny one and I could see the ridged muscle, taut as wound cable, running up his forearm.

"Cain't have it," he said, and the tone of authority caused all four of us to flinch.

"B-But, Mr. Brown, this . . . ," the big boy started to whine.

"Shut up," the old man explained.

All three of them exchanged glances and backed away, their necks in hangdog position. The old man watched the group move out of the entrance before turning to me.

"Nate Brown," he said, extending what I now considered a magical hand. "You're the one pulled Fred Gunther out of the swamp?"

"Max Freeman," I answered, shaking the hand, which felt for all the world like a bunch of rolled pennies wrapped in old leather.

"Walk with me, Max."

I followed him to the far corner of the room while those at the bar turned back to their card game. Back in the recesses of the room, at a round wooden table, Brown introduced me to three middle-aged men who rose to their feet in a polite fashion and shook my hand.

Rory Sims, Mitch Blackman, Dave Ashley.

I took the last wooden chair without comment. As I

watched them sit I noted that all but Ashley were wearing the same small knife scabbard on their belts.

Brown settled and filled a heavy, cut-glass tumbler with two fingers of sipping whiskey and pushed it in front of me. My glass matched the other four at the table. After he refilled his own, Brown reached down and set the bottle on the floor next to his chair leg.

"Fred Gunther is a good man. And we all call him a friend. So first off, we thank you for what you done," Brown started. "And goin' on Fred's advice, we agreed it would maybe help to speak with you."

The others nodded, with the exception of Ashley, who sat staring into the amber light of the whiskey in front of him.

Brown went on. His voice had a slow Southern cadence that made me want to sip from my glass.

"Ain't none of us too fond of the law out here, least of all me. But these here chile killins got a lot of folks stirred up and we are thinkin' it might do us well to have some kinda, you know, go-between."

I looked from man to man until I was convinced they were waiting for me to answer an unasked question. I slowly turned the tumbler of whiskey in a circle on the polished table.

"I'm not sure how I can help," I said, finally giving in to the temptation and taking a drink. The whiskey burned the open cut inside my mouth but slid warm and easy down my throat. The others followed suit.

"Gunther gave us reason to believe you might be in the same sort of, uh, position that we think many folks out here are in," said Sims, a balding, bearded man whose collared shirt and manner made him seem the odd man out in the group. "That is," Sims said, "he indicated you may have been a suspect yourself at one time but seemed to have proved your way out of that."

Billy must have said more to Gunther than I knew.

"Look, Mr. Freeman," Blackman said, pronouncing my last name like it was two words. "They're riding folks mighty hard out here and we just don't want to see an innocent man get caught in some damn government frame-up."

I took another sip of whiskey and looked over the rim of my glass at him. There was an agitation in his eyes that none of the others carried.

"I mean, look. I'm in the guide business just like Gunther. I spent my whole life out here and we don't need the bad publicity either," Blackman said, in a calmer tone.

"We thought maybe you might be a sort of liaison with the authorities, you being a former officer and all," Sims said. "Our expertise may indeed be helpful."

"Do you have any guesses who might be involved?" I said, looking at Ashley, who was the only one who hadn't spoken.

"If we knowed who it was, we'd of taken care of it already our ownself," Brown said, reaching down for the bottle.

"A lot of work has gone into protecting the traditions of these Everglades, Mr. Freeman," Sims said. "Something like this can do more damage than good."

Brown was filling glasses but I put a hand over mine.

"I'm not sure that I have the kind of access to the people investigating this that Gunther thinks I do," I said. "But I'm sure anything you might offer could easily be passed along."

The table went silent for several seconds. I had played snitches and informants and hustlers too many times not to see that we had hit a delicate moment. These men too had tracked and hunted and waited patiently with lures and bait too many times to jump before they were ready. I waited a few more calculated seconds before standing up. A chorus of scraping chairs joined me.

"Well, Mr. Gunther obviously knows how to reach me."

As I walked through the room, rag woman watched me from behind the bar where my change from the single beer lay untouched. I tipped my head as I passed her and I swear she tried to smile.

When I got outside the western sky was streaked in purple and red and the remains of a rain shower was dripping off the porch roof. The big boy's truck was gone, but as I walked across the lot I could see they hadn't left easy.

The passenger side of my front windshield was smashed, a spiderweb of fissures running out from a deep divot in the middle. Three separate scratches ran down the driver's side from the front cowling to the tailgate. I figured the only reason they didn't bust out the headlights was so I could find my way out of their part of the world.

CHAPTER 16

I waited until I was back on the Tamiami Trail and then called Billy, giving him a brief description of my meeting with the Loop Road group. I left out the encounter with the welcoming committee. I gave him the names of the four men at the table, knowing he could not resist his natural inquisitiveness.

Driving east into Miami, headlights and overhead streetlights flashed and splintered through my broken windshield and hampered my view of the skyline after dark. When I got up onto the interstate, I could see a curving neon light that snaked through the city, an artistic addition to the Metrorail line. The Centrust Building stood bathed in teal spotlights, a tribute to the Florida Marlins baseball team. Against the blackness of Biscayne Bay, the lights in the high-rise towers took on the look of manmade constellations. The contrast to the weathered pine of the Loop Road Hotel was not lost on me.

When I got back to Billy's apartment he was waiting for me with a fresh pot of coffee, a take-out order of jerk chicken and black beans and rice, and a sheaf of computer printouts, dossiers he called them, on Brown, Sims, Blackman and Ashley. He also had company.

He was on the patio with a woman he introduced as Dianne McIntyre, "a lawyer w-with an office in the s-same b-building as mine."

She was as tall as Billy and had a swimmer's figure, broad shoulders and narrow hips, and was dressed expensively in a pure silk blouse and a charcoal skirt. She was comfortable enough to have taken off her heels and was padding about in stockings.

As I ate at the counter they stood in the kitchen area, sharing a bottle of wine. When I looked up Billy was staring at me.

"W-What happened to your face?"

I self-consciously touched the swollen cheekbone.

"Door," I said.

The woman raised one of her fine dark eyebrows and indelicately probed at a molar with her tongue. Billy accepted my reticence and picked up the first page of the stack of papers.

"Dianne actually kn-knows this f-fellow Sims. S-She worked w-with him on an environmental case."

I could tell how hard Billy was trying to control his stutter and it made me anxious for him. But the woman seemed completely inured.

"It was several years ago in a dispute between a very influential developer who wanted to build some kind of mega sports complex in an area of the Everglades that had never been touched," she said, turning the wineglass in her hands. "Sims had been working with the naturalists and environmental groups for years and had marshaled some fairly strong support against the project. One of the shrewdest things he'd done was elicit the favor of the old Gladesmen by convincing them that their way of life would be threatened as much as the flora and wildlife of the area."

"N-No doubt men l-like your Mr. Brown," Billy said, leafing through the stack of papers.

"Apparently things got ugly and some of the developer's back-room people allegedly threatened Sims," McIntyre continued. "Shortly after, handmade posters started showing up at the public fishing ramps and even in some outlying suburban stores that if anyone harmed Sims, those responsible would be gutted and fed to the gators."

The attorney again seemed unruffled by the circumstances. Neither shocked nor amused. Just the facts, ma'am. I watched her closely.

"The project finally died and Sims seemed to move away from the mainstream. I haven't heard much about him for the last few years." When she finished, she sipped again at her wine.

Nate Brown's was a story in itself, much of it untold.

Billy had found some archived newspaper clippings and legal transcripts online that shed a little light on the wizened old man who could back down three pumped-up thugs with only the slightest flick of his Loop Road respect.

Nathaniel Brown had been born in the Glades and learned the skills of the back country with one motivation: survival. There was no record of his parentage and no official documentation of his life until a war record placed him in an infantry division in the army in WWII. There were notations of his award of two silver stars, for bravery beyond the call when he had taken out a group of specialized German mountain troops during an ambush, "single-handedly causing a number of casualties upon the enemy." He had then doctored a group of his own squad members wounded in the fight and kept them alive in the woods for nearly two weeks until they were found.

After his discharge, his name didn't surface again for more than a decade until he was arrested and charged in the death of a game warden. By then Brown had built a small reputation as an alligator poacher whose knowledge of the Glades made him impossible to catch.

But court transcripts showed that on a night in the early 1970s a warden was chasing Brown, whom he suspected of carrying several fresh gator skins in his outboard runabout. The boat chase led into a series of twisting tributaries on the edge of Florida Bay, and Brown reportedly lured the warden into an area of sand bars. Even in the dark the Gladesman was able to read the fine currents, water he had grown up on and traveled his entire life. The game warden was not. The officer ran his boat into a sand spur at high speed and was thrown from the boat, breaking his neck. Brown disappeared into the mangroves.

Three days later, after supposedly hearing of the warden's death, Brown turned himself in. His public defender pleaded him out to a charge of involuntary manslaughter. He served six years, his final two at a road prison near the isolated Ten Thousand Islands section of Florida's southwest coast. After his release, his official tracks again disappeared. No driver's license. No property holdings. Nothing.

"And you saw this guy?" Dianne McIntyre said, her first true sign of piqued interest. "He'd have to be near eighty."

Billy filled the wineglasses and I watched the woman cup her hands around the crystal. She had a near-perfect profile and her auburn hair fell across her cheek as she bent to the glass. She was oddly standing on one foot, her other brought up behind her like one of those 1950s movie starlets during a kiss. I guessed she liked her wine.

"This B-Blackman I actually kn-know of," said Billy, paging through the documents. "He is, or w-was, a guide like Gunther."

Billy said he'd tried to depose Blackman when he was handling the client suit against Gunther.

"Fred said he was w-working with him at the t-time. That he was the b-best guide in the G-Glades, but had an attitude."

Billy had sent several certified requests to Blackman's business P.O. address but got no response. When the people suing Gunther dropped the suit, he never pursued it.

Blackman had the typical paper trail of licenses, social security and business permits, but court records showed little in the past. But in the last few years he had had a handful of complaints filed against him by clients, including a charge of aggravated assault in which an upstate New York man accused Blackman of whipping him across the face with a fly rod during an angry outburst on a fishing excursion.

Blackman said it was an accident. The New Yorker settled for a plea of no contest to a misdemeanor assault charge and court costs. I set Blackman's face in my mind, recalled the agitation in his voice and the almost mocking pronunciation of my name.

Dave Ashley was an unknown. The silent member of Brown's cabal had no paper trail. Variations of his name and my estimate of his age in the early forties brought nothing. No licenses, addresses, court appearance, nothing. In this day and age, the blank sheet stunned the attorneys. It was difficult to believe any person could exist without leaving some imprint in the modern electronic tracking of every soul from birth to school to work to death.

"There was an Ashley gang, a notorious criminal family that roamed the South Florida region in the early nineteen hundreds," McIntyre said.

Both Billy's and my faces must have taken on the look of blank dumbness. A crinkle came to the woman's eyes, she took a sip of wine and began.

The Ashleys were a family of Crackers who had come to Florida near the turn of the twentieth century and found work providing the muscle and sweat to build Henry Flagler's railway line into then frontier South Florida. While the father and older boys chopped railroad ties, young John Ashley became a skilled hunter and trapper in the Glades. Then came a day in 1911 when the body of a Seminole Indian named DeSoto Tiger floated up in a canal. Word had it young John was the last one seen with Tiger, who was on his way to Miami to sell twelve hundred dollars in otter skins. The skins were eventually sold— by young John.

Ashley was eventually arrested and jailed but escaped and for the next ten years he and his family took up the business of robbing banks, running illegal rum from the Bahamas, and using their criminal wealth to buy off the local law.

"Then some old-time Palm Beach sheriff became the Ashley gang's sworn nemesis," McIntyre said. "He tracked them down for years and once came close, but one of his deputies, his cousin, was killed in a shootout.

"Then sometime in 1924 he laid an ambush on the Sebastian River bridge. When John and three of his gang went for their guns, all four were cut down. The rest were eventually killed or captured or run out of the state. But who knows about their descendents?"

When she was done, both of us stared at her in appreciation.

"Be a long stretch, huh?" she said, smiling over the rim of her wineglass.

I thought of Ashley, sitting slumped in his chair at the table, looking into the glow of his whiskey and turning the crystal glass in a circle as he'd seen me do. Could a genetic hate for the law and a throwback's love of a wild place fester into homicide? There have been lesser reasons.

* * *

I cleaned Billy's kitchen while he and his lawyer friend finished their wine on the patio. I flicked on the wall-mounted video screen and watched the news. A manhunt was growing. The lake behind the two-story pastel house in Flamingo Lakes was still being searched for any scrap of clothing or footprint or sign of a boat or body being dragged ashore. Neighborhood groups had rallied and, as in the other cases, were organizing to pass out leaflets with a photo of the missing girl.

News of the dead dog had been leaked and one reporter had "a source close to the investigation" confirming that a quick necropsy of the animal had been done and determined that a "razor-sharp blade" had been used to slash through the shepherd's throat and instantly silence the dog.

"My sources tell me that such an attack would have required great strength and a knowledge of animal anatomy to have been done so quickly and efficiently," the reporter said, laying it on with just the right tone of professional knowledge and solemn warning before tossing it back to the studio.

In the other abductions it had been three or four days before the GPS coordinates were sent to the police, and I knew Hammonds' people had to be scrambling. The feds were in full strength now and I vaguely remembered the craziness in Atlanta years before when they finally closed in on Wayne Williams after twenty-two children and young adults had been killed. Twenty-two.

I switched off the television report when Billy and Dianne McIntyre came back inside. She retrieved her suit coat from the back of the couch and slipped on her shoes while Billy set their glasses in the sink. I was caught in a bad place. The roommate that shouldn't be there, intruding.

"Billy," I started, "I was just thinking of going . . ."

"Max, it was a pleasure to meet you," the woman deftly interrupted. "I absolutely must go. Depositions at eight o'clock sharp."

She shook my hand and smiled. There was an intelligent sheen in her dark eyes that was not alcohol-induced. They went out into Billy's lobby, closing the door behind them. I filled a cup of coffee and went out onto the patio. A half moon, balanced on its tip, was sitting high in the summer sky and the clouds nearby picked up its light at their edges. The air was still. Below I could faintly hear the uniform rhythm of surf washing the sand.

Billy joined me in less than five minutes. He'd retrieved his glass from the sink and sat down hard in a chair, saying nothing. I stood at the railing.

"Nice lady," I finally said. More silence.

"Brilliant," he answered without a hint of stutter.

When I looked at him he was staring at the moon. I didn't ask which he was referring to and after letting it set awhile he finally took a sip of wine and changed whatever subject we might have been on.

"How d-did you get that n-nasty bruise?"

I told him about the backwoods boys, the altercation in the parking lot and how Brown had held an obvious provenance in the Loop Road world.

"So d-do you really th-think they need you to take the heat off them?"

"No. There's something else working there. Blackman's angry, Ashley's sullen, Sims is caught in the middle and Gunther's carrying around a load of guilt," I said, trying to grind the stones down to their essence. "And Brown is trying to save them all."

"Man in a foxhole full of w-wounded," Billy said.

* * *

In the morning I called a local auto-glass repair service out of the yellow pages. They came to you, so I gave them the tower address and the model of my truck. When I hung up the phone, my cheekbone seemed to ache more. There was a knot in my left forearm that felt like a small group of marbles under the skin. I took another sip of coffee and called Fred Gunther's hospital room.

"Yeah. Sorry about that. Sometimes with strangers it can get a little rough out that way," Gunther said after I spilled a little venom on him about my parking lot encounter and the vandalism of my truck.

"Hell, they still talk about the time some city boy came out there and started calling somebody at the bar a Cracker. Before he knew what hit him he had a blade cut from his scrotum to his rib cage, right through his clothes. There was a barroom full of people and of course when the cops got there, no one saw a thing."

"They do seem to have a thing for knives," I said.

There was a silence on the other end of the line that seemed heavy with meaning but hard to read. I wished I'd gone to talk to Gunther in person so I could see his face. He had not yet asked what his "acquaintances" had told me.

"You'll have to excuse my denseness, Mr. Gunther," I finally said. "But I'm not real sure why you sent me out there or what your friends want me to do for them."

"Acquaintances," Gunther snapped, the first response so far that hadn't been chewed and measured in his head before letting it out of his mouth.

"You never worked with Blackman?"

"That was a while back," he said. "I worked with him some because he'd been here forever and knew every damn fishing hole and hog-hunting patch in the Glades. But he wasn't so good working with people."

"So you were his partner?"

I could feel myself slipping into my old police interrogation mode but couldn't help myself.

"We shared some clients," Gunther said, getting careful again. "I would help him out with outfitters and new equipment that came on the market. He flew with me sometimes so we could spot out places to take sightseers and such."

"And that ended?"

"He started getting hinky with people, was less tolerant of folks. Clients didn't like him. It started hurting my business more than helping."

"But you were still friends."

"Acquaintances. Yeah."

I could tell I was starting to lose Gunther's tolerance, or sense of indebtedness, or whatever it was that had motivated him to confide in me. But I wanted more.

"What's with this guy Ashley?"

"Nobody knows much about Ashley but Nate. He lives somewhere out near Myersons Hammock in the middle of the northern Glades and just seems to show up, usually to trade off skins and to let the guides know what the fish and game are doing. He lives like the old-timers. Supposedly he's related to the old Ashley gang but no one knows if that's true. He'd hang around with the group at the Loop bar if Nate was there, and listen to the bull. I don't even know why he was there to tell the truth.

"Hell, I'm not real sure why any of us were there," he added. I could feel him tasting his words. "Doesn't matter, I'm outta here anyway."

"Out of the hospital?"

"Out of the state," he said. "I've got family back in upstate New York and I'm going home."

Now it was my turn to measure my words. There was more

going on in the big man's head than just getting out. Two days ago he was angry that someone had tried to kill him. Today he was chucking it all and running.

"Do you think any of your acquaintances have anything to do with these child killings?"

I could hear him breathing on the other end of the line.

"Thank you for saving my life, Mr. Freeman. Goodbye."

The line went dead.

* * *

I was putting my cup to my lips when the phone rang back to life and caused me to jump, sloshing hot coffee down my chin. The desk manager downstairs was on the line.

"Mr. Freeman, there is a gentleman from AA Auto Glass here. He is in need of your keys, sir."

When I walked outside through the front entrance, a step van with the Auto Glass logo was parked in the visitor's lot next to my truck. On the other side, Detective Diaz was leaning against the front bumper of his sedan.

He was dressed in his now familiar uniform: dark canvas Dockers and a white oxford shirt rolled up at the sleeves. His tie was pulled down, his sunglasses low on the bridge of his nose. He was talking with the glass installer like they were buddies, killing time in the shade of a bottlebrush tree.

"Good morning, Mr. Freeman," Diaz greeted me with too much familiarity.

"Detective," I nodded.

The use of his law enforcement title caused the installer to frown and cut his eyes at Diaz, who probably hadn't mentioned his status while asking the workman questions.

"What brings you way up here on such a hot and no doubt busy day for you?"

Diaz did not answer, and only motioned to the other man with a nod of his head.

I talked with the glass guy, gave him my keys. When he went back to his van I returned to Diaz, who was still leaning on his front bumper. He had backed into the parking space. It was standard practice for someone using an unmarked police car. If the detective needed to get his shotgun or bulletproof vest out of the trunk, his hardware wasn't so easily seen by passers-by.

"So what's up? You get any prints off that stuff?" I asked.

"No. None at all," Diaz answered. "They're still trying to trace the retailer on the GPS unit, but it could be hundreds of places and the guy would have paid cash. Hell, it was probably stolen anyway."

I nodded, waiting.

"So," I repeated. "What's up?"

"You have some trouble?" he asked, answering my question with a question, waving the back of his hand at my injured truck.

"Diaz," I said, losing patience. "What the fuck do you want?"

The windshield guy peeked up from his work. Diaz put his back to the workman and looked into my face.

"We've got a suspect, Max. He's in the house right now. Being interviewed."

The information wasn't something Hammonds would have necessarily shared with an outsider or that Diaz needed to drive here to tell me.

"Seems that during the interview, your name came up," he continued.

"Yeah?"

"Yeah. Hammonds wants you to join us down at the office."

"May I ask who this suspect is?"

"Name is Rory Sims. Some kind of environmental activist," Diaz said. "Familiar?"

I didn't answer. A new rock was in my head, its edges sharp and irregular. I uncrossed my arms and stood up.

"You want me to ride in front or in back?"

CHAPTER 17

I rode in front, but it was just as quiet as if I'd been stuffed in the back with a set of handcuffs looped through the D-ring on the floor.

When I asked Diaz what Sims had said and why they considered him a suspect, he stared into the passing lane and said: "Anonymous tip." When he refused to offer more, I put my elbow on the passenger's side armrest, matched his reticence, and tried to smooth the rock on my own.

If someone had dropped a dime on Sims, what could they have said to make Hammonds take it seriously? His team must have listened to hundreds, maybe thousands of crank tips and useless accusations by now. If the information was legitimate, it still didn't make sense. Would some environmentalist get so caught up in his cause that he would turn to violence? And how the hell would a guy like that slip in and out of neighborhoods and into a place like my river shack without leaving a trace?

From my quick encounter at the Loop Road bar, Sims seemed the least likely in the group to be scuttling through the swamp. It wasn't in his eyes. Killing children wasn't like picketing the EPA or marching on the White House. A brain would have to fester some time to find enough motivation for what this guy was doing. Sims didn't have the smell of it. But what had he told Hammonds about me?

When we finally pulled into the administration building lot, Diaz took three turns searching the rows for a spot under the withering shade trees. He finally gave up and took a slot in a middle row with the other unfortunates sizzling under the sun. The entire sky seemed white hot. When we got out, Diaz strode across the parking area like a man avoiding a downpour.

"I hate the summer," he said, more to himself than to me as we went through a side door and then into an elevator obviously not for public use.

The doors opened onto a room of cubicles and I was lost until we came through another door that led into the same half-glassed office of files and desks where I'd been caught staring at Richards' legs.

This time it was busier. A long folding table had been brought in and was stacked with new phones and laptop computers and half-empty Styrofoam cups. Three young men wearing the same careful haircuts and cinched ties were working the phones, all of them standing but bent to the task of typing in notes. Diaz gave the secretary outside the high sign and she picked up her own phone. None of the federal agents looked at us when she signaled back and we went into Hammonds' office.

This time the government had made no attempt to cover its encroachment into Hammonds' space. In front of his bookcases was a South Florida map showing the vast Everglades and the color-coded counties and municipalities along the east coast. There were plastic push pins jammed into the map board in a variety of places. The red ones I recognized as the spots were the first four bodies had been found. There was one stuck in my river. There was also a yellow pin downstream at the location of my shack. Along one wall the office furniture had been shoved out of the way and the space was now occupied by a table with two laptops, an exterior modem, a zip drive and a spaghetti pile of wire dripping down the back. Hammonds still had his chair, but I could tell that even that was in jeopardy.

Two FBI types were in the room, gathering up files, logging off one of the computers and looking unusually put out for FBI types. Hammonds sat behind his now cluttered desk, his fingers steepled, waiting. Richards was also there, half sitting, half leaning on the edge of the computer table. She was again dressed in a business suit of light gray material with a white blouse that had a prim, close collar. She had her legs crossed at the ankle and I noticed a thin gold bracelet there. I moved my eyes to the floor until the government boys were gone, then looked up at Hammonds when the door clicked shut. His eyes were closed.

"Let's be up front, Mr. Freeman," he started, his voice trying to reach a tone of authority that he was maybe beginning to lose. "You may not have been much of a cop in Philadelphia, according to your record, but you're smart enough to know the drill."

I silently agreed on both points.

"Proximity made you a suspect in the Gainey child's homicide. We never found anyone near the others. Your psychologicals from Philadelphia made you as unstable. There was the shooting incident up there with the minor involved."

I had to force myself to stay locked onto his eyes, which were now open and painful-looking in their swollen tiredness.

"When you came across with the GPS and the canoe tag we tried to reassess. Your input the other night at the scene was an acquiescence." He pushed himself away from the desk and crossed his arms over his chest.

"But dammit, Freeman. Your name keeps coming up in this godforsaken mess and I do not like that coincidence."

So I was wrong about the voice of authority.

"What do you want to know?" I said. If they were actually going to lay their cards out, it was probably time for both of us to play straight.

"How do you know this Rory Sims?"

I told them about the Loop Road meeting, arranged by Gunther, whom they had obviously interviewed at the hospital after the plane crash.

"You must have asked Gunther enough questions about me to make them assume I was trustworthy, in a suspect sort of way," I said.

"Loop Road's a tough place to have conversations for an outsider," Diaz cut in from behind. "We never get shit out there but nasty looks and Cracker drawl."

I didn't bother looking around.

"Who was at this meeting?" Hammonds resumed.

I gave them the names.

"Blackman we know about," Richards finally said. "He's a disgruntled guide who has a few minors, mostly tiffs with clients. But he's never been vocal or threatening to residents that we know of. But you actually talked with Nate Brown?"

The amazement in her voice made me turn around. For the first time she looked at me as if I was a human being instead of somebody in a lineup.

"Yeah," I said. "Crusty old guy who didn't say much but was obviously the man behind the meeting."

Richards filled in the others on Brown's criminal and military history, adding that he had been suspected by the DEA for using his knowledge of the Glades to help marijuana smugglers dropping loads in the wilderness areas in the late 1970s.

"But he's been off the books for years. Everybody thought he'd died."

I was impressed, and watched her looking from face to face in the room.

"So what about this Ashley?" Hammonds said. "What's his story?"

Richards shook her head. I had nothing more to offer.

"Let's get on that," Hammonds said. "One of you two."

Diaz scribbled on his pad. Richards just nodded. Hammonds cleared his throat and looked at me. It was his turn to share.

"We got Sims in here on an anonymous tip this morning. One of the FBI guys took the call. The voice was obviously distorted, but they weren't taping a random call anyway.

"When the agent told the caller a name alone didn't mean much, he dumped a reference to a herpetologist down in south Dade County. Said Sims knew where to get rattlesnake venom and hung up.

"Only the interior investigators are supposed to know that the first child was killed by snake venom. I know enough about information leaks in a high-profile case not to be too optimistic, but it was enough to get Sims in here."

"We'd already talked to the snake guy at the University of Miami. We got back to him and he and Sims go back. They share a lot of data on snake movements and Sims does some tracking for him after they stick these transmitters into the captured ones," Diaz said.

"Point is, we get him in here and he denies any involvement and then he brings your name up like you can vouch for him," Hammonds said.

"So is he still here? I'll talk to him. Let him explain it himself."

Hammonds turned away.

"Had to cut him loose. We had no corroboration. Plus he had a damn good alibi for the other night when the Alvarez girl was taken. His lawyers would have had him out in a couple of hours anyway. But what I want to know is, why you, Freeman? Why you and this crew of swampers?"

The words only put a voice to the same question I'd been grinding on ever since I saw the moonlight on the dead child's face on my river. Why me?

"I told you. They thought I could be some kind of link. I think they want to help," I said, the thought just coming into my head. "But I don't know what kind of help."

"There's another child out there now, Freeman," Hammonds said, holding my gaze with his red-rimmed eyes. "I think maybe the viper pit is finally feeling the heat and the snakes are crawling out one by one," he said, refusing this time to look away. "We need some damn help too."

Hammonds sat back in his chair. The meeting was over. Diaz led the way out and this time, as the three of us walked through the outer office, the FBI agents took no pains to conceal their interest. They were trying to read our faces, to interpret the body language. Suspect or ally? New information, or more bullshit?

"Let's go get something to eat," Diaz said. "Come on, we'll get lunch."

* * *

Diaz drove. A few blocks from the sheriff's office we came into a neighborhood where somehow a cluster of old live oak trees had survived and rose up together to create a large shady spot in the middle of a working-class block.

The trees' limbs were hung with the gauze of Spanish moss and under the canopy a handful of picnic tables were arranged. The natural shade must have taken ten degrees out of the air. At the side of the lot was a small, white, clapboard building and alongside were three split fifty-five-gallon drums fashioned for cooking. A cloud of the sweetest-smelling smoke I had ever drawn a breath on curled from the drums and gathered in the leaves above.

While Diaz went to speak to a small, wiry black man who was smiling and chopping at several slabs of ribs on a piece of raw butcher block, Richards tiptoed, somehow gracefully on her high heels, through the lawn of exposed roots and sand holes to a table. I followed.

"You're in for a treat now," she said, watching Diaz in animated discussion with the cook, who had traded his cleaver for a pair of tongs and was now flipping the slabs on one of the grills.

"Diaz is second generation Cuban and can't stand the idea of any unfamiliar food passing his nose without taking a taste. They say these are the best barbecued ribs south of the Mason-Dixon line," Richards said, watching the interplay between her partner and the bald little chef. "I personally think Diaz is addicted."

From the look of the line of folks waiting for carryout, Diaz was not alone. Trailing into the street was a line of people from white-shirted office workers to overall-clad laborers patiently waiting their turn at a card table where cash was being exchanged for Styrofoam containers of ribs.

Richards and I sat in silence. She had taken a seat opposite me at the table. I wasn't good at small talk with women. I thought we were both watching Diaz, but when I turned to her, she was focused on something beyond me. I looked back over my shoulder and in the distance across the street, children were playing on a school playground. They were climbing on big orange and blue plastic jungle gyms and chasing each other in a field of green grass. Now that I was watching, I could pick up the high-pitched ringing of their shouts and laughter like the sound of a neighbor's wind chime in an easy breeze. They didn't seem to mind the heat. They didn't seem to mind anything but getting to the top of the slide, catching the kid with the floppy red shirt, or pumping their skinny legs to get the swing higher and higher. They were true innocents.

"So, how long have you been down here?"

Richard's voice snapped my head around. She was now watching me, hands folded on the table.

"Uh. Over a year now."

"And you've been living in that place on the river the whole time?"

"Yeah. Most of it. I did stay with Billy, uh, Manchester, for a while when I first came."

"Your attorney?"

"Yeah."

"No family?"

"No. I'm alone."

Her eyes, now more green than gray, made me nervous. I watched her hands instead, fingertips moving slightly across her own skin. Her nails were cut short and polished a neutral color. She touched the simple gold wedding band on her left ring finger once.

"You were street patrol up there, mostly?"

"Yeah. Probably more than most."

"But I saw in your file that you worked the detective bureau for a little while. Didn't like it?"

"Not too much," I said, swinging my left leg up over the bench and under the table to fully face her.

"Too much hurry up to close cases. Not enough time to spend thinking about them, being sure. I wasn't very, uh, efficient."

I was looking into her eyes this time.

"You like going out? On cases I mean," I said quickly.

She let a smile slip and I grabbed it like it was real.

"I mean, you look like you're pretty good at it."

"It's been OK. Except for this case. But I probably liked the road better too."

"How long you been with Diaz?"

She half shook her head, the smile went into a wry grin.

"I've been in Hammonds' group for about twelve months. Since my husband died. They thought it would be better for me." She was looking past me again, off into the playground.

"Your husband was a cop?"

"Road patrol. Answered a silent alarm at a convenience store late at night. One of those you know is going to be a false alarm. When he got there three kids in jackets in the middle of summer were walking backwards out of the place and when they saw the squad car they bolted."

A strand of hair fell across her cheek, but she ignored it.

"His partner ran after the two older ones and left Jimmy chasing the little one. The kid went down a blind alley and got trapped by a construction fence."

Her eyes did not look down. She was re-creating the scene behind them.

"They found Jimmy lying six feet from the fence. Two shots from a half-assed .22-caliber. One hit him in the vest but the other went straight into his eye and tumbled. He never even took his gun out of his holster. They got him to the hospital, but he never regained consciousness."

My fingers had gone quietly to the spot on my neck.

"Sorry," I said. "They get the kid?"

She nodded, looking out at the playground behind me again.

"Middle-schooler. Eleven years old."

Diaz had walked up while we were both caught in our own silence, staring past each other. He sat three square Styrofoam containers on the table.

"What?" he said, looking from her to me and back.

"You bring an extra side of sauce?" Richards said, as if we'd been discussing the weather.

"Of course. The reverend with the magic sauce," Diaz said,

climbing into a seat next to his partner. "He always treats me right."

We ate with little conversation. Diaz asked for more detail on Ashley and Nate Brown. As I described them, the worn and washed-out look of their clothes, the deep lines in both their faces seamed by hours of looking out over open spaces in unshaded sun, I realized that neither man had worn any adornment. No rings or watches. No fancy belt buckles. But envisioning them again standing up to greet me, I remembered the small leather knife scabbard that each man, including Blackman, had worn on his belt. Sims was the only man in the group without one. I didn't bother adding that observation to the mix as we sat and ate.

"This is truly wonderful stuff, Diaz. But we gotta go," Richards finally said.

Driving back to the administration building Diaz suggested that Richards drive me back north to Billy's tower.

"I'd do it," he said, "but I better get on this Ashley profile, see if we can find anything."

Before she had a chance to respond I told them Billy was down at the county courthouse and they could just drop me there.

"I'll get a ride back with him."

Richards stayed silent, looking out into the sun through the front windshield. Diaz drove several blocks to the county justice center and swung to the curb. I thanked him for lunch and got out. Richards' side window whirred down and Diaz leaned over her.

"We'll be in touch?"

I tapped the hot finish on the roof, waited until Diaz pulled his head back and then answered his question to Richards' eyes.

"I hope so."

They waited until the automatic doors of the building entrance slid closed before pulling away. I stood behind the glass and watched them disappear into traffic. I wondered if Richards had just strung me a line with the story of her husband, using my own past to find a psychological connection to somehow loosen me. Then I thought of the look in her eyes when she was staring across the street at the kids on the playground. She might be a good investigator. She might even be a good liar, as a good investigative interviewer sometimes has to be. But there was something real about her. Not even a pro could lie like that.

I went to a bank of phones just inside and called Billy. Like the good lawyer he was, he told me to keep my nose out of it.

"Max, I thought you were off the hook, my friend. Don't let the idea of a setup get you vengeful enough to set yourself up."

"Whatever Sims told them already got them back on me. This guy Hammonds is playing a hell of a chess game."

"The more places you show up, the more circumstantial he's got to lay on you. Don't make it easy on him, Max."

CHAPTER 18

Sims had dropped a dime on me. Or maybe Hammonds had shaken it out of him. Either way I needed to get to him.

I had Billy contact his woman lawyer friend who came up with a phone number and the address of a lab on the property of Florida Electric in south Dade County.

When I got Sims on the phone, he hesitated at the sound of my voice.

"Jesus, I didn't mean for you to get in trouble," he said. It was impossible to tell how sincere he was over the phone.

"Yeah, well, what you meant and what it ended up being don't go together," I said, putting a bite in my voice, ad-libbing as we went along. "I just got myself clear of these guys and then on your word they pulled me in and put me through another round of interrogation. Is that what you and your friends meant when you said you thought I could identify with your harassment? 'Cause now you put it back on me."

There was silence on the other end of the line, but I could hear the man breathing, feel him thinking.

"Look. I didn't mean to get you in deeper. This thing is getting way too spooky," he finally said.

I could hear the same struggle going on in his voice as Gunther had shown in the hospital.

"Yeah? Tell me about it," I said.

"Not over the phone."

"Where do you want to meet?" I said, pushing him through the door that he had already opened.

"You know the way to the power plant?"

I told him to give me directions and after I punched him off I sat thinking about what Hammonds had said about sticking my fingers into his investigation. I decided I didn't care at this point. Members of the Loop Road gang were either deeply paranoid or something was truly scaring them and I'd stumbled into a position of loosening them up. Hammonds was never going to get that far. I rang Billy back, told him where I was going, listened to his objections, and then walked outside and hailed a cab from in front of the courthouse.

When I climbed in the back and told the driver that I needed to get to Turkey Point, he turned in his seat and said, "Dade County?" I nodded my head and handed him a hundred-dollar bill from my wallet. He smiled and turned up the air conditioning.

When we got to the end of U.S. 1 we went east on Palm Drive, toward the ocean but far south of the tourist beaches and oceanfront glitz of South Miami. Here the land rolled out flat with brown, dormant tomato fields lining either side of the roadway. An occasional tree farm with rows and rows of palms in various stages of growth took up more space. We followed a sign to a secondary road and ran into a chain-link fence marked with a Florida Electric sign: Private Property. All visitors report at the security entrance.

The cabby hesitated but Sims had told me to ignore the sign so I urged him on down a dirt road that branched away from the parking lots and led to a small block building sitting alone on a hump of land.

A dirty white van was parked near the front entrance and was the only vehicle in sight. The building was made of stuccoed cinderblock, windowless and painted in dull beige, with a thick metal door. I gave the cabby another fifty dollars and told him if he was here in an hour he could take me back to Palm Beach. He smiled again and in broken English said he'd be back.

When the cab pulled away I pushed a buzzer next to the metal door frame and Sims' voice crackled through an intercom. I answered and he buzzed me through.

Inside was a two-room lab: white tile floors, fluorescent lighting, sterile-looking walls. In one room two desks were knocked together and stacked with papers and folders and computers that were a few generations behind the ones Billy used in his office. The other room was lined with glass-fronted cabinets stacked with books and vials, plastic models and labeled containers. In the middle was a long, stainless steel table. Sims was standing there, next to a large blue and white ice chest.

I tried to look imposing, but my threatening manner on the phone was impossible to keep up in person. So I kept my mouth shut and let my silence build up on him.

"I, uh, could use your help here," he said, tapping the top of the cooler.

His request caught me off guard. He was either too nervous to talk or was effectively spinning our roles. Me help him?

He was wearing a long-sleeved denim shirt rolled up at the cuffs, jeans, and thick-soled hiking boots. My guess was about a size nine.

"Sure," I said, stepping up to the table.

"I'm sorry, Mr. Freeman. I didn't know how long it would

take you to get here and my inopportune visit to the sheriff's office this morning has thrown me off schedule. I've already started this procedure and I'm afraid it really can't wait," Sims said, moving to one of the counters and pulling open a drawer. From inside he brought out a tray of instruments and a box of latex gloves and put them on the table next to the cooler.

"We're tracking as many of our resident rattlesnakes as we can and this one is due to be released back where we found him," he said, tapping the top of the cooler. "So I've got to get this chip in him while he's still cold and slow."

Sims snapped on the gloves and then unwrapped a small package that contained a tiny microchip and a large-bore hypodermic needle. He explained how his study of the snake's movements was done by inserting the chip into its layer of scales. I nodded at the logic. It didn't take a detective to know what my role in all this was going to be. Sims loaded the chip into the needle and laid the syringe on the corner of the table.

When he was ready, he carefully opened the cooler a few inches and peered inside and then reached one hand into the space. His movements seemed too slow for what I knew was inside, but his arm came out with the spade-shaped head of an adult rattlesnake gripped in his hand. When three feet of the animal was out of the chest, he grabbed the middle with his other hand and gestured at me to hold on to the last three feet.

"Tight. But not too tight," he said. "Just keep him from wriggling while we stretch him out on the table."

I don't know why I followed his instructions. But now I had half of a six-foot poisonous snake in my hands. The skin of the animal was smooth and the body felt as hard as a giant hose under full pressure. As I worked to pin it against the stainless table it flexed, and when I tried to keep it from curving, my hand slid up against the grain of its scales and the edges scraped roughly across my palm. When I repositioned my hand, I laid it higher and then slid it smoothly down the cool body.

"He's been on ice for about fifteen minutes so he's feeling pretty sluggish," Sims said. "Just hold him here while I get this chip in."

I couldn't see the snake's head. Sims kept his left hand locked just behind the flanged jaws which, I assumed, kept the animal from twisting around and biting him.

"I honestly did not intend to raise more scrutiny from the police by revealing our meeting, Mr. Freeman," Sims suddenly said. He obviously wasn't as focused on the snake as I was.

"I guess it just sort of spilled out as they were questioning me. They are very persuasive. In an unsettling way."

"They do have that effect on people," I said, trying to concentrate on both the environmentalist's words and the shift in the lump of muscle under my hands. "But why do you think they called you in to begin with?"

"That's a bit of a mystery in itself," he answered. "They'd already talked to Professor Murtz, who is the head of the lab. They wanted to know about the milking of snake venom, which we do some of right here. The process is really quite easy. You see, the fangs are really like big needles themselves," he said, twisting up the head of the snake in his hand and somehow squeezing the jaws to make them open to expose the half-inch gleam of needle-sharp bone.

"You get them over a funnel with some rubber-like membrane stretched over it and let them sink their fangs in. They think it's something's skin and pump away.

"Most of the time they're more than anxious to bite. A snake is a survivalist, the venom is its protection and its means to a meal, so they're instinctive with it. You anger them, they're going to hit you. So the hard part is handling them over and over because, eventually, you're not going to be quick enough."

I watched Sims pick up the hypodermic and then hold the syringe in his own mouth while he probed the snake's skin, running his hand over the cream-colored diamonds, looking for a spot to stick it. He motioned for me to bend up the tail and decided on a place near the base. As he held the animal's head away, he slid the needle under a scale and pumped the chip in. When he finished, he swabbed the spot and then motioned to the cooler and we lifted the snake back into the ice chest and closed the lid.

"Professor Murtz already gave the police all of that information the first time, and how dozens of people from scientists to snake hobbyists to any good Southern snake hunter could do it," Sims continued as he stripped off the gloves. "We could never figure why they were so interested and I thought that was why they called me in this time. But somehow they kept turning me toward the meeting at Loop Road and when your name came up I got the impression that I wasn't telling them anything that they didn't already know."

"Yeah. My name just happens to come up a lot in places where I'd just as soon it didn't," I said, rubbing my palms together, still feeling the slick smoothness of the snake and the cool tingle of my own nerves.

Sims wrapped up the hypodermic and put the package back in the drawer and then washed his hands in a stainless steel sink built into the counter. I wondered if I should do the same.

"They knew you were there," he said, turning as he dried his hands with a paper towel and reading the flash of confusion that must have shown in my eyes. "At the hotel bar. I don't know how, but I'm positive they already knew it. They just wanted to know why."

It took me a second to gather myself. Of course they knew.

Why the hell wouldn't Hammonds know? He'd been trailing me ever since I pulled up to the ranger's dock with news of a killing.

"I don't doubt it," I said to Sims. "I'd still like to know myself why it was that I was there."

The environmentalist seemed to consider the question for a few seconds as he oddly and carefully folded the damp brown paper towel in his fingers. Then he tossed the square into a waste basket, walked over to grip both handles of the ice chest and lifted it off the table. He nodded his head to the door.

"Let's go drop this off," he said and I followed, holding open the door and wondering why I was letting him lead again.

We loaded the cooler into the back of the van and as Sims drove out to an empty asphalt road leading east he explained, as best he could according to him, what he knew of my invitation to Loop Road.

"You've got to understand, Mr. Freeman, there are generations of folks out there in the Glades that have lived lives far different than what modern-day people think of as Floridians."

"Yeah, I got that lesson from Gunther," I said, watching the road stretch out in a straight line into nothing but low-hanging green brush. Sims had no air conditioning in the old van and even the wind spilling through the open windows was hot. I was thinking about the warming state of the rattlesnake sliding around in the cooler behind us.

"What I mean is that, for some of them, the Glades is their neighborhood and you can't just move into the neighborhood without being noticed and without becoming suspect." He let the statement sit, waiting for my response.

"You mean my place in the old research shack?" I finally said.

"Glades folks notice something like that. People have used

that old place for years when it was empty. But they also have respect. Your presence was known but no one was really sure what you were up to. They knew you weren't a hunter, or a fisherman. There was speculation that you were doing some kind of night research, but the professor and I couldn't come up with anybody who knew you."

"And how exactly did all this discussion come up?" I asked.

By now Sims had turned off the pavement and pulled onto a dirt road. It too was posted with a no-trespassing sign and bore the logo of the power company. Sims downshifted and started south down a lane that was flanked on either side with mangroves and long finger islands that stretched out into standing water.

"These are cooling canals. Man-made for discharging the water from the reactor," Sims said, answering the question I hadn't asked and avoiding the one I had.

"The company has acres and acres of property out here but although they can keep the people out, they can't easily control the animals that find their way in here. That's why they employ Professor Murtz and myself. To keep track of the native populations and monitor their growth and migrations. It makes them look environmentally concerned and benefits us at the same time. We have even developed a breeding ground for the American crocodile in here that almost singlehandedly rejuvenated a species that was very much on the endangered list only a few years ago."

As we jounced down the rutted road I tried to pull him back to my invitation to Loop Road.

"And the discussion about me being the new mystery man living in the old research shack?"

"I don't know who brought it up first. Word gets passed along out there and you rarely know the source, or even the truth of the stories. But it got to the bar. And then Blackman said he'd heard that you had been questioned by the police in connection to the killings of the kids."

"I suppose that eased some of the pressure among the natives."

"I don't deny that," Sims said as he slowed and then stopped the van in the middle of the road, in the middle of nowhere. When he got out, I followed. "There'd been a lot of talk since the child killings started. Some of it working off the same whiskey-inspired threats that had gone on for years about stopping the western flow of the suburbs," Sims said as he opened the back doors of the van and hauled out the ice chest.

"It was crude stuff at first. Like 'It's about time' and 'More power to 'em.' But then the investigators and agents started questioning people at their camps and ranches and folks started getting nervous."

He set the chest down in the dust about ten yards away and came back to the van. I watched the lid like it was going to pop open like some jack-in-the-box.

"They would have loved to have an outsider like you get blamed. But then we heard about you and Gunther. And as far as I know, it was Gunther who said you'd been in law enforcement up north. That's when Nate Brown decided we ought to talk to you ourselves."

I watched as Sims reached into the van and pulled out a golf club. A putter I thought at first. Then I looked closer at the head and saw that the shaft had been sheared off and the end had been bent to form a hook.

He walked back to the cooler, and using the hook, flipped open the lid. I could hear a bone rattle echoing inside. The snake had warmed up. Sims stepped closer and probed in the cooler for a few seconds and then lifted the rattler out. Its body was cupped on the hook about one-third of the way down its length. The tail was curling and twisting in the air with a motion independent of the head, which stuck out straight as a stick from Sims' club.

With the animal dangling, he walked it closer to the edge of the road. The embankment dropped several feet down into the water weeds and mangroves. When he set it down, the snake curled into an immediate coil and the rattle intensified.

"He'll probably just set there awhile until the sun warms him up," Sims said, standing far too close to the beast if its strike range really was the ten feet that I'd read about. "This is about the spot that we found him a couple of days ago. So we're just hoping he's close to home."

We stood watching the snake's tongue flick the air and listened to the click of the rattles. Finally, it began to unwrap itself. We watched as it then slid softly into the grass and down the embankment. First the body disappeared, and then the rattling sound went quiet. I stood behind Sims as he walked over and peered over the edge.

"Gone," he said, and then turned to me. "I still don't know why they had any interest in the snake venom."

I was still looking into the grasses and mangroves, a bit amazed at how quickly the animal had simply disappeared.

"The first dead child," I said. "Died from an injection of rattlesnake venom."

I looked up at Sims. His mouth was slightly open, his face was caught in a mask of pure, dumbfounded thought. Yes, he had computer access. Yes, he had a van and enough knowledge of the Glades and enough expertise with tracking devices to make a GPS seem like a toy. He even had size-nine feet. But the look in his eye told me he hadn't known about the snake venom. He might have been in on it at some point, but not when the real killing began.

CHAPTER 19

My truck was waiting for me in the lot when the cab dropped me at Billy's tower. The new glass was shining but the three gouges in the paint brought up a taste of anger I couldn't keep down. My keys were at the lobby desk and the assistant manager cleared me to the penthouse. I made a pot of coffee, drank half of it while I put my bags together and then poured the rest in a huge, wide-bottomed sailing mug. I threw the bags in my truck and drove out west to the ranger station.

When I pulled into my usual parking space, I could see Cleve and his assistant had pulled the Boston Whaler out of the water on a trailer and were washing the hull, scrubbing the algae and dirt stain from the water line. Cleve tossed his brush into a galvanized pail, wiped his hands on his trousers and greeted me with a handshake.

"Max. Good to see you back."

The assistant was looking past us at my truck, his mouth had dropped open a bit and then he snapped it shut and turned away, shaking his head in disgust. Cleve and I walked up toward the office.

"I don't have a new canoe yet. But if the offer still stands, I'd like to borrow yours to get out to the shack," I said.

"No problem. But I'll have to get you the key," Cleve answered, moving through the office to his desk.

"After everything going on, I went out and put a hasp and lock on the door. Figured it might keep your stuff safe," he said, putting the key in my palm and then looking at it a second too long. "First time I ever had to do that."

I felt a pang of responsibility, like I'd taken something from him.

"I'm sorry," I said.

"Ain't your fault," he answered. "Things change."

We carried his canoe to the water. I loaded my bags from the truck and just before pushing off I called out to Mike Stanton, who was still working the waterline of the *Whaler*.

"If you want to fix her up again, I'll pay you."

He looked off across the ramp at my truck.

"OK. Yeah. Maybe."

I nodded, put my right foot in the middle of the canoe, grabbed the gunwales and pushed off.

My ribs were sore from the plane crash. My arms and shoulders knotted from the parking lot fight. And my lungs were dry and constricted from too much air conditioning and not enough exercise. Cleve's canoe seemed awkward and the paddle felt strange in my hand. I tried to get a rhythm going and got deeper into the flow of the current and around the first mangrove curves, but it wasn't working. I couldn't get the feel of someone else's boat. The trim felt wrong. The balance was off. The only thing that wasn't different was the river.

I still worked up a heavy sweat and a running heartbeat by the time I entered the mouth of the canopy. Inside the shade I stopped paddling and drifted into the coolness. A Florida red belly turtle stood guard on a downed tree trunk, his neck stretched out as if sniffing the air, the yellow, arrow-shaped marking on his snout pointing up the river. The white summer sky peeked through the leaves, its rays spattered the ferns below and in the distance I heard the soft roll of thunder. I re-settled myself in the seat and moved on.

By the time I reached the shack it was raining, hard. The leaf canopy sounded like cloth ripping and lightning sent a flash through the undergrowth and for an instant stole the color from the trees. I lashed the canoe to my platform and ran the bags up the stairs but when I twisted the knob and pushed, the door rattled and stuck.

I'd forgotten Cleve's new lock and dug through my pockets for the key. Once inside I dragged the bags through the door-way and stood dripping on the pine floors and squinting through the dusk. I had seen too much of Billy's airy and fash-ionable apartment.

I found my way to the kerosene lamp and lit the wick. Hammonds' warrant servers had been civil. With the exception of a few counter items out of place, it was the same as I'd left it. I started a wood fire in the stove and set up a pot of coffee. I found my old enameled cup that some officer had misplaced on the drain board.

Outside the lightning snapped and I could hear the water sluicing off the roof and onto the cinnamon fern below the win-dows. I took off my dripping clothes and sat naked in my wooden chair, tipped back on two legs, put my heels on the table and listened to the rain.

* * *

I lay in my bunk that night half dreaming and half recall-ing, my skin moist in the humidity, and every time I closed my eyes I could see blue and red lights flashing through the trees. I was back in Philadelphia. The concrete sidewalk was still wet from some early-morning drizzle and up high at the top of the hill in the distance loomed the huge, yellowish back wall of the

Museum of Art. In front were the tiered steps that the Rocky character had charged up and then shaken his fists at the world. In back was the Schuylkill River winding out through an urban park of maple trees and wooded lanes and granite cliffs. On that morning, between the museum and boathouse row, under a thicket of azaleas, lay a young woman with her running suit muddied and half pulled off, her Nike cross trainer on one foot but without a partner, and her throat cut from ear to ear.

I was working with a Center City detective squad, low on the totem pole and "learning the craft," according to my new lieutenant. We were on the first call out that morning.

It didn't take long to identify the victim. Although she wasn't carrying I.D. and the key she had strapped into a holder on the remaining shoe was unmarked, I recognized the store label on the running suit. It was a small specialty athletic place on Rittenhouse Square. It was five minutes away up the Benjamin Franklin Parkway and over to Walnut. When we got there the store manager went slack-jawed when he saw the Polaroid we'd taken of the woman.

"Susan Gleason," he said, turning away from the photo. She was a regular. A dedicated runner who lived across the historic square in a centuries-old building retrofitted into high-priced condos. He knew she ran from there down to the river and along the row early every morning. She went through a pair of shoes every twelve weeks. She was a very good customer.

We confirmed with the condo management. Gleason lived alone, a thirty-six-year-old stock analyst, loved the city and worked constantly. The running seemed her only outlet.

The blue lights were still spinning when we got back to the scene. The body and been removed and the other shoe had been found fifty yards away near a parking spot close to one of the rowing clubs along the river. Other members of the detective squad had interviewed several early morning runners. Some recognized the woman's running suit. Some also knew the parking spot was often occupied at dawn by a late-model, beat-up Chevy Impala with one of those orange, city employee parking stickers.

"A big, odd-looking white guy would just sit there with the window down. He's there every morning except on the weekend," a runner said. "You can see the Fairmount Dam from there. I figured he was just enjoying the view before starting the day."

The prints of a size thirteen work boot were found in the mud by the azaleas. The squad fanned out among city maintenance divisions in Center City. A supervisor at the City Hall–area subway division recognized a description of the Impala: Arthur Williams. "Yeah, big guy, kinda, you know, slow."

Williams worked in the underground subway access tunnels, sweeping trash and cleaning graffiti from the walls. He was in his 40s. Quiet. Didn't come in that day, which was unusual.

We got an address in North Philadelphia and another car went with us. An upper-class woman from Rittenhouse Square had been murdered while jogging in a popular park along the river. They weren't sparing any manpower at the roundhouse to button this one down by the evening news.

The house in North Philly was in the middle of a worn-down block of tired homes. They all shared a creaking roofline and were all connected so you could stand on the front porch at one end of the block and see your neighbor eight doors down standing out on his. Only a spindled railing separated your porch floorboards from the next guy's.

We were greeted by an elderly woman who talked through the screen door.

"Mrs. Williams?"

"No, sir. I am Fanny Holland. Mrs. Williams' sister."

"Is Arthur home, ma'am?"

She could see the other detectives moving about the Impala parked on the street.

"He's not going to lose his job over this is he?" the old lady said as she let us in. "He has never missed a day before."

Two detectives went up the narrow staircase. My partner and I went into the kitchen with Fanny Holland and sat her down at the table. She listened for sounds up through the cracked ceiling. The house was not unlike my own childhood home. It smelled of liniment and old cardboard, ancient comforters and soiled doilies. My mother had grown sick in such a place.

The others brought Arthur down. Big, docile, with a confused child's look on his face. They found him in bed covered with three blankets. He still had on his work clothes, including a pair of huge, mud-caked boots. He stumbled with his thick wrists cuffed behind his back and kept repeating in a low whine, "She was too pretty to die. She was too pretty to die."

I was left to explain to the aunt while the rest of the squad took Williams to the roundhouse. The old woman seemed confused and stunned and took the words from my mouth as something indecipherable.

Attack a woman? He could not. There was not a bully on the street, male or female, who couldn't slap the boy to shame since he was ten years old.

Cut her with a knife? He wasn't capable.

Weighing the situation, Fanny Holland let loose the family ghosts. And I listened.

Arthur had been a damaged child. A low I.Q., a momma's boy. A boy who fell further when his father left. His mother endured "until it got to be too much."

She'd committed suicide. Cut her wrists out in the garden. Her favorite place. Had carried the knife in her picking basket. She was dead when Arthur came home from school.

"You couldn't put a butter knife on the table since," the old woman said. "Cut a woman? Impossible."

Arthur's only habit was to leave his house early each day and find a green place. A garden of sorts. She herself went with him on weekends to the Longwood Garden's indoor arboretum in winter. It was the only thing he clung to.

When I got back to the roundhouse the TV news trucks were already stacked in the lot. Inside the bureau a knot of detectives was gathering in the hall opposite the interview rooms. I singled out one of the senior investigators and told him I thought I had some relevant information from the aunt on Williams.

"Good, Freeman. Write it up and we'll add it to the package. The guy already confessed."

The detective in charge didn't want to hear about I.Q.s and broken homes and mothers who cut their own wrists.

"The guy was stalking women on boathouse row. Gettin' his jollies watching 'em bounce down the jogging path every morning. It gets to be too much for his pants to hold, he grabs one, she fights, he cuts her.

"His footprints are next to the body. Her shoe is by the parking spot where people saw him this morning. Only thing we're missing is the knife, which is probably in the river and DNA, which we ain't gonna get cause he never finished the rape.

"Whata ya mean it doesn't make sense, Freeman? The guy confessed. He keeps sayin', 'She was too pretty to live. She was too pretty to live.' What more do you want?"

Charges were filed despite my suggestion that we rethink the case. The lieutenant listened politely to me and said:

"There's a sense of urgency with a case like this, Freeman. Sometimes you have to put it together quickly and act. You can't grind on every little aspect. That's the way it works sometimes."

I told him I thought we had the wrong man. Three weeks later he approved my transfer back to patrol. Arthur Williams went to prison. He may still be there.

* * *

I awoke with my finger on the dime-sized scar at my neck. I had been drifting most of the night between dreams and consciousness, caught between those two places and feeling like I didn't belong in either.

I got out of bed, lit the stove and then stood at my eastern window. An early light filtered in through leaves still dripping from the night rain. I heard the low grunt of an anhinga and spotted the bird swimming along small patches of standing water with just its head and long flexible neck showing. I watched him awhile as he stabbed into the water at fish and then I turned to start coffee. Padding across the room I stopped to pull on a pair of faded shorts and heard, or maybe felt, a soft thunk of wood against wood. The single vibration had shivered up from the foundation stilts, or maybe the staircase. I stood, listening, and heard it again. Paranoia got the best of me and I went quietly to my duffel bag and slipped my hand to the bottom, finding the oilskin-wrapped package and drawing it out. The warrant servers had indeed been careful. My 9mm handgun had been re-wrapped. The sixteen-round clip folded into the cloth so the two metals wouldn't scrape together. It was done carefully by men who knew weapons.

I undid the trigger lock and fed the clip up into the handle and held the gun in my right hand. I had not picked it up with purpose in over two years. I stared at the barrel. Despite the packing, a hint of brownish rust was oxidizing on the edges from the humid Florida air.

I felt the thunk again. This time it seemed too purposeful. I went to the door and opened it slowly with my left hand. At the base of the staircase, with his back propped against a stanchion of the dock, sat Nate Brown. The early light caught the silver in his hair. He had one bare foot flat on the deck and the other draped over into a sixteen-foot wooden skiff. With a subtle movement of that leg he thunked the bow against the dock piling.

"Ain't gotcha no alarm clock, eh?" he said without looking up.

I slipped the 9mm into my waistband in the small of my back and stepped out the door.

"I don't usually get visitors," I said, and quickly added, "this early."

I took two steps down and sat on the top landing. Brown remained where he was. He had a sawgrass bud in his left palm and was carving out the tender white part to eat with a short knife that had a distinctive curved blade. It looked too much like the blade I'd taken from Gunther's scabbard after the plane wreck and accidentally dropped into the mud of the glades.

"You ain't gone need that pistol," he said, finally looking up at me. I just stared at him, trying to see what might be in his eyes.

"I heard ya load it."

I took the gun from behind me where it was digging into my backbone and laid it on the plank next to me. In the rising light I could see the dark stain under Brown where water had dripped off his clothes. His trousers were wet through and there was a water line that changed the color of his denim shirt at mid chest. Somehow he must have walked through the thick swamp from the west to my shack and found it in the dark. There had been no moonlight in the overnight storm.

"How about some coffee?" I finally said. "I was just making some."

"We ain't got time," he answered. The tone of authority that had struck me at the Loop Road bar was back in his voice. "We got to go."

I started to ask where, but he cut me off.

"It's the girl. The little one. You're gonna have to come git her."

Now I could see his pale eyes as he stood up and there was an urgency in them that seemed foreign to his face.

"The kidnapped girl? Where?" I said, unconsciously picking up my gun. "Where is she? Is she dead?"

"Yonder in the glade," Brown answered, barely tipping his head to the west. "She ain't real good. But she's alive."

"Who's with her? Is there anyone with her? Can we get a helicopter out there?" Now the urgency was in my throat.

"Ain't nobody with her now. An' ain't nobody now who can find her 'cept me. You're gonna have to git her," the old man said, his voice flat but still holding strength. "You alone. Let's go."

I walked back in the shack and laid the gun on my table and quickly dressed, taking an extra minute to pull on a pair of high combat boots I rarely used. I picked up Billy's cell phone and punched his number, got his answering machine and left a hurried message that I was heading out into the Glades with Brown and would call him back with details. I stuffed a first-aid kit into a waterproof fanny pack and strapped it around my waist. As I clomped down the stairs I put the cell phone inside too. Brown didn't object.

I climbed into the stern of the shallow skiff and Brown crouched on a broad seat built about a third of the way back from the bow. Using a cypress boat pole almost as long as the skiff itself, he pushed us down my access trail and onto the river.

"It'll be faster goin' up the canal with two," he said, heading upstream.

The old man seemed like a magician with the boat, poling and steering his way up my river at a speed that I could match only on my best days in the canoe. Sometimes he would stand erect, working the pole its full length but suddenly slip to his knees to duck a cypress limb and never miss his rhythm. I watched him bend down and noted the short leather scabbard on his belt where he'd holstered his curved knife. It was then that I remembered my 9mm. I'd left it on the table. I had also not thought to fasten Cleve's new lock on the door. I had not needed the gun for some time and I hoped I wouldn't need it now.

We got to the dam in twenty minutes, half my usual time, and I helped Brown hoist the skiff over. It was a flat-bottomed craft, made of marine plywood in a simple but efficient way. The techniques of both building and maneuvering such a skiff had been passed down through generations of Gladesmen. When Brown pushed off again I watched him as we slid past the spot where I'd found the wrapped body of the dead child. He never hesitated, never turned his head, either toward the spot in memory or away from it in avoidance. He just kept poling, his taut shoulders and back moving under the faded cotton of his damp shirt like the smooth muscles of a racehorse under its hide.

"I believe she will be fine" and "We'll be there directly" were his only answers to my questions about the girl.

I sat back in frustration and watched him. The sun was up full over the eastern horizon now, deepening the blue in the sky and slicing through the river canopy like light through cheesecloth. We passed the canoe park and I stifled an urge to call out to Ham Mathis at the rental shack.

In another thirty minutes we pushed through a shallow bog of cattails and green maidencane to a canal levee where a culvert fed fresh water to the river. Brown jumped out into knee-deep water and I followed as he tugged his skiff up the grass-covered levee bank with a half dozen lunges. I tried to push from the stern but wasn't much help and I was again awed by the strength coming out of a small man who we'd already determined was nearly eighty years old.

From the high berm I looked out over the open expanse of Everglades and tried to get a fix on our direction, but Brown had the skiff floating again and his silence screamed, "Get your ass down here." I knew we were on the L-10 canal and headed deep into the Glades. The canal system had been dredged eighty years ago to transport commercial fish and produce from Lake Okeechobee, the huge liquid heart of Florida, to the shipping centers on the coast. But I couldn't tell how far or how fast we were going. Now in open water, Brown used the full power of the pole and could push the skiff nearly a hundred yards with a single stroke. He worked silently, except the times he spotted an alligator lying in the grass at the water's edge or a snout like a floating chunk of dark-colored bark in the distance.

"Gator," he would call out, not in warning, but like a cop in a prowl car might say "crackhead" or "eight-baller" to his partner as they cruised a drug area. This was Brown's work sector. The neighborhood he knew. I was on his turf and at his mercy.

As the sun climbed up the sky he did not seem to tire or slow or even sweat. I had to admire his ability to grind. After more than an hour he suddenly stopped poling and steered to the side. No marker. No trail. No indication that this spot was any different than the miles we'd already passed. When he jumped down into the water I followed and we hoisted the skiff to the top of the berm. To the west lay acres of freshwater marsh, stretched out golden in the high sun just like I'd seen from the cockpit of Gunther's plane. On the horizon was a faint line of dark green rising like a ridge and bumping the skyline. We had to pull the skiff some thirty yards through shallow water and around clumps of grass the size of small autos until Brown found a serpentine trail of deeper water that spun out toward the faint hardwood hammock in the distance. He tossed me a quart of water in a clear Bell canning jar. It was sealed with a metal screw-on collar and a rubber rimmed lid.

"We'll be there directly," he said, stripping off his shirt to expose a sleeveless white T-shirt underneath. I had taken off my own shirt and draped it over my head and shoulders as protection against the sun. We pushed off again and this time Brown took up a spot on a smaller poling platform at the back of the skiff. He started us down the middle of the water trail and I straddled the center platform, alternately looking ahead trying to keep my bearings and watching him, standing above me, framed in the blue canvas of sky and squinting into the distance.

"Who brought her out here, Nate?" I finally asked, wondering if he would let go of it.

"Ain't for me to say," he answered, and I wasn't sure whether the response meant he knew but wouldn't tell, or that he simply wouldn't speculate. But somehow I believed that it had not been him.

In short time I lost track of the turns and directions we moved. I had no clue why he took one watery path over another. On occasion I would stand up on the platform, wobbling the boat, and see that we were gaining on the line of trees. Then I would sit back down and take a drink from the jar. The heat was rising and the sawgrass smelled warm and close, like hay in a summer barn, but the sweet odor of wet decay mixed with it to create an odd perfume. It was not like my river where everything was dominated by moisture. Out here the battle between a drying sun and the soaking water was waged in the six-foot-high envelope of space we were sliding through.

I didn't know how much time had passed. An hour, maybe more, as the wall of trees grew taller and more distinct. Finally Brown shoved the nose of the skiff up into the grass and we stepped out onto semi-solid land. He yanked the boat up on a dry mound.

"Got to walk in," he said, and started off.

I stuck the water jar in my bag and followed, watching where he stepped and peeking ahead, hoping to see some sign of a destination. We walked thirty yards through ankle-deep mud, my boots making sucking noises with each step. Then we climbed a gradual rise onto a dry ridge and plunged into the hammock.

I slipped my shirt back on and it stuck to my skin with sweat and when we stepped into the shade it quickly took on the feel of a cold wet cloth. The place was filled with thick trees; reddish gumbo limbo whose limbs bent and curled at odd angles, mahogany that was native to South Florida but had been harvested out of most areas, and scaly, black-spotted poisonwood that was dangerous to the touch.

There was no trail. Brown made his own and I tried to follow but where he gracefully ducked past wide swathes of spiderwebs, I caught them full in the face, the sticky filament pasting across my eyes and lips. While I wiped at the strands I would trip over a root or knot of vines and then look up to see Brown fading into the vegetation and shadows ahead.

I struggled to keep up, slushing down through water-filled ditches and back up over downed trunks of mottled pigeon plum. But my eyes had adjusted to the filtered light and after several minutes I could see the unnatural shape of dark right angles in the trees up ahead. A structure became more defined, and when we got to the clearing, I could see it was a shack not unlike my own but in sadder shape. Balanced on top of a shell mound, it was built of rough-hewn lumber that was darkly weathered and rotting at its corners. The spine of the tar-papered roof was broken and sagged at the middle. A tall wooden rack that might have served as a child's swing in another world stood off to the side and was hung with alligator skins from four to six feet long.

Brown had stopped at the edge of the clearing and stood staring at the building, his eyes narrowed as if he was still in the sun, his shoulders slumped slightly. He was going no farther, and for the first time in the journey he seemed tired.

"You'll have to git her," he said with a nod at the shack.

CHAPTER 20

I strode across the scuffed incline to the front steps, looking back at Brown only once to confirm that he was not following. The first step up to the raised porch creaked under my boot. I hesitated at the hinged plank door and listened for several seconds to stone quiet. Then I turned the dull metal knob and went in low and quick.

The room was in muted darkness. The only two windows were so smeared with dirt that the little light that snuck through was yellow and dull.

I came slowly out of my crouch and could make out a three-legged table that had tumbled against the front wall without its balance. A small stone fireplace was to the left, its ashes dead. A chair was standing alone in the middle of the floor, the seat facing the door as if someone had been waiting. I picked up the glint of broken glass from an oil lamp that had been shattered, its pieces scattered in one corner. The room smelled of animal grease, rotted food and wet smoke. My eyes adjusted, but I still almost missed her.

She was on the floor, partly wrapped in a child's filthy blanket and tucked far under a wood-framed cot. Her eyes were closed but when I touched her I felt soft muscle quiver under my hand.

"It's all right, sweetheart. It's OK. I'm here to help you. You're all right now," I said softly.

I got my hands around her and slowly pulled her out from under the bed. She did not fight but I heard a tiny keening start up in the back of her throat and it was heart-wrenching to know that that was all the struggle she had left in her.

I pulled a cover from the bed and wadded it up and slipped it under her head. Her face was swollen under a layer of grime and a crust of dried moisture was gathered in her lashes and the corners of her eyes. I thought of dehydration and took the mason jar from my bag.

"Here, sweetheart. Take some water."

I tipped the water to her cracked lips but at first could only wet them. Most of what I poured ran down her chin and neck, leaving streaks through the dirt on her skin. Then she began to take it, her mouth opening slightly like a tiny fish trying to breathe.

I felt her for injuries. I looked for blood. She did not recoil at my touch but kept her eyes shut. Maybe she couldn't open them. Maybe she never wanted to open them again. After the cursory check I got on the cell phone, punched in 911 and before the operator could tie me up with questions, I identified myself as a police officer and asked her to put me through to Vincente Diaz with the FDLE special task force in Broward and, yes, it was an emergency. I kept repeating myself and it still took three more dispatchers and what seemed like ten minutes to get to Diaz. The public's perception of police technological efficiency is always skewed by TV and movies. They are never that good.

"Vince Diaz," the detective finally answered.

"Diaz, this is Max Freeman."

"Max. When did you rejoin the brotherhood?"

I ignored the sarcasm.

"Diaz, I've got the girl, the Alvarez girl."

There was silence and I thought we'd been cut off or had lost the satellite connection.

"Diaz?"

"OK. OK, Freeman. Take it easy, all right? Slow down man. Tell me what's going on."

Diaz's voice had slipped into negotiator mode and I realized I'd used the wrong words.

"I found her, Diaz. I found the kid and she's alive. But you gotta get some help out here now."

"Jesus. You found her? How the hell. . . . Where are you, Max?"

I could hear him talking out into a room, spreading the word before coming back to me.

"OK, Max. She's alive? Right? You said she's alive? Where the hell are you?"

I got up and walked outside, hoping for better reception. Nate Brown was gone. If the old man had been in on it, he'd turned by bringing me here. If he'd truly been trying to find the killer, as his group at Loop Road had indicated, maybe they'd succeeded, and taken care of it on their own. Either way, I had a feeling Brown wouldn't be back and I had little clue to where the hell I was.

I looked up into the tree canopy as if there'd be a damn street sign. This was not Thirteenth and Chestnut. You couldn't call in an address.

"We're in the Glades," I said. "Somewhere south of my river off the L-10 canal. West of the canal and in a long hardwood hammock somewhere."

I could visualize them going to the map in Hammonds' office, tracing their fingers from the yellow push pin that was my river shack. It was quiet on the porch. The air in the trees had gone still and the smell of rotting animal carcass drifted from the gator rack. There was no bird sound. No leaf flutter. Just dead silence.

"Jesus, Max. That's a lot of area," Diaz came back. "Can you give us some mileage? Some landmark?"

I stepped back into the cabin, repeating, I knew, the too vague directions off the canal. That's when I saw it. I don't know how I missed it the first time. Maybe I dismissed the chair at first because it was non-threatening and then because I saw the girl. Now I looked down at the dark cloth on the seat and on top of it was a GPS unit. It was nearly identical to the one I'd found in my river shack.

"I think I can do better than that," I said to Diaz, carrying the unit back out into the light. "I've got a GPS unit."

Billy had shown me how to operate the unit we'd had before. This one had power and I called up the present location on the read-out. I repeated the longitude and latitude numbers to Diaz and asked if I was doing it right.

"That's got to be it, Mr. Freeman."

It was Hammonds on the phone.

"We're dispatching a TraumaHawk helicopter. Is there anyplace for it to land when it gets there?"

Hammonds' voice was taut, but in control.

"Yes," I answered, thinking about the dry ground that Brown and I had walked across to enter the hammock. "There's dry ground to the east of my location." I went outside, walking around for the first time to survey the land around the cabin.

"We're in the middle of the hammock, but the marsh is only a hundred yards or so out."

In the back of the cabin the high ground sloped down to a twenty-foot-wide ribbon of water. A natural canal wound off into the thickness of the tree cover. Pulled up on the bank was a wooden skiff, almost identical to Brown's, and a pitted, flat-bottomed aluminum boat with an ancient Evinrude outboard motor mounted on the transom.

"And you may also be able to get a boat in here," I said, now moving, slower, to the other side of the cabin.

"We've got some logistics people working on that with the coordinates now," Hammonds said.

The other side of the building was in shadow and along the outside wall I was looking at a long split trunk of raw cypress set on the ground behind the gator skin rack. The meat of the wood was stained nearly black. Flies were buzzing around the surface and also around a stump the diameter of a barrel and half as high. It was where the gator butchering was done. A hatchet was half buried in the stump, its blade sunk deep. Next to it a small knife had also been planted in the wood. Its handle was worn smooth and polished with use. Its blade was short and shiny and had a distinctive curve to it.

"Mr. Freeman?" The cell phone was still at my ear. It was Hammonds. His voice was careful. "Mr. Freeman, are you alone with the girl?"

"Yes," I said. "It would appear so."

"All right. Stay on the line."

Diaz came back on the phone. I had left the stump and was moving down a narrow path that appeared worn and led slightly down and into a thicket of trumpet vine and fern.

"Max, we're coming out there. What kind of shape is the kid in? How's she doing, medically?"

"She's breathing OK, but she's probably got some dehydration going on," I said, pushing the branches and vines away with one arm as I followed the path down into a small clearing.

"How about injuries? Any injuries?"

In the clearing the stench of animal gristle was overwhelming. On the ground was a rotting pile of entrails that had been dumped there after the butchering. I was about to turn back when I saw him from the corner of my eye.

From the thick limb of a poisonwood tree hung the body of David Ashley, a yellow nylon rope around his neck, a plain wooden chair that matched the one in the cabin tipped over beneath his feet. He stared down at me, his head cocked at an angle. But his eyes had gone opaque.

"And Diaz," I said. "You better bring a body bag."

"A what? I thought you said she was . . ."

"She's OK, Diaz," I cut him off. "But you got somebody else out here who's not."

I stayed on the line and backed out of the clearing. Diaz was also moving. The phone signal kept fading and I heard shouts and commands in the background.

"All right, Max. We're on our way. I got your number. We're bringing a team. Max? You all right?"

"Yeah."

I punched him off and worked my way back to the front of the shack and went inside and sat on the floor next to the girl. She hadn't moved. I fed her more water and she still wouldn't open her eyes. When I touched her the quiet, high-pitched keening started again. I stayed nearby but only held the phone and kept my hands to myself.

* * *

I heard the rustling of birds in the trees five minutes before I heard the helicopter. I went out to the porch in time to see a group of green herons sail out of the trees and head out to the marsh and then I picked up the flat sound of blades chopping the sky. There was a scratching sound of nervous scrambling on the wood below me and I heard a splash in the canal behind the cabin that was too loud for a fish.

The mechanical noise grew and the leaves in the canopy

started spinning and then thrashing as the chopper came in overhead, hovered, moved off toward the marsh and then sank down below the tree line.

A new quiet returned and I waited in it for fifteen minutes before I heard the snapping and crashing of someone on a headlong rush through the underbrush and vines coming hard from the direction of the chopper. Richards was the first one through. Her hair was tucked up under a baseball cap, the ponytail flashing behind. She was coming through the tangle like a swimmer, arms reaching and sweeping anything in the way behind. Her jeans were soaked to mid-thigh and as she got closer I could see fresh red welts across her face where the branches had whipped her.

"Where is she?" she said as soon as she got within range. The words were urgent but not harsh. I stepped aside as she started up the stairs and her eyes were bright green with adrenaline and checked emotion as she swept past me. Diaz was five minutes behind, in high boots and picking his way with more care.

"Jesus, Max," he said, out of breath when he reached the porch. "This is fucking out here."

He looked around, assessing the scene and narrowing his eyes at the sight of the gator-skin rack.

"The medical guys are coming up," he said, and then stepped to the door.

Inside the cabin Richards had gathered the child in her arms and was holding her on the bed, rocking. I thought at first that she was singing some kind of lullaby, but realized she was repeating the same phrase, "You're safe now, you're safe now," over and over. The girl's head was pressed into the detective's neck and now she was sobbing, her small body vibrating. Her eyes had opened and she was staring, and I hoped that what she was seeing would someday go away.

Richards rocked with her and I saw her look at the child's blanket, its pattern partially obscured with dirt, and the sight seemed to confuse her. She pulled it off the girl and set it aside.

I hadn't paid much attention to it at first, but something about the size and color of the blanket now sparked a memory of a mother's anguished words. The Alvarez girl had been abducted from her backyard. But it was Alissa Gainey who was all ready for bed when she was taken.

"She was already in her pajamas. Her little blanket was gone. She never put it down. Oh God, she's gone."

I filed the small rough stone away in my head and watched Diaz as he stepped around the room, absorbing with a cop's eye but touching nothing. I couldn't tell if he was using crime scene protocol or was just repulsed by the filth. I told him about the chair, how the GPS unit had been set on it. He looked at it.

"It's like he was putting a sign on the door. Like he was saying, OK, you found me. But it's too late for the girl."

I started to offer a different theory, thinking of Nate Brown, who might have left the GPS as the only way to bring in help quickly, but stopped and only nodded. Maybe Hammonds was right about the snake pit. But now the snakes had given up escape and started feeding on themselves.

But if Brown had been in on the abduction, why not finish the job? Or at least walk away? If he stumbled onto this scene, what would his options have been? Pole his skiff to the nearest pay phone and call 911? He obviously knew the way to my river shack. Had he been in my place that day and left the other GPS to frame me? I somehow couldn't picture the old man in smooth-bottomed "booties."

Outside the sound of the medivac team hacking and stomping through the hammock grew. We went out and Diaz directed them in with their portable litter and two huge orange carrying cases of medical equipment. They clomped up the steps and I wondered if the floor of the place was going to hold the weight of all David Ashley's new company.

Diaz and I watched through the doorway as the team started unpacking. Either the child wouldn't let go of Richards or it was the other way around. The detective held the girl while the techs examined her. I turned away feeling useless.

"So where's this DOA?" Diaz asked and I led him around to the back of the cabin. He was still recording with his eyes, mapping the layout, studying the access, trying to put himself in the place. He was a good cop, but I doubted if anyone could put themselves in the world that Ashley lived in out here.

The sun was past high noon now and a natural wind had set the high leaves turning, fracturing the light that dappled the ground cover of dead twigs and leaf husks.

"Jesus. What kind of person could live this way?" Diaz said.

I didn't offer an opinion and kept on walking, but Diaz reached out and caught my elbow.

"Look, Max. I'm not talking out of school here by telling you you're moving back up on Hammonds' shit list," he said, looking in my face as if he were trying to be an ally. It was another good interview technique and when you were good at it, it was hard to see through it. I couldn't tell now.

"This is the second time you find a kid. It's going to be hard to prove that you're not in it."

He was right. But now I was in it.

"The man's gonna think whatever he needs to think," I said, trying to be nonchalant about my own suspicions about Hammonds' surveillance of me. "I think you've got higher priorities right now, regardless of what your boss thinks of me."

Diaz shrugged and looked away. Maybe he was on my side.

When we got to the back of the cabin, the detective noted the two boats, wondering aloud if the old Evinrude on the rowboat worked. When we got to the butchering site, he put his hand to his nose, surveyed the scene, then turned away. He made no comment on the knife stuck in the stump.

"How the hell did you get out here anyway?" he asked.

I told him about Brown appearing at dawn on my river and about the trip up the canal and through the marsh.

"The mysterious Gladesman? The war hero? And you didn't think there was a chance that this old guy, strong old guy I might add, would just whack you during this trip through the wilderness and leave you for the gators?"

"Yeah. I thought about it," I said, and kept walking.

I led him down the trail to Ashley's body. A cloud of insects had gathered in the midday heat and their buzzing set up a low hum. The sight of a hanged man didn't seem to bother Diaz as much as the animal slaughter. He'd seen dead men before and this one held no pity for him.

"I couldn't find a damn thing on this guy while he was alive," Diaz said. "No paper trail of any kind. No arrests. No property. Nada. We're not going to have any prints on him until they take them at the morgue. What's he look? Forty? Forty-five? How does anyone live in the world these days, even out here, without leaving a trace?"

When I didn't respond Diaz reached out and pushed a leg, setting the corpse in a slow spin.

"So he gets threatened by the encroachment of civilization and like some animal protecting its turf he starts killing off the enemy's young to scare them back."

Diaz's spoken theory turned under the unseeing gaze of marbled eyes. The detective might be wrong, but no correction would come from Ashley's blackened lips.

"Then he sees it isn't working and his psychosis gets to him and he does himself and leaves the kid to die out here in this godforsaken place."

Ashley stopped spinning.

"Murder-suicide," Diaz said, turning away. "Seen it a dozen times. Not as weird as this," he said, raising his palms to the hammock. "But a dozen times."

It was a good theory. Made for a neat, plausible package. But I didn't believe it. As Ashley's body had turned I'd seen the scabbard still laced through his belt, the short knife clipped inside. The one stuck in the stump wasn't his.

In the distance we heard the low grumble of powerful outboard motors rolling through the trees from the direction of the creek.

"That's gotta be Hammonds and the bag boys," Diaz said, starting back up the trail.

As Diaz passed the butchering area and rounded the corner, I took a wet handkerchief from my pocket and pulled the curved knife from the stump. If it wasn't Brown's and it wasn't Ashley's, whose was it? I folded and wrapped the blade and tucked it down into my combat boot. I was again corrupting a crime scene, harboring evidence. But I also knew the one we were really after had finally slipped up, left something behind he couldn't afford to lose. But we'd need him to come after it. The knife was useless without the hand of the owner.

Hammonds was jumping from the bow of a center-console Whaler when I came around the corner. A second identical boat was still trying to get up the shallow sloping bank, the driver jabbing the throttle and churning up the creek bottom with the propeller. There were five men in each boat. I could tell the two with Hammonds were FBI even before they turned around and showed the bright yellow letters sewn onto the backs of their navy-blue windbreakers.

Hammonds was also wearing a light jacket despite the steaming heat. At least he'd taken off his tie. But he was still wearing black wingtips, now sunk to the laces in mud. Diaz was talking to him, his hands pointing: The kid was in there with Richards, the DOA back there.

The FBI guys were next to them now, listening but looking up into the trees as if they were spotting for snipers. Diaz took the crime scene crew from the second boat and waited for them to assemble their gear before going back to Ashley. Hammonds started toward me. The mud sucked at his shoe and nearly pulled if off before he reached down and rescued it. He didn't seem flustered when he finally approached. In fact, he seemed damn near jovial.

"Nice place, Freeman," he said, and the jocularity of it caught me off guard. "When we get back you can tell me in your own words how you came to find it." I was silent. The FBI was silent. We all moved on to the cabin.

The medical techs had the girl on a stretcher. An IV was taped to her hand, the line being fed from a plastic pouch of clear liquid that I was familiar with. They had wiped her face clean with swabs and covered her with clean white blankets. They were ready to move back to the helicopter. Richards was still stroking the child's hair and quickly briefed Hammonds.

"She's shocky and suffering from dehydration and exposure. Probably hasn't had anything to drink since he took her. They're not sure if she would have stayed conscious much longer, but she should be all right now."

I could tell Richards was trying to keep the emotion out of her voice.

"They don't think she was abused."

"I want you and Diaz in the hospital with her until she's stable," Hammonds said, touching his detective's shoulder.

She nodded and the techs picked up the litter and started out. As they passed me, Richards looked up into my face. Her eyes were shiny with tears and I thought she tried to smile when she said, "We got here in time."

* * *

Hammonds was watching me when I turned back into the room. The FBI guys were moving through the place. One of them had unpacked an expensive digital camera and was shooting the room from different angles, recording the world of a monster for their academy classes, I thought.

The medical team had left behind a scatter of torn paper and plastic wrappings from the syringes and instruments they'd used. I made a mental note that someone, Richards I assumed, had put the child's clothes and the tattered blanket into an evidence bag and left it for the crime scene guys. The chair on which I'd found the GPS unit had been shoved away.

Hammonds studied the place for a few minutes, apparently showing no interest in the broken table or the shattered oil lamp.

"I'm going to check on the late Mr. Ashley," Hammonds said, and the FBI, unusually dutiful, followed him out.

I stayed on the porch listening to the TraumaHawk engines. The man-made gale again whipped through the hammock, this time stripping a shower of leaves from the tree canopy as the machine climbed and swung away toward the east. I wondered where Nate Brown was. I knew he would not be far, sitting down in the tall sawgrass perhaps, seeing the chopper come and go, hearing the whine of the boat engines grinding through the shallow creek, smelling the ripe clouds of exhaust.

I called Billy on the cell phone and got him at his office. He listened patiently as I described the events of the day.

"They're going to call it a murder-suicide and close the book," he said.

"Yeah. I know."

"So you'll be off the hook. They'll probably keep your file open and know they didn't finish it, but if another child doesn't disappear, it ends."

"Yeah. Happily ever after."

I didn't tell him about the knife in my boot. He said he needed to work on some records he'd been researching and that he'd meet me at the police administration building where we both knew there would be a frenzy of media when we got back in.

"My advice is to duck it," Billy said.

"Thanks," I said and punched him off.

When I got around to the back of the cabin the crime scene guys were carrying the black vinyl body bag containing David Ashley out of the trees. The wiry Gladesman had weighed barely 150 pounds alive. The team was strong and experienced and it was hardly a chore. One of them was working a small video camera, carefully documenting the scene and would have spent extra time on the noose and the tipped-over chair in Ashley's clearing. I wondered if he would be as careful inside the cabin. No one would want to make a return trip out here. The team seemed particularly stone-faced. Everyone was slapping at the following clouds of mosquitoes that were swarming around their heads and necks. The scene techs had put on long-sleeved shirts that were already soaked through with sweat, leaving dark Vs on their backs and rings under their arms. Mud was caked on their boots and no doubt some animal gristle they couldn't avoid. But their job was rarely easy and they went about it stoically.

No one else was carrying around the sheen of relief that was subtly, but unmistakably, coloring Hammonds' face. He stood with his arms folded across his chest, sweating like the rest. At one point I could see at least three or four mosquitoes light on his face but he seemed unaware as he watched his team pack up. He would answer a question from one of the men with a short sentence or order and turned occasionally to talk softly with one of the agents. But mostly he stood silent. He looked to me like a man who could envision a cool, soft bed and a long, untroubled night's sleep in the near distance and he wanted it badly.

The sun was going orange in the western sky by the time they were finished. The boats were reloaded. Ashley held an inglorious spot on the floor in the stern and the team members pointedly avoided looking down at the black bag. The bank to the creek was now trampled into a lumpy oatmeal of mud and grass, and two obvious paths led from the bank to the front of the cabin and to the thicket where the hanging took place. Each was littered with wrappings and film containers and discarded latex gloves. Before we pushed off, a scene tech stretched a three-inch-wide streamer of yellow tape across the landing from the trunk of a gumbo limbo to a pigeon plum that read: CRIME SCENE. DO NOT ENTER. I was sure that none of these men would ever return. They had all they needed.

Our boats ground and churned their way through the narrow channel until we cleared the hammock on the opposite side from where Nate Brown and I had originally entered. When the waterway opened up into the sawgrass the Florida Marine Division driver inched up the throttle and we began making time.

Out of the hammock the moving air was cooler and from my spot near the bow it smelled clean and tinged with the odor of fresh-turned soil. The rain had held off and the sky was strung now with clouds going pink and purple, their edges still bright and glowing in front of patches of blue. The whine of the engines covered any other sound and most of the men rode with their faces turned up into the wind, their eyes glossed over with the colors of the sunset.

CHAPTER 21

The last light had left the sky by the time we reached the public fishing camp that Hammonds used as a staging area. I could see the glow of unnatural lights from a distance, but we still had to use hand-held spotlights to find our way to the boat ramp docks.

When we hit solid ground the group moved with a familiar efficiency. Others who had been waiting throughout the afternoon in boredom jumped to help unload the boats. A large white crime scene van was parked nearby on the shell parking lot and next to it was a black Chevy Suburban from the medical examiner's office. I could see a sheriff's helicopter sitting fifty yards behind it.

The techs moved the evidence and the equipment first and then let the M.E.'s people retrieve Ashley's remains. As they hoisted the black body bag out of the Whaler a floodlight suddenly flashed on, its brightness causing everyone to squint and turn their faces or shield their eyes. Billy had been right about the media. At least one news crew had staked out the staging area and now was getting "exclusive footage" of the body being removed from the Everglades.

No one was surprised. Little could be kept from the media.

Every newsroom had a variety of police and emergency scanners or contracted with a sophisticated service that did nothing but monitor the array of radio traffic and dispatch instructions being sent twenty-four hours a day. Some agencies had even given up on the traditional signal codes, a now archaic attempt to broadcast a homicide as a Signal 5 or a rape as a Signal 35 in hopes of keeping some eavesdroppers at bay. Reporters and the freelance listening service operators knew the codes by heart and the game was useless.

Since the child killings began, any radio traffic sending cops out to the Glades would have caused an immediate heads up. By this time there would be TV crews at the hospital, the Flamingo Lakes neighborhood and outside the task force headquarters. Out here a young woman reporter and cameraman had gambled on following the crime scene and M.E. units, and had spent the day waiting to see who or what would come back in on the boats. Their payoff was the body bag footage. And I knew it would make prime time on the news.

I stood on the other side of the Whaler, just outside the cone of the camera's light, watching as the M.E. guys lifted Ashley out. The boat's stern was still rocking in shallow water and as one of the techs stepped over the gunwale he stumbled and a strap on the bag got caught on one of the stern cleats. As the camera rolled, the two men struggled to free the package. Another tech came to help but they couldn't pull it loose. The scene was getting awkward under the glare of the television lights and I thought of how it was going to play on the eleven o'clock news. It might be my only opportunity.

With one quick move I bent and pulled the wrapped knife from my boot, snapped it open and stepped into the boat. The camera lights flashed on the blade and with one motion I cut the strap clean.

One of the M.E. boys said thanks, and they continued up the slope to the Suburban, the cameraman following. Now he had even better footage.

As I climbed back out of the boat I saw Hammonds watching me but he was quickly distracted by someone calling his name.

"Chief Hammonds. Excuse me, Chief."

The woman reporter approached and instead of raising his palm and walking past her, Hammonds stopped. She was short and thin with high cheekbones and brown eyes that held Hammonds' attention and seemed to simultaneously assess the others in his group, including me.

"Chief, can you give me anything on where you've been and maybe who's in the bag?" she asked in an informal way. The cameraman was still across the lot and she was being both polite and disarming. Hammonds seemed to know her.

"Donna, you know the drill. First I have to go in and brief the sheriff. These guys have to speak to their people," Hammonds said, hooking a thumb at the FBI agents. "And then we'll most likely have a press conference for everybody at the same time for the eleven o'clock." He too was being polite.

"OK. Off the record then," Donna said, turning back to her cameraman as if to emphasize that he wasn't filming. "Just so I didn't wait out here all day being eaten by mosquitoes for nothing."

"Off the record, Donna," Hammonds said, the grin I'd seen earlier now undisguised. "I think we got our guy."

The agents turned their heads and began walking with Hammonds toward the helicopter and the reporter turned to me.

"Mr. Freeman? Right?" she said. "Coming out of the swamp again. How you doing?"

I looked in her face, a foolish confirmation. I shouldn't have been surprised that a smart reporter would recognize me from the plane crash with Gunther only a week ago. I didn't respond.

"Mr. Freeman, are you on loan from Philadelphia?" She was again polite. "Does any of this tie in somehow to Philadelphia?"

Billy was right again. There would always be one who did their homework.

"No comment," I said, feeling a flush rise in my neck.

"You coming?" Hammonds called from the parking area where the helicopter blades were just starting to spin. I turned and jogged after him.

We were all strapped in and the helicopter was beginning to wobble and rise when Hammonds turned and yelled over the engine whine: "We'll have a briefing in the conference room as soon as we're in."

He was talking to all of us and looking at me. As the machine rose he pulled a headset over his ears and no one said a word during the trip in. I stared out the window and shivered at the thought of the last time I flew. But this time there was only an ocean of black below. For thousands of acres there was not a light. Without a moon, even the canals that did run through the sawgrass could not show themselves. The windows of the chopper only reflected the pilot's green instrument board.

It was hot and close inside the cramped space and I sat trying to imagine Ashley somehow moving the girl out into his old and rusted rowboat and making it out here in the dark four nights ago but the vision wouldn't come. His navigation through this part of the wilderness I didn't doubt. His ability to steal her away from the backyard and through the man-made lake was also plausible for a man of his talents. But there was no waterway or wood that led from the surrounding streets of Flamingo Lakes into these dark acres. How would a man like him make that leap? How would a man confined to oil lamps and animal skinning send an e-mail of GPS coordinates from a downtown Radio Shack?

I was convinced he hadn't, but I wasn't sure what Hammonds believed. As I ground the edges, a false dawn and then a sliver of light put a border on the eastern horizon. The glow of the coastal city. Minutes later we crossed highway 27 due west of Fort Lauderdale. It was the boundary. On one side was blackness, on the other lay a blanket of lights webbed all the way to the ocean.

The pilot brought us in on a straight heading, following a line of orange tinged lights that flanked a boulevard running through suburbia. You couldn't see the trees at night, only dark splotches interrupting the pattern of street lamps. The broader dark areas I knew had to be golf courses. The light grids thickened as we approached what I could now see was the glowing gray belt of the interstate, and we started down. The pilot swept us in a banking circle and we hovered over the neighborhood that tolerated the sheriff's administration building and he eased down to it. I wondered what the citizens thought of the chopper's occasional wind and noise assault, the sight of a machine so familiar but so far from their experience. They would never ride in it, or sit in it on their way to some important meeting. They surely weren't asked whether they had objections to its boisterous comings and goings. Maybe they didn't give a damn. Maybe they just watched TV and became oblivious to its sound, just like the night train whistle or the hum of interstate traffic. That's just the way it was. You just live in it.

The helipad was next to a motor pool and as a group we climbed out of the settled helicopter and walked along the now-closed garage bays and through a set of fenced gates. Hammonds' key card let us through an unmarked metal door into the big building. He was slipping us in the back way. We all knew the TV crews and reporters were staked out in front.

We went up an elevator that may have been the same one Diaz had taken me on, but it was a different ride.

We stank. We were four men who'd spent a day in the humid Everglades in the company of rotting entrails, decaying plants and a ripe corpse. We had sweated through clothes that were soaked in swamp water and smeared with mud. Our faces were insect-bitten and sunburned. Hammonds had pushed number six when we got on, but the elevator stopped at four and opened. A woman in office attire carrying an armload of files started to get on but either the sight or smell hit her and she backed off and flipped the back of her fingers mumbling something that sounded like "go on." We got off at six.

It was nine o'clock but the office pods and aisles were still filled with investigators in shirtsleeves and with uniformed aides. A wave seemed to push out in front of Hammonds, causing a silence as it went. He nodded at several people. An older detective reached out and briefly shook his hand and said, "Congratulations."

When we got to the glassed office, both Diaz and Richards were waiting. The FBI broke off to their computer table and Hammonds crooked his finger to the detectives and to me as he entered his office. Diaz closed the door behind us.

Without a word Hammonds went through another small door in the back corner of his office. I heard water begin to run.

I sat down in an upholstered chair, mud and all. Diaz was still wearing his clothes from the swamp, minus the boots. Richards had changed her shirt and was wearing a tight knit top tucked into her water-stained jeans. She'd brushed her hair to a gloss.

"How's the girl?" I asked, an excuse to look at her face.

"She's fine. Her family's with her." A small smile touched the corners of her mouth.

Hammonds returned, wiping his face with a towel and then dropping heavily into his chair and leaning back.

"OK. Update me."

"The kid's all right," Diaz started, looking at a small notepad. "She was dehydrated. Her, um, potassium levels were down. She was covered with insect bites and there was a small bite, maybe a rodent, the doc said, on one foot." He flipped a page as if it had to come from some official record.

"There was no sign of sexual assault and the only sign of physical injury was some bruises on her arms where the docs think she was grabbed and probably picked up and carried. And they took some adhesive out of her hair and off a cheek that looks like it came from a strip of duct tape he used to gag her.

"They expect a full recovery, but they said she was really on the edge." He finished, looking at me.

Richards was again half sitting on the edge of the table, her arms crossed.

"Her parents were brought in and they were all put up in a hospital suite on one of the upper floors. The doctors want to keep her at least a couple of days for observation," she said without the aid of a notebook. "The newsies were waiting for us and were camped out for hours until hospital public relations got the E.R. doctors to issue a brief statement that she was in guarded condition and they were optimistic for a recovery."

Diaz checked his notes and nodded at the precise language.

"The parents are holding off on the press. They don't want to say anything yet," Richards continued. "They were grateful. We gave them a vague description of where she was found and told them we thought the kidnapper had killed himself." She looked up at Hammonds, wondering if she'd overstepped.

"All right. Fine," he said, turning his eyes on me. "Now, Mr. Freeman. If you wouldn't mind explaining again how you *found* this situation."

I knew the grilling was coming. It was the only reason Hammonds had brought me along. While he began to twist the small towel in his hands, I went through the same description of Nate Brown's appearance and the boat ride to the cabin I'd given Diaz. They listened. I gave the same description of the girl and of finding Ashley's body. They listened. Then I went out on a limb.

"There was some evidence of a struggle. The table and lamp broken. That bit with the chair under the tree was too pat. And why does a loner like Ashley even bother to bring the kid all the way to his place? It wasn't for rape. It wasn't for torture."

They listened. Diaz moved uneasily behind me. Richards studied the carpet. Hammonds twisted the towel and the lines at the corners of his eyes were tightening again.

"What the hell's your theory?" he finally asked.

"Someone else was there."

"Brown?"

"Yeah. But someone else too."

"You have proof of that?"

I thought of the knife, still stuck inside my boot.

"It just didn't feel right," I said.

All three of them let it set. Maybe they were thinking about how it felt. Hammonds broke the silence.

"Look, Freeman. I'm not sure you aren't in deeper shit than even you think. Sure, we'll try to find this Brown and talk to him. Hell, we don't even have a damn autopsy on Ashley yet. But in fifteen minutes I have to go in front of the sheriff, the FBI's regional director, the county mayor and who the hell knows who else and spin a logical string of events."

He had rolled up to his desk. The towel was stretched between his hands like a thick rope.

"We've reached a point of urgency here. And I cannot entertain any goddam conspiracy theories at this point in time.

"We've got a damn good suspect who's damn good and dead. We saved a kid from becoming victim number five. Now if you want me to make you out to be the hero in that, fine. But I don't think you're up to the scrutiny that that would bring. Am I right?"

I was thinking of Donna the reporter. Maybe he was too. I nodded my head in agreement.

"So we go with what we have for now."

The others nodded. Hammonds stood up and started for his bathroom as we began to file out and stopped.

"And Freeman," he said, again in control of his voice. "Don't leave the state."

The FBI agents watched us as we headed for the hallway. Each time I saw them it looked as though they expected to see me in handcuffs. I couldn't tell if they were disappointed or not.

"Jesus," Diaz said, again leading us with his voice. "I never heard the old man cuss before." We reached the elevator and he punched the down button.

"If he expects us to be at the press conference, I gotta change down in the locker room," Richards said, looking at her mud-flecked boots and jeans. She couldn't see the fine red welts still glowing on her forehead and cheek from the branch whippings. "I'm a mess," she said, more to herself than us.

As we rode down Diaz asked if I had a way back north.

"My attorney's downstairs," I said.

"That was probably good planning," he said, smiling.

When the doors opened at the second floor, Diaz punched the lobby button for me and shook my hand before stepping out.

"We'll be talking, right?"

Richards started to follow him out, but put her hand on the door guard. I thought she was going to say something but instead she stepped in close, reached up on her toes and kissed me on the mouth.

"Thanks," she said. Her eyes were an unmistakable green.

CHAPTER 22

When the elevator doors opened on the lobby it took me a few seconds to recognize the action. My head was still softly swimming. The doors started to close again and I reached out and clanged back the metal guard, tripping them open. I started across the marble floor, admittedly a little glazed, and my hand seemed to involuntarily come up and touch my mouth.

Across the lobby I saw Billy in a dark tailored suit standing before a large piece of public art, studying the shape and color as if he were deeply interested. The young woman at the raised reception desk didn't turn at the sound of me bashing the elevator door guard. She was watching Billy with an authentic interest. Billy turned before I got to him. "M-Max," he said softly. "Shall we go?"

As we started to the front entrance the woman called out pleasantly, "Good night." Billy smiled and tipped his hand and we went out.

Through the door he took me on a hard left. The TV trucks, their mechanical necks stretched high, swarmed at the near sidewalk. The standup reporters were under portable lights, filming their introductions to the press conference. I did not see

Donna. We got to Billy's car with only a few curious looks, eased out of the parking lot and headed for the interstate. Billy made a call from his cell phone, said, "We're on our way," and hung up. I was quiet for twenty minutes and my attorney indulged me. As he drove north in the far left lane I stared out the window, watching the inside line of sedans and minivans and tractor-trailers slip behind. Billy did not let a single vehicle pass us. He was doing eighty-five. It was his way. But neither his patience nor his impatience was limitless.

"And?" he finally said.

I started the retelling with Nate Brown on the deck of my shack and took him through the day. Billy interrupted only once, when I began to describe taking the knife from the stump and putting it in my boot. Before I got it out he raised his hand to stop me.

"M-More evidence?" he said, in a tone that wasn't pleased. "Max, you're out of it. What's left to p-prove? Why bring a link to yourself?"

I slipped the knife into the wet and muddied fanny pack on the floor in front of me and said nothing.

"So you d-don't think it's done?"

"It could be," I said. "Unless another kid comes up missing."

* * *

It was near midnight when we reached the tower. For the last few miles I could almost see Billy's analytical, lawyerly mind working. We were not so different. He just did his grinding in a different way. When we came through the door of the apartment, Dianne McIntyre was in the kitchen, again in her stocking feet, but this time she had Billy's chef's apron tied around her. The rich aroma of paella was coming from the stove behind her and she was just sprinkling a touch of chardonnay over the mixture of seafood and rice.

"Good evening, boys," she said as we walked in. "You are just in time for dinner and a movie."

She reached up and plucked a wineglass from a suspended rack and filled it for Billy and when I sat on a stool at the counter she put her palms on the surface and affected an Old West accent:

"What'll it be?"

I ordered Boodles, but before she turned she scrunched her perfect nose and said: "Hot bath upstairs for two bits."

I looked down at my crusty clothes and smiled. Billy slipped his suit-coated arm around McIntyre's waist, tasted his wine and raised an eyebrow. We had indeed been an interesting pair leaving police headquarters.

"Yes, ma'am," I said and headed for the guest suite.

I showered and dressed in a pair of jeans and a loose Temple University T-shirt that had been snatched up by Billy's maid during my last visit and cleaned and pressed by his laundry service.

I then had my drink and we all sat in the living area with steaming bowls of the paella and watched McIntyre's "movie."

Billy had asked her to tape the television news and she had recorded Hammonds' press conference.

Billy pressed a button on the remote and a panel hung with one of his oil paintings slid silently up into the ceiling to expose a flat, wide-screened television. He punched on the set and hit the play button, and the head of an anchorwoman filled the wall.

"And our top story tonight, the dramatic rescue of abducted six-year-old Amy Alvarez and the discovery of a body in the Everglades of the man police are now saying may be the Moonlight Murderer.

"Tonight we have team coverage including this exclusive footage of the medical examiner's office removing the body of the man police say could be responsible for the abduction and murder of four children from South Florida neighborhoods over this long, hot summer."

It was the video shot at the boat ramp by Donna's cameraman and it opened as the M.E.'s team was hefting the body bag out of the Whaler. The camera caught the men struggle and slip with the load as it hooked on the boat cleat and showed one man go down on a knee. Then in the glare it caught my back as I stepped in and used the knife to slice the strap free. The angle only showed part of my face but the light glinted sharply off the knife blade before the cameraman panned up the slope of the ramp following the body bag up to the black Chevy Suburban.

As we watched the footage I could feel Billy's eyes on me, but I didn't turn from the screen as the report cut back to the anchorwoman.

"More in a moment. But now we take you live to the sheriff's administration building where lead investigator Jack Hammonds is holding a press conference."

The screen changed to show Hammonds standing at a podium flanked by several men in suits, clasping their hands in front of themselves like ushers waiting to take up the collection at Sunday church service.

Richards was the only woman in the bunch. She had cleaned up and was wearing a skirt with a jacket that looked too large. Her blond hair made her stick out even more and I could tell she'd put on some lipstick. I picked up my gin and took a deep draw.

The camera tightened on Hammonds, who had begun to speak.

"As you are already aware, through the joint efforts of the FDLE, the FBI, the Sheriff's Office and the FMD earlier today we were able to ascertain the whereabouts of six-year-old Amy

Alvarez at a location in the far Everglades. With the quick action of a medical-response team from the county rescue center we were able to airlift the child to Memorial Hospital where she is now listed in guarded but stable condition."

Hammonds cleared his throat and took a drink of water before continuing.

"Subsequent to our arrival at said location, we were also able to locate the remains of a suspect we have now identified as David Ashley, a thiry-eight-year-old Florida native. The deceased was found hanged in a location nearby."

You could hear the press corp squirm in their chairs and then someone in the back yelled, "Are you saying he committed suicide, Chief?"

Hammonds paused again and seemed reluctant to look up from his notes to face the gathered cameras.

"Mr. Ashley did not leave any correspondence or suicide note to indicate his mindset or motivation, but there were indications at the scene of a troubled and potentially psychotic individual. Evidence was also collected at the scene linking Mr. Ashley to another victim in this summer's string of abductions and although we will continue our investigative efforts into this matter, it is our hope that today's developments put an end to this long and difficult case."

Hammonds gathered his one-page address and turned to his team as some politician took the podium and began, "First of all we want to share in the joy of the Alvarez family in the safe return of their child, but our hearts also go out to the families . . ."

I stood up and Billy stopped the tape and punched off the set. I made myself another drink and stood at the kitchen counter thinking about Hammonds' "linking" evidence and how even he wouldn't hang himself out that far unless they picked something up at the scene. I was running my memory through the inside of Ashley's cabin when I remembered the blanket. Richards had peeled it off the child and someone had put it in an evidence bag. Hammonds would not have missed it. Every piece of evidence in every abduction would be stuck in his head. He could easily use it as a strong tie-in, proof that Ashley was the right suspect.

Billy rolled the painting back in place over the television screen and McIntyre started for the kitchen.

"What they like to call a slam dunk case," she said, stacking the bowls in the sink. "Especially tidy since the suspect is dead."

"At least *they* k-kept you out of it with that 'able to ascertain the w-whereabouts' c-crap," said Billy, carrying his wineglass to the counter.

"Yeah, at least there's that," I said, avoiding a reaction to his emphasis on the word *they*.

"Do you think it's over then?" McIntyre asked me.

"Possibly," I said, thinking of the knife. "Maybe they're just hoping that if there were more snakes in the bucket, they crawled away for good."

She raised another exquisite eyebrow to me, her only response. I picked up my drink and moved out to the patio where I stood at the railing in the high ocean breeze and looked out on the black water. The moon was down. I could see a few dots of light far out from shore, boats at anchor or trolling so slowly they appeared stationary. I sat in the lounge chair and closed my eyes. I was trying to remember the kiss in the elevator but visions of Ashley twisting under the tree canopy and the black-stained butcher stump and Nate Brown standing high in his skiff kept invading my head. I could hear the tinkling of glass and china inside and the low voices of Billy and McIntyre in conversation.

Then the lights went out and I heard Billy step to the door.

"Can I get anything for you, Max?"

I could tell from the cleanness of his words that he must have still been just inside and that it was too dark for him to see my face.

"No thanks, Billy. I'm fine."

"I hope you know what you're doing."

"I've given it some thought."

"All right. We're going to bed."

I had always thought there should be more joy in such a statement. But what did I know?

"Good night," I said.

I sat for a while, thinking of my friend. I wondered if he stuttered when he was in the arms of his lover, in the darkness of his room. If he couldn't see her face, could he whisper his words without hesitation? I suppose it didn't matter. In the arms of a lover your faults and failures were supposed to be inconsequential. Sometimes you're supposed to be a hero. Even if your armor is somewhat tarnished. But I knew that was fantasy too.

I sat listening to the surf eighty feet below and the sound of water took me again to that jumpy place in between dreams and consciousness.

* * *

It must have been a dream because I could see my breath billowing out like thin smoke in the freezing air. But I could hear the voices of men screaming as clearly as if they were standing below on the sand looking up. I had never heard men scream before that day, not with such panic and helpless ache.

It must have been a dream because I could see the woman, really only a girl, not much older than I was as a second-year patrolman. She was standing on the outside ledge of the Walnut Street Bridge, leaning out over the water forty feet below, her arms reaching back to the cold concrete abutment. She had tossed her coat into bridge traffic before we could cordon off the area, and it lay there now with a brown stain of a tire tread across the back. I was watching her hands, gone white with the cold and fear. Her long fingernails were blood red in contrast as they dug into the gray stone.

It must have been a dream because I could see Sergeant Stowe in front of me and my partner, Scott Erb, who had first spotted the commotion and wheeled the patrol car up the bridge access lane into one way traffic. We'd run up within fifteen yards of the woman before she stopped us with a wordless look of such desperation it was like taking a punch to the heart.

Now Sergeant Stowe was talking to her but she refused to see him. She kept looking down into the half-frozen water, the skin on her face stretching so taut across her bones that I could see the blue veins below the surface.

We had never seen a jumper actually go, Scott or I, though we'd been called to a few attempts on the Ben Franklin. I sneaked a look at the current below. The distance was not great. Both of us had jumped off higher points into the Schuylkill off the old Girard railroad bridge as kids. But this was mid January and the river was running hard and cold with chunks of gray ice spinning on its surface and its white banks closing in with hardening edges.

The sergeant was still talking when the scratching sound stopped him. It was the girl's nails. Maybe she was trying to change her mind as they dug into the concrete, red slivers splitting off as they scratched against the weight of her body pitching forward.

And that's when the men below screamed. And that's when Scott peeled off his thick blue police jacket and went over the side after her. And that's when I followed my friend.

When I hit the water it seemed oddly thick. The impact was

hard, but dull through my heavy shoes, and when I looked up into the bubbles and light from below the surface, the water looked green and boiling. I rose with the buoyancy of my jacket and broke the surface and that's when the cold bit my chest and refused to let me draw air. I was panicking, but looked around and found Scott and he was already to the woman, trying to get a grip on her sweater and turn her on her back. I finally gasped for a breath and it felt like a razor going down my throat but I started swimming.

I know it had to be a dream, but I could hear Scott's voice saying "I got her, I got her," though his lips were like two hard lines and not moving. I swam to them and got a fist of the sweater and started pulling and kicking and I could see the snow covered bank but my clothes were heavy and my free hand was starting to feel like a solid mitten. I saw Scott start to lose his grip and slip back and I yelled for him to hang on, god-dammit, hang on, but his eyes were starting to glaze. His blue shirt was pasted to his skin and he said he was losing his arms and I told him to keep kicking. The cold had left my own limbs nearly numb and I could feel it creeping toward my heart but I could also hear someone yelling now from the bank. Sergeant Stowe had scrambled down from the bridge and was up to his waist in the water and reaching out. I took a few more slapping strokes and now he was only six feet away. I was still hanging on to my partner and the girl but losing them both when through the numbness of my legs I felt my foot kick the bottom. I had to make a decision. We were too close to give up.

I'm not sure if I was even thinking but I got behind both of them, took as deep a breath as I could, and went under. I planted my legs in the hard mud, tried to concentrate on the feeling I still had in my shoulders and then drove the pile up with as much force as I could.

The effort pushed me deeper and I hung there, my energy

spent, a darkness closing in from all sides. From inches below the surface of the water, I could see the sergeant's face shimmering through the current. Bubbles from my own lips began to rise and the ice seemed to close in, going black around the edges when he bent and got me by the jacket and yanked me up onto a slab of ice. Several men were around us now and one had thrown his coat over Scott, who was on his knees looking down at the woman stretched out on the snow. Her eyes were closed and her face was inhumanly pale. A snowflake landed on her lips and refused to melt.

I crawled over to her and put my hand under her neck and tilted her head back. I fit my mouth over hers and blew air into her lungs and it came back warm. I waited, pinched her nose with my frozen fingers and blew again. The third time she coughed and shuddered and then threw up a handful of river water onto the snow, and then another, and another, and then she curled up into fetal position and continued to gag. Another bystander draped his overcoat on her and then the professional voices of the paramedics were shouting their way through the circle.

When I woke the warm ocean breeze had kicked up but my arms were covered in goose flesh and Billy's patio felt chilled in the wind. I rubbed my hands over my face and I was out of the dream but could remember every part of that rescue nearly a decade ago.

Sergeant Stowe and Scott and I were wrapped in emergency thermal blankets and watched as the paramedics loaded the woman into a rescue basket and carried her up the embankment to the ambulance. A freelance photographer caught the scene, the three of us, hair plastered and tinged with ice, all soaked and shivering and looking up the hill. The photo ran on the front page of the *Daily News* the next day with a headline: PHILLY'S FINEST BRAVE FROZEN SCHUYLKILL TO SAVE PENN STUDENT.

A cutline gave our names and a brief description of the time and location of the incident. The woman was described only as an eighteen-year-old freshman at the university. There was no story since it was the newspaper's policy not to do stories on suicide attempts. Their rationale was that publicity might encourage others to make such attempts. It always seemed to me a naïve logic, that someone would look at a story of suicide and say, "Hey, there's an idea." But it also seemed an incomprehensible world where an eighteen-year-old would decide there was nothing left in it for her.

Of the three heroes that day, the sergeant was soon promoted, Scott left the force for engineering school, and I went on to the detective unit where I fell on my face.

The girl lived but we never heard from her. Maybe she resented our interference. Maybe she went back home, recovered, turned her life around. I didn't think of the incident often, but more than once on the edge of my dreams I have tasted her cold lips, blown air into a dark throat and felt my own warm breath come back to me.

CHAPTER 23

The sound of water pulled me all the way back into the world. The surf below was so clean and uniform, each wave crested and then ripped down the sand with a sound like paper tearing. I listened for a few minutes and then got up and went to bed. There were no sounds from the other rooms and I lay on top of the covers in the guest room for a long time, staring at a dark ceiling and thinking about the taste of Richards' kiss, and thinking about Megan Turner and how I'd let her go without a fight. Sometime late in the night, my memories let me sleep.

Billy's girlfriend was gone by the time I got up and made my way to the coffee pot. Billy was out on the patio, the sliding doors opened wide to the ocean and the rising heat. The AC was kicked up to accommodate the fine paintings and fabrics. It was Billy's way of enjoying both worlds and to hell with the cost of electricity. He was sitting in the morning sun, a laptop popped open on the glass-topped table. He was holding the *Wall Street Journal* folded lengthwise once and then halved again, reading it like a subway commuter. But he was wearing a pair of shorts and an open white linen shirt and his bare feet were propped up on a chair.

"And how's the market today?" I said, knowing his early morning inclinations.

"The w-world is a new and wonderful p-place," he answered, peeking up from his paper, a satisfied schoolboy look on his brown, *GQ* face.

Billy had somehow foreseen the tumble of technology stocks, and those clients who trusted him, and most of them did, let him put their substantial gains in commodities before the fall.

"Sleep well?" I said.

"Very w-well. Thank you."

The sun was throwing a wide sparkle on the dimpled Atlantic and the sky was stealing some of the blue from the Gulf Stream.

"I thought I might go out today and buy a new canoe," I said. Billy nodded.

"B-Back to the sh-shack?"

"Why not? Can't live with my attorney forever."

We both listened to the sea for a long minute.

"Your p-portfolio is d-doing well. You c-could afford a reasonable p-place on the beach."

I let the thought sit awhile as I watched the broken line of early boats making their way east, out past the channel marker buoys and onto the horizon where their fiberglass superstructures stuck up small and white against the sky.

"You d-don't have to keep h-hiding out there," he finally said and the sting of the logic, the harsh taste of the truth gathered at the top of my throat.

"Oh, so I could hide up here in a tower like you, Billy?"

He turned and stared out at the ocean, a look of thoughtful recognition on his dark face but not a glint of offense. He was a black man who grew up on some of the hardest streets in urban America. He'd made his way past a million slapdowns from subtle to raw to get out of the ghetto, get through law school, gain the respect of his profession and make it to a place where he made his own choices. He made no apologies or excuses for those choices. It was that truth that made our friendship work.

He went back to his paper. I went back to my coffee. We both let the truth sit there for a while.

"Y-You th-think it's done?" he finally asked. "The killing?"

"It's officially done," I answered. "Sometimes that's enough."

"Enough f-for who?" he said, looking at me like a lawyer who knows too much about his client to let it pass. He let me stare at the ocean. But his patience had limits.

"What are you d-doing with the knife?"

I shouldn't have underestimated Billy's ability to put the signs together.

"He's a hunter," I said. "Knows the wilderness. Knows animal tendencies. Thinks like one himself."

"Yeah?"

"Bait," I said.

I could feel Billy's eyes on the side of my face.

"Hunters use it, and they are also susceptible to it," I said. "They'll bait their quarry, but they'll also enter into places they know their quarry is, even if it's dangerous, because that's where the goal is. It baits them."

"So w-what's the b-bait. The knife, or you?"

I wasn't sure of the answer. My hunch was the knife. But I needed to be attached to it. The killer was too afraid of the cops. He might be an animal, but he wasn't a stupid animal. Even a brash hunter won't expose himself too much. But this one had already been bold enough to come into my space, creep my shack, leave a violent piss marking on my territory by smashing my canoe.

Billy's eyes were still on my face.

"S-So you d-don't think it was Ashley?"

"Maybe."

"S-So why not let Hammonds have it?"

"Hammonds won't flush him. He can't get close," I said finally turning to Billy with what I knew was that stupidly confident grin we used in the patrol car in Philly.

Billy met my eyes and said: "Let me show you s-something."

* * *

I followed him into his study and while he went into a file room I wandered to the floor-to-ceiling corner windows that looked out on the city. Billy loved high views but the thing about South Florida from a height was its complete lack of borders; no mountains or hills or even small rises, nothing but the horizon to hold it in.

"I know you're fighting with the idea of this thing being done," Billy started, talking from the filing room and out of sight. "But your comment about someone having the capacity to kill started me thinking about your known band of Brown's 'acquaintances,' so I dug a little deeper into the case I handled for Gunther when he was being sued by one of his fishing clients. He had told me it involved a family and he mentioned that he and Blackman often partnered up on trips. But when the case was suddenly dropped by the complainant, I never went much more into it."

"And now?" My attention had wandered to a museum-quality Renoir hanging on an interior wall under its own spotlight.

"S-So I p-pulled the whole f-file," Billy said, coming back into the room and placing a stack of files in the middle of his broad, polished walnet desk. The attorney for the family had taken depositions from the father and mother.

"Hers is m-most interesting," he said, pushing the bound transcript across the desk.

The trip had been a fishing excursion into the waters of Florida's Ten Thousand Islands on the southwest coast. The family, including a ten-year-old boy and a thirteen-year-old girl, were from Michigan and wanted an overnight wilderness trip. They hired Gunther to be their outfitter and guide. He in turn brought in Blackman, who knew the twisting waterways of the mangrove islands better than he. Many of the so-called islands were little more than a mass of mangrove roots that clung to the bottom of Florida Bay. It took an experienced guide to get through the confusing spins and fingers of shallow water and to find those few small islands dry and high enough on which to camp.

The tarpon fishing had been excellent and all were satisfied until evening when they made camp on a narrow sand beach on a small shell mound. They'd cooked dinner on camp stoves and the odor of pan-fried fish attracted a resident raccoon.

"The children thought he was cute and tossed a bit of fish to him to eat," the mother stated in her deposition.

"It seemed harmless enough but Mr. Blackman became very angry. He snapped at the kids and told them to stop. He said they were turning the creature into a garbage hound."

"Did his demeanor bother you?" read the question from the attorney.

"Well, I certainly don't like other people yelling at my children, especially hired help. But I told them it might not be such a good idea."

"And did they stop?"

"I believe Mathew tossed one more piece. You know, to spite us both. You know how boys can be."

"And then what happened?"

"Well, my God. The raccoon came out to get the piece and, well, it was a blur. I've never seen a human being move so quickly.

"Before we could turn to see it, Mr. Blackman had the creature by the back of the neck and had cut its throat with a knife."

"Did the animal squeal?"

"It never made a sound. But my daughter and I certainly did. It was appalling and I told Mr. Blackman so."

"You registered your displeasure?"

"He said the animal was useless now for anything but a hat. Then, in front of us all, he held the poor thing up and sliced it open like a wet bag."

"He skinned it? In front of the children?"

"Exactly."

As I read, Billy had gone out and refilled my coffee and set the cup in front of me. I took a substantial swallow but did not look up.

"And then what happened?" read the attorney's question.

"Well, my husband came back into the campsite with Mr. Gunther and when he saw this, this, atrocity, he confronted Mr. Blackman."

"And what was Blackman's reaction?"

"He pointed his knife at Henry."

"At your husband?"

"Yes."

"In a threatening manner?"

"I thought so."

"Did Mr. Blackman say anything threatening?"

"He said something about how the children ought to learn about the real wilderness instead of pretending. Then Mr. Gunther stepped in and calmed everyone down."

At that point in the deposition the attoney steered the woman away from any more talk of Gunther's peacemaking efforts and went on about the children's mental anxieties and recurring nightmares and other bullshit to bolster his case. I closed the folder and took another long swallow of coffee.

"W-Want to g-guess what the sk-sk-skinning knife m-might have l-looked like?" Billy said, leaning back in his chair.

Brown, Ashley, Gunther, Blackman, I thought. One moved in and out of the world like a ghost. One was dead. Another I had saved from dying. And last turned out to be as odd as any of them.

"G-Gunther n-never t-told me the details. He said the clients w-went after him because he w-was the owner of the b-b-business.

"I tried to call this f-family but the wife r-refused to talk. She said her husband told her to f-forget it."

Billy said he'd tried to call Gunther but he was out of the hospital and his business and home phone had been disconnected. The pilot had apparently made good on his vow to leave the state.

"So you've been busy, counselor," I said, smiling at Billy.

"Only l-looking up alternatives," he said. "In case y-you were the only suspect they s-settled on and p-pushed into an indictment."

And they'd had enough to get their indictment. But the most recent target was now on a slab. It was neater that way. Maybe it was over. Maybe they got all they needed.

"M-maybe you could s-second guess the bait thing?"

"Kinda late," I said. "Right now, I'm going to get in a beach run and then go shopping," I said. "You game?"

"I w-will drive."

* * *

I finished my coffee and went running. The tide was out and the sand was packed but nothing like the South Jersey shore beaches where the tide could run out and leave a swath of hard brown sand thirty yards wide on the barrier island beaches of Wildwood, Cape May and Ocean City. I'd tried for months to run Lavernious Coleman's dead face out of my head on those beaches. But his ghost was always waiting for me back on the city streets.

The Florida beach was not nearly as wide but twice as hot, and within a mile the sweat was dripping into my eyes and had glossed across my chest. The nights of little sleep, the drain from my bout with dehydration and the ache from my fistfights with the Glades and its oddballs had left me weakened. At the two-mile mark I turned and headed back, my legs already feeling tight and my calf muscles stinging in the too-soft sand. The last mile I had to push through, my lungs grabbing for air instead of using it, my throat rasping and burning instead of letting my breathing flow. The blood was singing in my ears over the last fifty yards when I tried to sprint it home. The exercise gurus talk about the release of endorphins that bring true runners a high that keeps them hooked on such self-punishment. If it's true, I never met them, the chemical or the pure distance athlete.

After I showered and dressed and ate a breakfast of toasted muffins and fruit, Billy drove us to an outfitter's store well out on Southern Boulevard.

Southern was like the majority of South Florida, it wasn't Southern at all. It could have been a summertime road through any growing sprawl from Des Moines to Sacramento to Grand Rapids. If you've driven down a four-lane flanked by mini-marts, McDonald's, Amoco self-serves and Jiffy Lubes, you've been down Southern Boulevard. Hell, there weren't even any Florida-looking palm trees except where they'd planted some near the international airport to fool the tourists.

I watched overhead as a 757 came rumbling out of the sky on a landing approach. It seemed ungodly close to the road traffic and improbably large to be floating down on the air like that. There were probably two hundred souls aboard and no doubt a few coming to relocate in a warm climate where there were already too many people and too few resources to match their dreams. Yet they came. Just like I had.

In the outfitter's parking lot was a collection of four-wheel drive pickups and SUVs, more than a few with trailer hitches. But it was also not devoid of the occasional family sedan and a couple of obvious company cars, guys playing a little hooky on a Wednesday afternoon during their sales call time. Billy parked the Grand Cherokee and we went in.

Such places draw an interesting crowd, men with serious looks who will stand for an hour inspecting fishing tackle with the tips of their fingers and practiced eyes. Wannabes who will keep asking the clerk at the gun display to "let us see that one there," and then inexpertly handle a rifle or handgun that they might admire for its dangerous look but have no capacity for its true use. These are decidedly manly places. The colors are earthy and subtle, the stitching in clothes and fabrics is thick and obvious. The zippers are oversized and even if they're plastic they're made to look metallic. This particular store held a clean smell of oil and new cardboard.

I went to the far back of the store to the marine area. Billy walked around, absorbing and looking only slightly out of place in a pair of pressed slacks and starched white shirt but without a tie. He was comfortable in one of the few places where he didn't have to worry about being assessed or hit on by the opposite sex.

The same guy who sold me my first Voyager canoe was in the back and recognized me. I could tell by the quizzical look.

"Let me guess," he said. "You like the first one so much you want two."

There is no such thing as boat humor.

When I told him a vague story about the vandalism, he looked personally hurt.

"I guess I shouldn't be surprised anymore, but that gets me," he said. "That's such a fine piece of craftsmanship. I could maybe see some asshole stealing it, but not just smashing it up.

"If you bring in the old shell, we can ship it back up to Ontario and see what the home factory can salvage," he said, searching for a positive.

He had another Voyager in the back, same model as I had. I filled out the paperwork. The salesman said again how sorry he was when he handed me back my credit card and a receipt for thirty-eight hundred dollars.

"Drive around back and we'll tie it down on your truck."

I went to search for Billy and found him back toward the front of the store, looking down into a glass case along one wall. His hands were in his pockets and he was staring, absorbed in the way he usually became in art galleries or in front of computer screens. The clerk was helping a couple of twenty-somethings look at a trio of black, brush-finished 9mm handguns. He had the guns out on a cloth on the glass top at the far end but he kept looking down at Billy, more concerned it seemed over a dapper black man staring at a display than with the customers in front of him.

When I stepped to Billy's side I could see he was looking at knives, the store's collection of antique and historic blades. I scanned the case and saw the short curved edge that had caught his eye.

"Didn't y-you say it was s-similar t-to that?" Billy asked, knowing that I'd recognized the piece. The trophy knife was sharpened and shined to a brutal gloss. Its handle was of dark mahogany or walnut and was polished from years of use, the oils of who knew how many working hands.

"More than similar," I said, bending to look at the word Meinstag printed on a gold-plated tag under the knife. It was exactly the same as the knife from the stump that I now had tucked away in my fanny pack in the truck. And although no expert, I would have bet it was an equal brother to the blade Nate Brown was using on the sawgrass bud as he sat on my dock yesterday morning.

"Gentlemen. Anything I can help you with?"

The clerk had put the guns away and shed the boys-with-toys couple. I hoped it was because he could see the more appreciative demeanor in Billy's eyes and the real money in his clothes.

"What's the history behind this piece?" I asked, pointing out the German knife.

"Ah, the Meinstag," the clerk started. "German-crafted as only they could do it back in the thirties."

I knew we were going to get a sales pitch, but the guy wasn't just spinning a rehearsed speech. From a deep pocket, he pulled out a ring of keys attached to a long rope chain and unlocked the display case.

"This was a special knife. Handcrafted long before the German war machine started cranking out weaponry in mass for World War II."

He took the knife out like a jewelry salesman showing an expensive tennis bracelet and put a black piece of felt down before setting the knife on the glass counter.

"There were probably a thousand of them made at most." He picked it up after neither of us made a move to touch the piece and held it lightly in his thick stubby fingers.

"Very high quality German steel," he said, drawing a finger down the backside of the blade. "And the curve in the blade made it especially versatile for everything from hunting and skinning to cutting lines and even carving. The folding style was well ahead of its time."

We watched him snap the hinged instrument closed and then easily reopen it.

"The bulk of them were issued to Germany's elite mountain

troops, fighters who were skilled woodsmen and would spend weeks in the wilderness on advance missions out past the front lines."

The salesman was a short, fleshy man, probably in his late forties with a shiny pate. His jowly face was so closely shaved I could see the high red capillaries just below the skin.

"And they got here . . ." I spoke each word slowly, trying to urge the story on.

"They were coveted by American soldiers in battle. After a fight with the mountain troops the GIs would go over the bodies or disarm the survivors and pocket the knives for themselves, especially the guys who could appreciate them. They brought them home when they got discharged and there's still a few of them out in circulation. Collector's items. Like this one."

He put the knife back on the velvet and stood back, folding his forearms over his broad belly and patiently waiting for the inevitable question of price.

Neither Billy nor I made a move to touch the knife.

"Well, thanks for your time," I said. "It's certainly an interesting piece."

I could see the disappointment in the man's face. He prided himself on reading serious customers.

"I could let it go for thirteen hundred," he said as we started away.

"Thanks," Billy said, smiled his *GQ* smile, and turned with me.

"You're not going to find another one like it," the clerk called out, not knowing how wrong he was.

* * *

Neither of us spoke on the way to the Cherokee. When we got in I got my fanny pack out of the backseat and took the knife out of the sealed plastic bag I took from Billy's kitchen.

"Nate Brown?" Billy said.

"World War II hero who takes out a whole nest of German mountain troops and brings back a few mementos," I said, running it through my head.

"S-So who d-does he give them out to?"

"Three that I'm pretty sure of. Gunther, Blackman and Ashley. But who knows who else? He could have brought back a dozen. He could have a lot of so-called acquaintances out in the Glades. But I doubt there's too many wacked out enough to get into a plan to kill kids."

"There was at l-least one."

"Yeah, but he's dead," I said, putting the knife back in my pack.

CHAPTER 24

The late afternoon rain clouds had walled off the western sky by the time we reached the ranger station boat ramp and the air blew warm and moist out of the Glades. No one was at the station and Cleve's Boston Whaler was gone from the dock. It seemed odd that he'd be out on the water this late.

My truck was parked over in the visitor's lot. I had to smile when I saw that the scratches from my Loop Road encounter had been buffed out and the chrome was shiny and even the wheel hubs had been cleaned. I'd have to give the kid an extra fifty bucks when I saw him.

Billy helped me take the new canoe down and we set it at the water's edge. He'd tried to convince me to stay at his place, but it hadn't worked. A good hunter, even an urban one, doesn't bait too close to the things he cares about.

Billy said he'd turn the information about Blackman and the encounter with the tourist over to Diaz.

"M-Maybe they will w-work it."

"Maybe," I said.

I loaded my bags, strapped the fanny pack with Billy's cell phone inside and stood taking the measure of the new polished pinewood paddle I'd bought.

"You're s-supposed to christen a new boat on it's m-m-maiden voyage," Billy said.

"Yeah?" I shrugged, looking at the boat as if I was actually considering it.

Then Billy stepped up, spit in the palm of his right hand and slapped the triangular bow plate with a wet smack.

It was the most uncharacteristic thing I'd ever seen him do. My mouth was probably still agape like a beached wahoo when he grasped my hand with the same damp palm and said, "Luck," and then turned and walked away.

"Christ," I muttered to myself. "What the outdoors does to people."

I pushed off onto the river and right away the water felt wrong.

The new canoe seemed oddly different as I sat in the rear seat and shifted my weight, feeling the bottom roll from side to side. The new paddle felt awkward in my fist as I took the first few strokes. I'd lost my familiarity, I thought. It was that new car syndrome. Same model, but still a different feel. I shook away the uneasiness and tried to put some muscle to the paddling and worked my way out toward the middle channel. The western rain wall was moving to the coast and the light was already going gray with the cover. I concentrated on the sliding current and setting up a rhythm: Reach, pull, follow through. Reach, pull, follow through.

I could still feel the ache in my ribs and the knots in one forearm, but I fell into a pace and the sweat and flow of oxygen and blood through my veins loosened my joints and I started to get a sense of the new boat's tendencies.

But there was still something wrong. The water didn't seem to swirl in the right direction off the shallows of the mangrove banks. The eddies didn't pull right. The air from deep in the river didn't smell right.

I was tired when I got to the canopy entrance to the upper river. It had started to rain lightly and I let the boat drift in. The water was running at me harder than before. The rain, I figured. It was filling the canal and the slough at the other end, the excess water flowing heavy, looking for the easiest path to the sea. The water was a reddish color, thickened by the sediment it pulled along with it. There were no osprey overhead. No wood warblers chirping from the low limbs. No turtles standing guard on the logs.

I was thirty yards into the canopy when I saw Cleve's Boston Whaler up around a sweeping corner in the distance. Even in the low light its white hull glowed like exposed bone.

It was settled, nose first, into the crook of a downed cypress log and the current lightly rocked its stern in an unrhythmic way. I watched it roll as I approached and scanned both shorelines for movement or noise. When I got close I realized I was holding my breath. I had to back paddle some to get up beside her and when I reached up to grab the gunwale and started to stand, I could see streaks of smeared blood on the middle of the center console. My legs began to tremble and I had to sit to keep myself from falling back into the water.

I tried to breathe. I tried to blink sight back into my eyes. I tried not to push off the side of the Whaler and paddle back down the river and disappear into the night.

I don't know how long it took me to gather myself, but I finally stood again and pulled myself back up and onto the starboard side of the Whaler.

On the floor lay Cleve and young Mike Stanton. Both had been shot at least once in the head. They were in their ranger uniforms. Cleve was partially on top of the kid, as though he might still be protecting him. Blood had run from their bodies with the natural slant of the boat and had collected in the stern with the rainwater. The reddish, tea-colored mixture was sluicing out the self-bailing scuppers and into the river.

I had seen enough dead bodies and didn't need to check for thready pulses or burbling breath sounds. So I just stared. Trying to understand. But the newest stone was too jagged to grind, the edges too sharp to even let it into my head. I sat on the gunwale and pulled my fanny pack around to get the cell phone, but when I twisted 'round I began to retch and couldn't stop.

Crime scene, I thought, or maybe I said it out loud, to no one else who could hear. "Crime scene, crime scene, crime . . ." The mantra brought me back.

I stood up and wiped my face with the bottom edge of my sweaty T-shirt and fell back on old habit. I pulled out the cell phone. I punched in Diaz's cell phone number and he answered on the fifth ring, his voice quick and busy sounding, a thumping mix of salsa and jazz in the background.

"Yeah, Diaz here."

"It's Max Freeman, Diaz, I . . ."

"Max, Max, Max," he cut me off with an admonishing sing-song cadence. "Man, we're trying to get a deserved rest here, Max. It has been a long hot summer you know, and . . ."

"And it isn't over," I said, cutting back in on him. "You've got a double homicide out here on my river."

The silence lasted several beats and I could hear him cupping the phone.

"What? Christ! What?"

Now I had his full attention.

"Not kids, Max. Tell me it's not kids."

"Two park rangers," I said, turning to look down at the bodies, trying to be professional. "They're in their boat, just south of the entrance of the upper river. Both of them head shot from close range. I'm not sure what else."

I looked down at Cleve's hand on the deck, trying to judge the lividity, how much blood had settled to the lowest body part. His fingers were dark and bloated and there was a bullet wound in his palm where a round had gone clean through. It was a classic defense wound where he'd raised his hand in vain to stop a bullet. The entry hole left behind was the size of a middle-caliber round, quite possibly a 9mm.

"It looks like a couple of hours ago," I said into the phone, staring at my friend's hand. "And it might have been my gun."

"Christ. Hey. Hey, Mr. Freeman. Take it cool now, OK?" Diaz was trying to be calm now. And I had become a "Mister" again. The coincidences were stacking up to be way too much, even for him.

"Mr. Freeman?"

"Yeah."

"Look, we're on our way out. OK? We'll get a team out there. OK?"

"Yeah."

I could tell he was moving, could imagine him leaving a group of cops in a bar somewhere, maybe even looking around for Richards, digging for his car keys. I could hear the music begin to fade.

"Freeman?"

"Yeah."

"Look, sit tight. OK? Don't do anything. It's a crime scene, right?"

I wasn't listening now. The rain was coming heavier, starting to ping off the white fiberglass and fill the scuppers where the rangers' blood was draining.

"Mr. Freeman?" Diaz was trying to keep me talking. "What are you doing now, Mr. Freeman?"

"Going home," I said and punched off the phone.

I climbed back into the canoe and pushed out away from

the Whaler. Before taking up the paddle I tucked the phone back into my pack and felt a smooth slickness of worn wood that had settled on the bottom inside. The short, curved knife from the stump was still in my possession. Had my stupid gambit with the bait led to this? I had meant to draw him to me, challenge him with the hope that he'd slip up, make a mistake, leave something more substantial than the footprint. But now he'd turned ugly, unpredictable.

I zipped the bag and spun it around on my waist and started up river, paddling hard and grinding.

* * *

It was dusk now and the light was leaving but I didn't need it to find the way. Rain was swirling through the tree canopy with a soft hissing sound as it spun through the leaves. I tried to think back to Nate Brown and yesterday morning. He had surprised me when he'd said I wouldn't need my gun after I'd tucked it in my waistband. Then I'd picked it back up after he'd told me about the girl and when I'd hurried to gather the first aid kit and get dressed, I laid it on my table and left it there. I could see it there, black and tinged with rust on the worn wood. Somehow I knew it wasn't there now.

I had also run out to join Brown and out of habit had not fastened the new door lock Cleve had installed for me. He'd been worried about the gun falling into the wrong hands after he'd seen the warrant servers find it. And now I'd made it all too easy.

I pulled the strokes harder. Twice I thunked the new boat into partially submerged cypress knees in the shadows. In twenty minutes I was sliding into the curve where the channel to my shack branched off. I glided, trying to listen. Raindrops tapped on the leaves and ferns. The current bubbled over a stump. Did it matter if he heard me? I pushed up the channel and stroked up to my dock. I was beginning not to care. My fight-or-flee reactions were gone, overridden by another cocktail of human emotion: anger and a raw dose of vengeance.

I eased myself out of the canoe and looped a line from the platform post around one seat to secure it. I could see the outline of the staircase in the dark, but it was useless to try to detect any footprints. I went up quietly. The door creaked when I pushed it open.

This time I didn't miss it. The first place I looked was the table where I'd left my gun. Lying in its place was a GPS unit, same as the one in Ashley's cabin, same as the one planted here only days ago. I took another step inside and glass crunched under my feet. Another step and I kicked a piece of silverware across the floor. When my eyes were fully adjusted, I found my battery powered lamp and snapped it on. This time whoever did the searching had been just as thorough as the warrant team, but carried an exotic anger. Drawers were emptied onto the floor. Shelves yanked from the walls. The armoire was ransacked and then toppled. The bunk-bed mattresses shredded. This time he hadn't bothered with soft-soled booties either. My coffee pot lay crushed on the floor, stomped under a heavy boot.

The destruction didn't bother me. I had little attachment to any of it although I desperately wanted a mug of coffee. I knew he had not found what he came for. But the GPS was a bad sign.

I picked up a chair and sat at the table in the ring of lamplight to study the unit. The numbers displayed on the readout were familiar. They pinpointed the spot upriver where I'd found the wrapped body. The air went out of my throat again. Was there another child there now? Had Cleve and Mike Stanton interrupted his work and been killed for it? Was he trying to leave more evidence to put Hammonds back on me? Or did he just want what I had? I didn't have the time to work it out. The answers were upriver. If I went now.

In minutes I was back on the water, working the canoe south, digging the paddle on my reach and splashing the follow-through. I was hot and inefficient, unmindful of what could happen and purely driven by anger. I was breathing hard and foolish most of the way and barely noticed that the rain had stopped and sprays of moonlight were sneaking through the ragged cloud cover.

I slowed more from fatigue than from good sense and in the dark I could hear the sound of the water rushing over the old dam. Thirty yards more and I could see its outline. Then a sliver of moonlight broke through, illuminating a white line of foam at the base of the falls. I fought against the spinning eddies and with some effort made it up to the stained concrete. I rested for a full minute, listening to the hiss of spilling water, then set my feet and yanked the canoe up over the abutment and onto the upper river.

With the canoe floated, I stepped in and pushed out onto quiet water. I took six or seven strokes to get upriver from the falls and looked deep into the tangle of root and ferns for the spot where I'd first seen the floating bundle. The moon broke away again from its cover and flickered on the river surface.

Hoo, hoo.

The double notes of a barred owl sounded so close behind me the skin on my neck shivered.

* * *

I half turned my shoulders to look but my weight shifted in the unfamiliar boat and it started to roll. At the same instant, the first gunshot roared out of the darkness and I let the momentum of the canoe spill me into the water.

It was an ungodly noise in this quiet place and even though

I was three feet underwater I heard the second shot explode the air. The round crackled through the shell of my overturned canoe and I swear I heard it sizzle through the water before it smacked hard into my thigh. The bullet felt like a dull iron poker. I could feel it sear through muscle and stop, trapped there. I thought about my neck. How I hadn't even known the first time I'd been shot. The pain in this one was different, hot and cutting, but I stayed under, holding my breath, waiting for the next one.

He was up high, I thought. Maybe in the trees. I knew that with the moonlight, he'd see my white face the instant I came up, if he hadn't already.

I looked up but could see nothing through the surface water. Blackness. A soft swirl of moonlight that wiggled and disappeared. I was still underwater, my lungs starting to ache. I couldn't stay down but how do you raise your head when you know a bullet's waiting for it? I felt for the canoe and my fingertips found the gunwale.

Could I come up under it? He had to think of that. My feet were in the soft river bottom. Could I push the boat to the river bank where I'd have some cover? My lungs were burning now. All the choices were bad.

I reached to touch the other side of the canoe and took the chance he knew I would, and came up into the trapped pocket of air. Now I was truly blind. But he didn't fire.

"Just like shootin' fish in a barrel, Mr. Free-man. Isn't this just how the tourists like it?"

His voice sounded dull and muffled, bouncing off the hull of the canoe, echoing in the air inside. But there was no mistaking it. The smartass inflection. The way he broke my name into two words. I could see his bearded face in my head. The hard, sharp cheekbones. The dark sullen eyes with the flash of anger. It was Blackman.

"How's it feel in there from the fish's side of things, Free-man? You know, the tourists want to think it's sport. But there ain't much sport to it, is there?"

It was impossible from under the shell of the boat to tell the direction of his voice. But I could feel the current swirling around my legs. He would logically be upriver of the dam. I hung onto the edges of the boat and let it slowly drift.

"All them folks out for the *wilderness* experience. Hell, they don't know wild until it comes up and really bites them. Right, Free-man? How's wild feel under there, Free-man?"

His voice sounded different now. Louder. But closer? I was on my knees now. My foot caught on a root as I moved back with the current. The bullet wound was singing with pain. My right knee ground into a rock.

"Oh, they all want to feel the wild. 'Take us out in the Glades so we can *feel* what it's like.' Shit. They don't belong out here any more than you do, Free-man. All they do is steal it. Piss in it and spoil it. You're no different, Free-man. Coming out here trying to live in my country."

I could hear the water spill at the falls behind me. I couldn't tell how close I was. I dug my feet into a wedge of rock. Shit. Why didn't he just shoot?

"How about it, Free-man? You pissin' in there?"

Thump!

Something hard and heavy hit the canoe hull and the trapped noise cracked inside and snapped in my ears.

"Huh? How about it, *tourist*?"

The force of wood on the hull rang again. This time dead center on a middle rib. It had to be the paddle, I thought. He had to be knee-deep in the water in front of me. He had to be close. I could hear him sloshing in the water, setting his feet. I cocked my knees and gripped the sides and imagined him on the backswing, wielding the paddle like an axe.

"HOW ABOUT IT, FREE-MAN!" he screamed again and I waited for that hard fraction of a second, the draw of breath that always betrays the amateur fighters before they swing.

"YOU THINK . . ."

I powered the boat up, driving its weight up with my legs and back and launching it forward with a spray of water. When I felt it hit something solid, another gunshot rang up into the cypress canopy and I turned and dove away.

My arm hit the top edge of the dam with a sickening thud. Momentum and current took me over the side and I fell the four feet, landing hard on a concrete edge below.

My feet seemed to scramble on their own and I pushed myself back inside the curtain of falling water and onto the shelf of concrete. I froze for several seconds, maybe in fear, maybe in pain. I was lying on one hip but when I tried to use my arms to prop myself up against the inside wall the left one buckled and I heard an ugly wail escape from my own throat. I reached for the arm and felt the bone sticking up under my shirt like a broken broomstick handle in a sack. I leaned back against the wall of the dam and held the arm in my lap. The hiss of falling water was all around me. I could see nothing beyond the moving film of the falls.

"Hell of a fall there, Free-man."

Blackman's voice was almost calm. A steady, clear inflection as if he were giving a nature-trail talk.

"And by the sound of that yelp, you might be in a bit of pain too. Oh, I've heard enough wounded animals in my time, Free-man.

"But you're a tough one. That little plane crash proved that. And the way you pulled that fat ass Gunther out of there. Now that impressed even me, Free-man."

The rush of the water made it impossible to pinpoint him. First the voice seemed to come from the left. Then the right.

Even through the occasional gaps in the water curtain, I could see nothing.

"Course, a smart animal doesn't mess with the weak and wounded at his own expense. Especially a pussy like Gunther who didn't have the balls to do what needed to be done."

Now the voice seemed to be coming from above.

"Oh, Gunther was a talker all right. Just like the rest. But when it came down to the doin'? There's always got to be a strong one."

"You mean he wouldn't kill innocent children," I finally answered him, hoping he'd talk enough for me to figure his position.

"Territory and survival, Free-man," he said, more agitated now. "Even a wild animal wouldn't take its young into territory where they couldn't survive. They all knew that. They all knew what the answer was. But hell, even old Nate was too damn old to do what needed to be done."

I saw the rip in the water curtain just before the edge of the paddle came through but I still couldn't raise my arm fast enough. The lacquered pine caught me across the temple and a flash of white seared through my head. Suddenly I was yanked out of the falls and thrown facedown in the river. I tried to get up but a hard boot kicked me a few feet forward. Then I felt a knee drive hard into my back and water already seeping up my nose and into the back of my throat.

I coughed but it only let more water into my mouth. Then I felt my head being yanked up out of the river. Blackman had a fist full of my hair.

"Shit. I knew you wouldn't be as hard to kill as Ashley. But this is too easy, Free-man," Blackman growled.

I tried to push off the bottom but the broken arm folded like a weak straw.

"I figured a tough cop who didn't mind shooting down some black kid on the street might put up a blood fight."

He grabbed the shoulder of my broken arm and spun me. We were in knee-deep water now. My heels were scraping the bottom, but he had me by the shirt front again and I wasn't moving. I shook the water from my eyes. The moonlight was splashed behind his head. I could see he'd lost the paddle but still had my 9mm in his hand, the dark eye of the barrel was pointed directly into my face.

"You got my knife, Free-man. I've got your gun," he snarled. "I like the blade a lot more. But this has already been good twice tonight."

I knew then that he'd seen the knife on the news, just like I'd hoped. But it had flushed him out the wrong way. I'd taken him for a coward, a psychotic who would always work the shadows. It wasn't meant to go like this. But one thing that had brought him here, that had run him into Cleve and young Stanton, was still in my possession.

He had me straddled now and jammed his knotted fist up into my throat. The fanny pack was still strapped to my waist, twisted behind me, and I used my good hand to rip at the zipper. Inside, my fingertips found the smooth wooden handle.

Blackman pulled me closer.

"Even if I don't get the knife back, it won't be much good without you alive to say where you got it."

Then he leaned into me, forcing me under. I hung there. From inches below the surface of the water I could see a blue, backlit outline of his shoulders and head, but I couldn't see his eyes. Bubbles from my own lips began to rise. I was at an edge too close to give up.

I planted my knees in the mud, tried to concentrate on the knife in my hand and the feeling I still had in my shoulder and then drove the blade up with as much force as I could.

Through the shimmer of current I saw my fist lumped hard
against his neck. It held there, trembling, and I felt his grip
loosen. Then dark drops of what looked like oil fell onto the
surface in front of my face and lost their shape in the swirl of
water, and the night went black.

CHAPTER 25

I heard the hiss of falling water and then felt the odd, involuntary rise of my own chest. Another mouth was on my own and when the seal of lips broke, I felt a small rush of warm air leave my lungs.

My throat gagged with the vacuum left behind and then caught and sputtered and a wash of water boiled out. I rolled my knees up and coughed out water for a full minute before I could open my eyes.

I was out of the water, up on the concrete dam abutment and Nate Brown was on his knees beside me. The moonlight was against his face and he wiped his whiskers with the back of his hand and said, "Been a long time since I breathed life into a man."

All I could do was look at him.

"You lay still, son," he said. "I gotta go yonder and git your boat."

I rolled onto my side as he climbed down into the water. The bullet wound in my leg seemed dull and thick. My thigh had gone numb. The pain in my broken arm felt like a deep nerve that had screamed itself into a hard buzz.

"Blackman?" I said, the word coming out rough and quiet.

"He ain't no more," the old man said and stepped away into the river.

I tried to focus my eyes but gave up and pressed my face down on the cold concrete, could feel the pebbled surface dig into my cheek and stared instead into foaming water.

When Brown reappeared, he had my canoe in tow. From inside the boat he brought out two short lengths of cypress stripped from a branch and tossed them up on the concrete. Then he moved out of my field of vision. I didn't want to turn my head for fear of throwing up again. The world was not quite straight, tipped on its axis at a hard angle while water ran through it. I still refused to close my eyes.

Back in sight, Brown had collected a handful of long vines. He stripped their leaves with a single pass through his fist and then quickly spun them together to create an instant length of twine. Then he came near and gripped my shoulder with one hand and my broken arm at the elbow with the other. I flinched and he said, "Holt on." With a short powerful yank he set the bone and I heard the animal yelp again and again. I passed out.

When I regained consciousness my arm was in a crude splint and somehow the old man had picked me up and laid me in the canoe. He stripped off his shirt and tucked it under my head and then climbed in the stern seat and got us moving in the current headed downriver. He had no paddle but guided the boat with his shifting weight and by pulling at an occasional low limb. With my head tipped up, I watched the canopy float by, the moonlight flickering through the leaf openings. I drifted in and out, afraid to close my eyes, trying to keep up with time. The river had gone quiet, as if the gun blasts had flushed out every sound. No bird call. No cricket. No night prey or predator. Only the sound of water sloshing intermittently at the edges of the canoe.

At one point Brown got out to push and then I felt the bow

bump against something solid and we were back at my shack. With some help from my one sound leg, he got us up the staircase and inside. I lay on the slashed and tattered bunk and watched the dark room spin. Brown found a match, struck it with a fingernail and lit my kerosene lamp.

Somewhere he came up with a mason jar of water and held it to my lips. He sat in my one chair and I focused my eyes on him. The yellow light fell on one side of his face leaving dark creases in his leathery skin and setting his real age.

"S'pose she's over now," he said, his voice devoid of any trace of authority. I let the silence sit.

"You were part of it?" I finally asked, the words husking in my raw throat like dry gravel.

"I s'pose I was," he said, looking past me. "It wasn't nothin' but talk at first. Them young ones sayin' how the land was ruint an' city folk was the cause. Course, we always knowed that. Same words been tossed 'round with whiskey for lifetimes."

He was talking at the wall. The same stare was in his eye that I'd seen as he looked at the front of the cabin where the girl had lain and didn't want to go inside.

"But these ones started talkin' 'bout actually doin' somethin' about it."

"Blackman, Ashley and Gunther?" I said.

"An' some others at first," he answered, feeding me more water and taking a sip himself.

"They wasn't bad men. I hunted and fished with all of 'em at one time. But you know how some things will just catch fire and burn out fast and others will smolder on like the peat under the soil. It just burns on until it's all black and burnt rotten."

There was nothing for me to add. Sometimes it was beyond understanding. I'd seen groups of cops do it, talk and talk and talk. Then one or more would finally step over the line and there would be hell to pay for us all.

"Once them kids started turnin' up dead, we all started lookin' at each other. Some removed themselves from it. Some weren't sure," Brown said. "I guess one liked it."

"But you didn't know who?" I said.

He shook his head and looked down at the floor.

"I s'pected Ashley for a time. He was always an odd one. I tracked him some. Then I found him out at his place. The girl was inside. I must have chased Blackman off. Dave Ashley wouldn't never of hanged hisself."

The old man got up and stepped quietly outside. I coughed and it felt like ground glass in my lungs. When Brown came back in he had my bag in his hand. He set it down beside the bed and zipped it open and took out the cell phone.

"They gone have to come git you," he said and put it near my good hand. I looked up at him.

"What about the knives," I said, and thought about the one I'd buried in Blackman's throat.

"I brung 'em home from the war," he said. "I give a few out to some of my . . . acquaintances."

He put the bag down next to the bed and turned to go.

"You might better keep that one there," he said, nodding at the table where I could see he'd laid one of the German blades. Without another word he slipped out the door and was gone.

I lay in the flicker of the lamplight for some time. My head spinning with Blackman's mad defense of territory and survival, half dreaming of green water and the pale dead faces of children.

* * *

I heard the motors first, deep downriver, the sound burbling and groaning through the trees and slipping through the dense fern and slowly growing loud.

Then I saw the flashes of light through my windows and heard their careful voices. I felt the thunk against the dock piling and the tread of feet, more than a few, coming up.

"Max?"

It was Diaz, unsure of my sanity, not wanting to put himself or his people in danger if he'd totally misjudged me.

"Max? You in there?"

"I'm here," I called out, my voice weak and watery.

I heard him whispering.

"It wasn't me, Diaz. You're going to have to trust me," I said, trying to reassure him.

I lay still, knowing movement would only spook them. Diaz finally came through the door, low, following the muzzle of his own 9mm. I didn't move. Sudden movement only makes them shoot you.

"Sorry I can't get up and spread 'em," I said, looking yet again at the wrong end of a gun.

"Christ, Max," Diaz said, holstering his gun.

Richards was the second cop in. The kerosene light caught several strands of blond hair that had come loose under her baseball cap. Behind her was an officer I'd never seen before. He was carrying an MP5 assault rifle, standard issue for SWAT teams. All three of them were wearing bulletproof vests.

"We're clear inside," the SWAT officer said into a radio microphone that was Velcroed to his shoulder. "Looks like we're gonna need an evac litter and a med tech up here."

Richards popped on a flashlight and sat down in the chair next to me. She did a once-over with the light, stopping at the crude splint and then moving it on to the blood-soaked pants leg.

"Bullet wound?" she said, probably knowing the answer. I could smell her perfume, so odd in this setting that it didn't take much to stand out.

"Yeah."

"You've got some bad habits, Freeman," she said, but I could see the small smile at the corners of her mouth.

More SWAT officers appeared in the door, their night-vision goggles hanging loose around their necks. They called Diaz over and spoke in low voices.

"Christ!"

He gave them some instructions and came back to stand over me.

"They found another body upstream. This one looks like a knife to the throat."

He said it as information to her and a question to me.

"Blackman," I said and then went into a spasm of coughing from the effort.

"He the shooter?" Diaz said.

All I could do was nod.

"All right, Max, let's get you out of here. Hammonds is going to have to hear this firsthand."

They loaded me onto a litter, got me down the steps and then into a Florida Marine Division boat. A med tech had cut away the backwoods splint and encased my arm in an inflatable cast. My leg wound was bandaged and wrapped tight. I heard them say something about blood loss. I was drifting in and out again. I thought I heard other boats but the rocking set my head sloshing even more. Spotlights were slashing through the trees. Radios were crackling with traffic. There were too many people in my shack, too many on the river. I heard the grumble of engines and watched again as the canopy sailed by.

Sometime down the river, I thought I recognized the spot where Cleve's boat had been. The trees around it were draped in yellow tape. From low in the boat I had lost the moon and I asked where it was and my voice sounded like I was speaking into the bottom of a pail.

"What?" It was Richards.

"Where's the moon?" I said again.

"What?" She bent her cheek to my lips.

"The moon. Where's the moon?"

"Save your strength, Max," she said, and squeezed my hand.

I thought I saw red and blue lights flashing at the boat ramp, spinning like a carnival ride. I thought I saw people standing in line to see. I thought I saw a black Chevy Suburban and I was sure that I was lost.

CHAPTER 26

Richards was right about my bad habits, hospitals and gunshot wounds among them. This time I stayed at least half conscious through most of it; watched the paramedics hover over me in the ambulance, taking vital signs and pushing IVs, felt the rocking back and forth with the turns and stops and slow-downs and accelerations through every intersection, heard the siren whining and then chattering through traffic.

I was awake when they wheeled me into the E.R. of yet another hospital; saw the ugly fluorescent lights, heard the rake of curtains on steel rods, listened to the repeated questions that I could hear but could not get my throat to answer. I heard a doctor ask the paramedic if this was it.

"Yeah, the rest were dead at the scene," he said.

I was conscious when they dug the bullet out of my thigh, heard them comment on how shallow it had penetrated into the muscle, heard the metal click into a hard plastic container, heard someone speculate on how misshapen the round was and that it must have hit something first and tumbled.

"Made a messy entrance wound, though," I heard the doctor say. "Not nearly as clean as this old one." And I felt his cold gloved finger touch the scar tissue on my neck.

I was awake when they x-rayed my arm, heard the metallic buzz and clack of the machine. Heard the orthopedic guy say, "Jesus, these guys didn't try to set this in the field, did they?"

I guess I slept some then. I still did not want to close my eyes, but they must have slipped something into my blood to make me sleep.

I was in another hospital room when I awoke. Sunlight was pouring through a window and painting an obtuse rectangle of light on the wall. Hammonds was sitting in a chair at the end of the bed, looking down at his folded hands. I watched him for several minutes before I cleared my throat and spoke.

"You need me?" I said, the words coming out softer than I wanted them to.

He looked up without lifting his head and met my eyes.

"No," he said. "Probably not anymore."

He stayed in the chair and talked. His tie was pulled tight. His elbows rested on his knees and his hands remained folded as he talked.

They'd recovered my 9mm from the river bottom just below the dam. Forensics was doing a ballistics test and lifting prints. They had also recovered the GPS unit from my shack and printed that.

Blackman's body was at the morgue and the preliminary cause of death was a knife wound to the throat. The M.E. had noted that the cut appeared to have been made with a blade similar in style to the one used on the Alvarezes' dog.

Hammonds looked up at me when he said this, and this time I looked away.

"We also collected a certain piece of cutlery from the table in your, uh, home. I'll assume you won't mind that we run some tests on that particular piece?"

I nodded my assent. There was a long awkward silence, but

Hammonds wasn't leaving. We were both trying to smooth some still rough stones.

"We had Blackman down as a suspect for some time," he finally said, talking into his hands. "We weren't sure, but it was impossible to tail the guy. We couldn't follow his movements, we couldn't bring him out."

I could see the investigator's hands start to tighten and then relax in a fidgety rhythm.

"Then you came along and at first we thought we finally had an accomplice coming out of the bucket. Then it looked more like you were set up. And after the plane thing, a target. After a while, we didn't know which side you were on but we figured you might draw somebody out."

"Bait," I said, with neither accusation nor surprise in my voice.

"Better if he were after you than the kids," Hammonds said flatly.

"Even after Ashley?"

"Ashley could have been our guy. But I couldn't bet on it."

"So you gave him a little confidence with the press conference," I said, trying to see his eyes.

"Sometimes," he said, looking up with no shame, "you have to use them."

I couldn't tell if he meant me, the press, the system, or all of us. Hammonds finally stood up, re-tightened the knot of his tie and smoothed his jacket.

"I know you're thinking it wasn't worth it. You could have stayed out of it. I could have locked you up and kept you out of it. Maybe the rangers would be alive," he said, looking too tired for a man of any age. "But he would have kept feeding on the innocents, Max."

He reached out and offered his hand and I took it.

"Now it is over," he said and I watched him walk out of the room.

A quiet minute after Hammonds left, Billy knocked at the door. He was followed by detectives Richards and Diaz. It was as if they were waiting for some sort of clearance from their boss.

"You're l-looking good," Billy said, standing at the end of the bed, cynically shaking his head.

"Good like runover dog shit," Diaz said, putting a hand on the bed covers and smiling his big-toothed smile.

It was Richards who stepped up to my side and touched my right arm just above the IV.

"How you feeling, Freeman?" she said.

"I'm OK," I said, looking for a brief second into her eyes. Her closeness was making me nervous. She took her hand away and cupped her elbows.

"Well, take your time lying here getting all that sweet nursing care," Diaz said. "The press is going ape-shit out there and there's no way to keep your name out of the public record.

"Right now you're a surviving victim who was wounded by some psycho committing a double homicide. Hammonds isn't even linking it up with the kid killings yet."

I looked at Billy but he stayed silent, not willing to speculate with two cops standing there.

"There's some reporter out there whose name is Donna. Says she knows you," Richards said, raising an eyebrow. I shook my head. "Says she's not really pressing, but knows you've got a story and she's willing to wait for it. I know I don't have to tell you that those are the ones to look out for."

"In the meantime, we got a ton of paperwork to file," Diaz said, butting in and giving me a reason to look away from his partner's eyes.

"You find any, uh, witnesses out there?" I whispered.

"None. After you called about the rangers we moved as soon as we could. We came upriver and got to the Whaler. The second team came down from where you showed me your smashed-up canoe. They were all in night vision. Only thing they saw was Blackman's body."

I knew the two SWAT teams coming in from both ends was a tactic that would have been used if they thought I'd gone psycho, killed the rangers and then holed up in my shack. I didn't say anything. It was good police work. You can't take it personally. But even with that kind of coverage and technical advantage, Nate Brown had slipped through unseen.

"And how is Hammonds going to play Blackman's death?" I finally asked, wondering if they even knew.

"You put up a hell of a fight, Max," Diaz said, his cop voice back on.

I shook my head, thinking of Brown poling his skiff out over the Glades in the moonlight.

"Anyway, Hammonds has already told us to find your pilot buddy Gunther," Richards said. "Seems he left the hospital and disappeared. But we think he might have headed home to New York State. We'll find him. It's not so easy to hide in the civilized world. But I guess you knew that."

"Yeah," I said. "I guess I knew that."

Both of them turned to leave, but Richards hesitated at the doorway and caught me with her green gray eyes. For a heartbeat I thought I felt an old emotion start to flicker across the room and then I watched as she loosened a strand of her blond hair and tucked it in place behind her ear.

"See ya," she said, and slipped out the door.

I heard Billy ask me if I was all right, maybe twice, before I finally turned to him as he pulled up a chair.

"You are a l-low maintenance cl-client, Max. But a high maintenance f-f-friend."

I tightened my mouth to a grin and thanked him.

"You m-may convalesce at m-my place," he said. "Ms. McIntyre and I are g-going on vacation to Paris. She w-wants to walk the c-city."

I didn't answer. I was staring at the sunlight painted on the wall and was already half in a dream. I must have been on the ocean because the horizon was curved and I could no longer hear the grinding. I must have been dreaming because I could feel a soft sea breeze and see Gulf Stream water the color of blue you could hold in the palm of your hand.

ACKNOWLEDGMENTS

I would like to thank magazine editor Dave Wieczorek for years of lessons, Russ and Marlene for allowing me a quiet place to write, Michael for his reading and guidance and, most of all, Lisa for her deep patience.

ABOUT THE AUTHOR

Jonathon King, a journalist for twenty years, began his career at the *Philadelphia Daily News.* He has covered crime and criminal courts and is now a national award–winning news feature writer for the South Florida *Sun-Sentinel. The Blue Edge of Midnight* is his first novel.